# On the Line

## A Second Chance Sports Romance

Julia Connors

*Sometimes you have to leave behind the life you thought you wanted to open yourself up to the life you deserve.*

# Chapter One

## LAUREN

*Park City, Utah*

Today is going to be a great day. I can feel it in my bones. Things are starting to come together, to line up in just the way I need them to.

I pull out into downtown Salt Lake City traffic, and the office where I just verbally accepted a job offer fades away in my rearview mirror. After several years staying at home, first as a newly married wife and then as a new mom, I've finally made my way back into the world of sports marketing.

And I've done it on my own: no handouts, no nepotism, no connections. I got this job solely based on my own merit, and it's the best feeling.

"So you haven't even told Josh yet?" Petra's voice carries through the speaker in my SUV as I approach a stoplight. Petra's one of my three best friends, but she's the only one who knows the struggles Josh and I have had over the past year and a half as we adjusted to being the parents of twin girls.

1

Well, I've adjusted. He's slowly pulled away.

"He hasn't exactly been reachable these past few days," I tell her.

"Where is he this time?" she asks.

Petra and Josh are both former professional ski racers. When she left skiing many years ago, she started a new career, first as a model, then as an event planner, and now she's the host of a well-known TV show.

Josh retired more recently, and in the couple years since, he's made his living skiing—traveling to ski resorts all over to promote different brands that sponsor him, filming videos and ads, and generally relishing the fact that he still gets paid to ski even though he's no longer competing.

"Somewhere in Washington. They were at Stevens Pass, then I think they headed somewhere near Spokane a couple days ago. He'll be home tonight, but I texted him earlier and haven't heard back yet. At least after this trip, he'll be home until Christmas."

"Well, that's a good thing," she says encouragingly.

"I don't know how you handle the load when Aleksandr is away," I say. Her husband plays in the NHL, so he's gone a fair amount during the season and together they have a seven-year-old adopted daughter.

"I just do." I can practically hear her shrug over the phone as I change lanes to head toward the on-ramp for I-80, the road that will take me into the mountains and back to my home in Park City. "He was already traveling when we got together, so it's all I've known."

Josh was also already skiing professionally when we met and got married. He traveled a lot then, but since I'd quit my sports marketing job in Boston in order to move out to Park

2

City with him after we got engaged, I was able to travel with him to his races that first year.

And I'd made some great girlfriends in Park City— starting with his physical therapist, Jackson, and her best friends Sierra and Petra. They brought me into their group and we were all so close, but all three of them have moved away and gotten married over the past two years, right as Josh and I were starting our family. With him still traveling a lot, I'm now often on my own with the kids, so his travel is hitting me harder than it used to.

But that's on me, because I don't have anything else in my life except for him and the kids—which is why the job is going to be such a big deal for me.

Having something to focus on besides my family will help me feel like a more well-rounded person, able to bring more to our relationship and our family than just my role as a mother. I'll finally have things to talk to my husband about again—things besides nap schedules and the infinite minutiae of what our girls did each day. Plus, with my background in sports marketing and my general passion for hockey, getting to work for one of the NHL farm teams is a perfect mix of my interests and abilities.

But I thought the interview and offer process would take longer than it had, so I assumed I'd have more time to figure out how to tell Josh.

"Sooo," Petra says when I'm so lost in my own thoughts I forget to respond, "how are you going to tell him?"

"It's like you're reading my mind right now," I say.

"I'd hardly have to be a mind reader to know that's what you're thinking about. I know how he feels about you working."

I didn't know he was so old-fashioned about the role of wife and mother before I married him. I guess that's what happens when you have a whirlwind romance and marry someone you've known for six months. At the time, it was all so romantic, and he was so attentive and passionate and protective. Completely unlike any of the guys I'd dated up until that point.

I used to joke that I was going to marry the first nice guy I dated, and I held true to that—I just wish that the Josh I'd dated and the Josh I'd started a family with were the same person.

"He's going to have to adjust," I say. "We'll work out childcare. Morgan mentioned that one of her friends might be looking for a part-time nanny position, so I'm going to talk to her as soon as possible."

"That's great," Petra says. Morgan is my younger cousin and Petra's personal assistant. She does most of her work remotely and because her schedule is so flexible, Morgan has been immensely helpful in watching the girls when Josh is out of town and I need to be somewhere else, like at today's final interview when they offered me the job.

"When it comes to talking to Josh," she continues in that husky voice she's literally famous for, "I've found that a good meal and good sex can convince a man of just about anything."

"I must finally be learning," I say with a laugh, "because that's pretty much exactly what I have planned for tonight."

"Yes." The word is a low hiss. "I've taught you my ways and you're going to have Josh eating out of your hand before the night is over."

My smile spreads. "I mean, the man's been gone for a week and a half, so there's a good chance you're right."

Petra's one of the few women I know who is as unabashedly driven by sex as most men. She's also straight-forward to a fault, strikingly beautiful, powerful in her own right, and intimidating as hell. If you'd told me years ago when I met her that we'd end up being incredibly close, I'd have laughed.

She intimidated the shit out of me when we first met. But love, marriage, and an adorable daughter have softened her hard edges just enough, without dulling the intense, passionate aspects of her personality.

"When are you going to tell Jackson and Sierra about this new job?" she asks.

"Probably tomorrow. I just want to talk to Josh first."

Not knowing how Josh is going to feel about me going back to work is taking a bit of the shine off this victory, but I remind myself not to let that dull my joy in this moment.

"Lauren," she says, and there's a warning in her voice. "Do not back down. Don't let him talk you out of this. Don't let him convince you that you're not a good wife or a good mom if you go back to work part-time. It's only three days a week. Everything will be fine."

I take a deep breath through my nose. "I know. And don't worry, it's going to be fine. He knows I need this. I really do believe that me going back to work is going to bring Josh and I closer, and I'm positive I can make him see it that way too."

"Good. But if the conversation doesn't go well, or if you need anything," she says, "just call. I don't care about the time difference."

"Thanks, Petra. I really couldn't have taken these steps without your encouragement."

"You one hundred percent could have," she says, her voice emphatic. "You're a badass, and you're doing the right thing taking this job."

Her confidence in me is often the boost I need to believe in myself. "You're right. This is the perfect job, at the perfect time. Things are going to be great."

———

I toss the bottle of balsamic glaze into my cart on top of the flank steak and come around the end of that aisle into the produce section. Josh always eats like crap when he's on the road and loves to come back to a good home-cooked meal. I hate cooking and don't do it often, but tonight I'm making his favorite: seared flank steak stuffed with spinach, garlic, butter, and Parmesan, along with creamy mashed potatoes, and green beans sautéed with garlic and topped with a balsamic glaze.

I still haven't heard from him, which is a little odd. Normally, he texts me when he gets on the road to head home. Maybe he lost his charger again, like on his last trip. Sometimes he's a little scattered like that.

It's a long drive from Washington, so I figure I still have time to get home and spend a little time with the girls, get the food prepped, put the girls to bed, and have dinner waiting when Josh walks in the door.

I'm pushing my cart through the produce section toward the front of the store when it happens—it feels like the floor drops out from under me, and I have the sensation of falling.

The moment replays in my mind, so vividly that I'm forced to relive it.

*The music is pumping, and the crowd is clapping in sync with the beat as I finish a sequence of artistic moves and then go through a series of backward crossovers to gather the speed that will take me into the most difficult jump in my routine: a triple axel.*

*I've landed it in competition before, but never on a national stage—this is going to make me a household name. That's what I'm thinking about as I turn forward, push off the outside edge of my left skate, kick through with my right leg to get the height I need for the three and a half rotations of the jump, hug my arms to my body, and spin through the air on the perfect axis. And when the blade of my right skate hits the ice and I'm about to kick my left leg out behind me, I know I've executed a textbook perfect jump.*

*Then the ice is coming at me with alarming speed, and I don't know what happens after that. Dozens of experts have analyzed the footage and no one can quite say why, instead of sticking that landing and clinching my first national championship, I end up on the ice, the side of my head connecting with the rink hard enough that I'm completely knocked out.*

I come to a full stop in the middle of the aisle, relieved that the store is so empty. I've broken out in a full-body sweat, and I bend at the waist, resting my forehead on the bar of the grocery cart and taking a few deep breaths to get my bearings.

I don't know what it means when I relive that moment like this. It's only happened a few times since I recovered— and each time it has felt like a terrible omen.

That's when Josh's name lights up my phone screen.

"Hey." I take a breath, ready to launch into the story of what just happened.

"Is this Lauren Emerson?"

The unfamiliar voice has me standing up, gripping the phone so hard I'm surprised I don't bend it.

"Yes. Who's this?"

"Ma'am," he replies with a steady, deep voice, "this is Lieutenant George Marshall from the Blaine County Sheriff's Office in Sun Valley, Idaho."

I'm pretty sure my heart stops. Josh isn't in Sun Valley, Idaho. He's in eastern Washington. This has to be a mistake. Except, he's calling from my husband's cell phone.

"Is everything okay?" Even as I ask it, I know how ridiculous the question is. The sheriff's office doesn't call because everything's okay.

"Are you somewhere where you can sit down?"

"I'm in the grocery store right now." I glance around self-consciously, but the only other person in the produce section is an employee stocking apples along the far wall.

"Do you want to go somewhere more private so we can talk?"

"No!" My voice is shrill even to my own ears. "I want to know why you're calling from my husband's phone!"

My words are verging on hysteria. I need to talk to Josh. I'm going to tell him about this new job, and he's going to be proud of me. We'll get back to everything being good between us again.

I can hear the concern in his voice when he responds, "Okay, ma'am. Your husband was skiing out of bounds at Sun Valley Resort with a small group of people. We've had heavy snowfall over the past five days and the avalanche threat was considerable. Their group triggered a substantial slide earlier this morning."

An avalanche is a skier's worst nightmare, especially if you're skiing in the backcountry. Josh was a ski racer—he's best on smoothly groomed trails where he can go as fast as he likes. He's not a backcountry skier. What the hell was he doing out of bounds? And why was he in Sun Valley?

A sob bursts out of me as I consider my husband buried under all that snow, like being trapped in frozen concrete, injured and in pain. "Is he going to be okay?"

On the other end of the line, he pauses, and let's out a shaky breath. "I'm sorry ma'am. He didn't make it."

I sink to my knees still clutching my phone to my ear. "What?" This doesn't make any sense. Josh is too smart to ski out of bounds when there's an avalanche threat. Isn't he?

"Rescue crews got to them as quickly as possible, but they were buried under too much debris. No one survived."

My body feels frozen in shock and my chest heaves as I try to draw a breath. Everything around me seems to be spinning. I think I'm hyperventilating, but I have no idea how to calm myself down.

"Ma'am?"

"I'm here," I squeak out, then take a few ragged, gasping breaths.

"I'm going to have someone in my office call local law enforcement and get them to come to you and make sure you get home safely. Please stay on the line with me until they arrive." He asks the name of the grocery store I'm at and where in the store I'm located, and, while he keeps me on the phone, he answers my questions to the best of his ability given that "the investigation is ongoing." All he's able to tell me is what time the avalanche happened, and how long Josh and his fellow skiers were buried before rescue crews were able to dig them out.

There were no survivors. That sobering piece of information is winding itself around my brain. I have so many questions—about why they were in Sun Valley and why they skied out of bounds when there was an avalanche warning—but anyone who could answer them is dead.

I feel like I'm trapped, suffocating, as I sit on the floor shaking uncontrollably. It feels like an hour, but is probably only a few minutes, before two police officers are walking up the aisle to me. The older one helps me up while the younger one takes the phone and speaks to the officer in Sun Valley.

"We're going to get you home," he says as he puts his arm around my waist to support me. The wrinkles around his eyes crinkle as he smiles a sad smile. The younger officer says something to him, but while his lips are moving, it sounds like he's talking underwater. I feel like I might pass out. "It's going to be okay."

And in that moment, looking up at the older officer, I'm certain nothing is ever going to be okay again.

# Chapter Two

## JAMESON

*Boston, MA*

Could this day get any worse? I highly fucking doubt it.

"Two days?" I ask the Pre-K teacher as I look down at my Italian leather shoes that are now covered in puke from my four-year-old nephew.

"At least. He can't come back tomorrow because he has to be symptom-free for twenty-four hours before he can return." She has the no-nonsense approach of an elderly aunt who's seen it all and has no time for your issues.

"Great."

I consider the three remaining meetings I have this afternoon—one of which includes signing an eight-figure endorsement deal with an international athletic wear company for my highest profile hockey player. We're supposed to be meeting in my office in an hour.

I don't know what I'm going to do with Graham during

those meetings, but at least his mom—my sister, Audrey—will be back in town tonight.

I do feel bad for the little guy. I carry him out of the school because he's too weak to walk at the pace I need to be moving. I don't have a choice but to hurry. When we get to my car and I take in the custom leather upholstery with the detailed stitching, I wonder if I can possibly get him home without wrecking the interior of my Maserati.

There's really no other option, so I buckle him into his booster in the back seat.

"How you doing, bud?" I ask as I ruffle his hair back from where it's plastered against his forehead with sweat. The kid is burning up.

"Awful."

"Yeah, I can tell. I'll get you home and in bed, and hopefully that'll help."

He leans his head back against the seat and closes those big brown eyes, so I shut the car door, come around to the driver's side, and get in. Then I crack my window despite the cold temperatures because I can hardly breathe through the stench of our soaked clothes.

Every time I peek in the rearview mirror, Graham's eyes are closed. And by the time we get back to the South End and turn onto our street, I breathe a sigh of relief. We made it.

"I don't feel good." Graham groans.

*Oh shit.*

"We're almost home," I assure him, giving him another glance in the mirror.

He's thrashing his head back and forth like he does when he doesn't want to do something you're telling him to do.

"I'm going—" his words are cut off by the projectile vomit.

I glance over and watch it trickle down the passenger seat, where it runs along the white stitched seams of the dark gray leather.

My stomach roils and then clenches in disgust, and I'm dry heaving. I take the turn to the alley that leads along the side of our brownstone a little too quickly and come to a skidding stop in the space next to the side entrance of our house. I push my car door open and run around to the passenger side to get Graham out before he can do any more damage, and as soon as I open the door, he vomits all over me. "Fuck!"

"That was a *very* bad word, Uncle Jameson," he says somberly as he unbuckles himself.

"Yeah, well, this is a *very* expensive car you just threw up in," I mutter as I lift him out of his seat and set him on the ground. His little body weaves back and forth like a boxer who just got clocked in the head. "You going to throw up again?"

"I don't know." He looks down at his abdomen, then back up at me. "My stomach says 'maybe.'"

———

"I need three huge favors right now," I say quickly, hoping that Derek, my personal assistant, is in a forgiving mood today.

I sigh, thinking back to thirty minutes ago in the school nurse's office when I didn't think my day could get worse. It feels like maybe I was inviting disaster.

"You already owe me big for last week."

"Like hell I do." Last week I gave him five hundred dollars to show up in my place to a fancy dinner at an outstanding restaurant, because I had somewhere else I needed to be: taking Graham to a Boston Rebels hockey game.

"Listen, this is very much not within your role as my personal assistant, but I need you to get your ass over to my place as quick as humanly possible. Then I need you to stay with Graham until Jules gets home."

"Why isn't Graham at school?" he asks. Over the speaker-phone, I can hear him putting on his coat and gathering his things.

"Stomach bug. Audrey is flying back from that conference in Chicago, and Jules is at a jobsite in West Roxbury."

Together, my sisters run the construction company that's been in my family for three generations now. Audrey is the architect, and Jules is the structural engineer and lead contractor.

"I talked to Jules a few minutes ago and she'll get here as quickly as she can, but I suspect we're looking at a minimum of forty-five minutes and I don't have that long. I need to get back to the office for the signing in"—I glance at my watch—"thirty minutes."

I hear the elevator ding over the phone and Derek says, "If I get the stomach bug, I'm taking three days of sick time and not feeling bad about it."

"Understood. But you're invaluable to me, so don't get too close to Graham, and you'll be fine."

As he gets in his Uber, I give Derek some more instructions about scheduling the dry-cleaning pickup for my suit and finding a detail place that can pick up my car and have it back to me before I leave for work tomorrow morning.

"I'll be lucky if I can find someone to pick it up today," he says, "much less get it back to you by tomorrow morning."

"Make it happen." I have full confidence in his abilities. It's amazing what he can accomplish when he's throwing my money around.

I set my phone on the coffee table and bend down to feel Graham's forehead. He still feels hot and clammy. "Hey, Derek is going to come and hang out with you until Auntie Jules gets back, okay? I have to go into the office."

"Okay," Graham says, his eyes never leaving his episode of Spider-Man. He's lying on the couch on his side with his iPad propped up on the coffee table and a garbage can sitting right between him and his show. Hopefully, if there's any more throwing up, he can aim it in the can. I already got him cleaned off as best I could and took a record-breaking fast shower myself.

"I'm going to run upstairs to my place to grab a tie." Converting our childhood home into a two-family house— where my sisters and Graham live on the first two floors, and I have my own place on the third floor—was one of the smartest things I've done. "I'll keep the door open so I can hear you. If you need me, just call. And if you need to throw up again, make it—"

"In the trash can. I knooow," Graham says.

He must be starting to feel better if he's already getting back to his normal smart-ass self. Audrey blames that part on me, saying I'm a bad example. Which always leads me to remind her that if she hadn't gotten knocked up in college, I wouldn't have to help raise my nephew after I already raised my two little sisters. She always appreciates that reminder.

I'm walking back down the stairs and tightening the knot on my tie when I hear the doorbell. Derek is less pissy about being here than I expected, probably because I tell him to get himself a nice dinner tonight and expense it.

Whereas many of my colleagues complain about not being able to find good assistants, I've held onto Derek for the last four years through a combination of paying him well and rewarding him when I ask him to do stupid shit that shouldn't really be part of his job, like today.

Because he's good at what he does, Derek even booked his Uber to take me back to the office, so I'm sitting back down behind my desk before Colt arrives.

"I'm about to sign the biggest endorsement deal of my life," he says, his huge frame filling my doorway as he walks into my office, "and you don't even have Derek here to help us celebrate? He should at least be here offering me a beer or something!"

"He's taking care of my sick nephew. I'll take you out for celebratory drinks another time."

"What's wrong with Graham?" At this point, Colt's been my teammate, client, and friend long enough that he knows my family.

"Stomach bug."

Colt has virtually no experience with kids, so I assume his grimace as he sits down in the chair across from me is in response to the thought of a kid throwing up. "And you made Derek go babysit him?"

"Yes, well, I pay him accordingly. And it's just until Jules can get back from a jobsite." I pick up the stack of papers on my desk and slide them across my desk toward him. "You ready to sign?"

"No," Colt says, the sarcasm evident in his voice, "I'm having second thoughts about all those zeros."

———

"Are you fucking kidding me?" I growl as Derek's name lights up my phone. It's easy to see the screen since I'm curled up on my side on my bathroom rug with a wadded up towel serving as a pillow. I reach over and tap the phone to answer it. "What part of don't contact me before noon was unclear?" My voice is more of a moan than a bark.

I'd texted Derek around two in the morning when I woke up sick. I told him I wouldn't be in and that unless someone died, I'd better not hear from him.

"So, about that text . . ." Derek says.

"What time is it right now?" It's still dark out, but I can see the orange-pink light of sunrise starting to filter through the seam between the shade and the frame of my bathroom window.

"Almost seven."

"Why the fuck are you calling me this early?"

Derek takes a deep breath. "Josh Emerson was killed yesterday in an avalanche."

"What?" I sit up so fast the whole room spins. I curl into a sitting fetal position, with my forehead resting on my knees. My stomach is still flipping over, though not as badly as it has been for the past several hours.

"He was skiing out of bounds in Sun Valley," Derek says,

17

then gives me the very few details he was able to find out so far.

"Shit." There is nothing else to say.

"What do you want me to do?" he asks.

"Print out a copy of his trust. I'll be in as soon as I can fucking walk."

"Do you want me to contact his family?"

"No!" The word hurtles from my mouth before I can stop it. "No," I say more calmly, "It's too soon."

When we disconnect the call, I sit there with my head on my knees for a few more minutes. The thought of having to talk to Lauren about Josh, seeing her devastation—it's more than my virus-addled mind can handle.

*Fuck*, I think to myself. In my whole portfolio of clients, there's only one person whose significant other I would do just about anything to avoid. And now I have no choice but to go see her.

The thought of coming face-to-face with her after all these years is apparently more than my stomach can handle, and I barely make it to the toilet in time.

# Chapter Three

## LAUREN

*Park City, Utah*

Petra scoots past Aleksandr, where he stands blocking me from the crowd of people milling around the restaurant, to hand me a glass of water.

"Here you go, sweetie," she says, taking up residence on my other side. Together, they've made it their mission to shield me from everyone as much as possible.

The last two weeks since I got the news about Josh have been a hellish blur of phone calls and funeral plans and paperwork, and at this point I am too mentally and emotionally exhausted to talk to people any more than I already have today.

I'm barely holding on. I'd prefer to have some time alone with just my closest friends and family, but I need to get through this next hour, because I know it makes people feel better to be here supporting each other and giving me their condolences, no matter how heartbreaking they are for me to hear.

*Such a tragedy. Such a beautiful young family. So many more memories for you two to make. A true loss. You deserved a lifetime together.*

All of those are true, and none of them are helping reconstruct my shattered heart.

Today I also heard the incredibly unhelpful *At least he died doing what he loved.*

I'm still trying to let that one go, because what he should have been doing was loving his family from the comfort of the beautiful home we built together in Park City.

Instead, he was chasing the high of skiing out of bounds after a massive early-season snowstorm, and it killed him. He was too smart for that. He was a ski racer, not a backcountry skier, and I will never know or understand why he took that risk when he had to have known the avalanche threat. I may never even know why he was in Sun Valley, Idaho instead of in eastern Washington, and all this not knowing is its own special kind of hell.

My eyes burn from crying so much, but I scan the room, checking on everything. There is still an enormous amount of food along the bar where the buffet was set up. However, people have mostly finished eating and are chatting in small groups.

Josh's parents are holding court at a large table at the front of the restaurant, surrounded by family and friends. I cannot imagine their pain, losing their only child.

They were parents, and now they're not.

I was a wife, and now I'm not.

And still, we can't connect, even over this tremendous loss.

Josh was always the only link between us. In the four

years we were married, they never made the slightest effort to get to know me, to make me feel welcome, to treat me like a daughter. Instead, I was more like an accessory he brought along to family functions.

"You're staring at them," Petra says, her throaty voice so low she's barely audible.

I glance over at her and sigh. "Do you know they haven't said a single word to me today?" Not an ounce of compassion, even in our moment of shared suffering. They sat next to me in church and never even spoke to me. Four years married to their son, the mother of their only grandchildren, and all I got was a nod of recognition.

Petra readjusts the long, black cardigan that's slipped off her bare shoulder to reveal the thin strap of the black, knee-length bustier dress she's wearing. Even at my husband's funeral she's her natural sex goddess self, which at least tugs a small smile from my lips. God, I love her and all her unshakable confidence.

"You know," she says, "it's possible that they're so wrapped up in their own grief that they can't acknowledge your suffering."

"Probably true," I say, my voice low so no one can hear me. "Except they're always like this."

The pain of losing Josh is magnified by how totally alone I feel now.

All my family is in New England, and now that Jackson and Sierra both live in Blackstone, NH, and with Petra now in New York City, my friend group in Park City has shrunk to the small moms' group I joined when the twins were babies. Those women have been wonderfully supportive about parenting and over the past twenty months we've grown together as new moms, but our kids are really the only thing I have in common with them. We're friends by circumstance more than choice. It's just not the same as having my best friends and family surrounding me, and right now I need their love and support more than ever.

In this moment, it becomes crystal clear to me that with Josh gone, there's nothing left for me in Park City.

Petra squeezes my hand in a silent show of friendship, and my eyes drift over to the table where my moms' group sits. They've all got their phones out and seem to be showing each other photos and videos, which is par for the course when we're together. *Look at my kid going down the slide for the first time. Look at this DIY project I completed entirely during my kid's naps. Look at this sweet thing my husband did for me.* Watching them, I feel lost—does any of that even matter anymore?

As Aleksandr tells Petra about a text they just got from their nanny, I let my gaze continue to slide across the room until I find Jackson and Sierra. They're standing at the bar with their husbands, talking to a man I don't recognize from behind. He's as tall as Jackson's husband, Nate, with dark hair that's closely cropped along the back and sides, and slightly longer and wavy on top. His black suit jacket shows his very broad shoulders tapering to a thin waist.

"Hey," Petra says as Aleksandr walks away from us, toward the bar. "What's wrong?"

I haven't got a poker face—something that Josh always teased me about—so I'm sure my confusion is written plainly across my features. This man is at my husband's funeral, and talking to my friends, so why can't I place who he is?

And then he turns toward Sierra's husband, Beau, and I

suck in a sharp breath as that perfect smile spreads across his face and recognition dawns. I gasp, and as Petra turns toward me, I mutter, "What is *he* doing here?"

"Who?"

"Josh's agent."

"Why wouldn't Josh's agent be here?" Petra is right to be confused. She doesn't know him, or know that we go way back—back to before I knew Josh.

Aleksandr approaches the group at the bar, walking right up to Jameson and they shake hands. No, no, no. Of all the people in this restaurant, how has Jameson found my closest friends to talk to?

"I . . ." I stutter, not knowing how to answer her question. "It never occurred to me that he'd come all the way from Boston."

"Of course he'd come if he's Josh's agent. Which one is he?" she asks, her eyes roaming the room.

I note the way Jameson and Aleksandr have their heads tucked into conversation, almost like the larger group isn't there. "The one talking to your husband."

She sucks in a breath. "Jameson Flynn was Josh's agent?" she asks.

"Wait, how do you know him?"

"He's Aleksandr's agent," she says, and now that she mentions it, it rings a bell. I think Jameson was already his agent when we both worked together at Kaplan Sports Management years ago. Back then, Alex Ivanov was still relatively new to the NHL, having played in the Kontinental Hockey League before that. "In fact," she continues, "he's responsible for getting me into the Honda Center for that playoff game last year. He kind of saved our relationship and my husband's career."

"*You* saved your relationship and his career," I remind her. And apparently Jameson helped.

I turn toward Petra, making sure to keep my back to him. The fact that he's here has knocked me off-kilter, and I will avoid looking at or talking to him as long as I can.

"You don't seem too fond of him."

"Because I'm not. He's arrogant, competitive, and self-absorbed." I only mention the qualities I observed at work and keep everything else out of the story.

"You know him that well?"

"We worked together at Kaplan. I was in sports marketing and he was an agent, obviously. All we did was fight." The statement is mostly true. For years, he was my work nemesis, and then one night that all changed. And the next night he introduced me to my future husband. "He's the one who introduced me and Josh, actually."

Petra takes a sip of her drink and eyes me skeptically. "Why would he do that if you two disliked each other so much?"

I shrug. "It wasn't like he set us up or anything. We were just at a work function together, and he was Josh's agent, so he introduced us."

The idea of Jameson being *just* "Josh's agent" is almost amusing. He was a big deal even then—not yet as powerful in his career as he is now, but he'd only been out of the NHL for about five years at that point, so there was still a lot of star power behind his name. Everyone in the hockey world knew who Jameson Flynn was. And for reasons I still don't understand, Josh was the only athlete he represented who wasn't a hockey player.

Petra glances over to where Jameson stands next to Aleksandr, and when I turn my head in their direction, I see that her husband is motioning us over. "We have to go over there," she insists. "You can just say hello, thank him for coming, and never see or talk to him again."

It's not like there's much choice in the matter at this point. But as we walk over, the last words he said to me— almost five years ago, on my last day at Kaplan—are running through my head and turning my blood to fire. I don't anger easily, but when I do—watch out. I have that temper redheads are known for, and unfortunately, Jameson Flynn has always known how to rile me up.

As Petra steps up next to her husband, I'm left between her and my former nemesis. I nod toward him. "Thanks for coming."

"I'm so sorry this happened, Lauren," he says. His face is somber and his voice matches, and the way he says my name lacks any of the vitriol it once had. He sounds . . . truly sorry.

I press my lips between my teeth, willing myself to not start crying again, especially not in front of this man. I take a deep breath through my nose before I speak. "Thank you. I see you've already met my friends, so I won't bother introducing you."

I look away right as Petra elbows me in the side.

He's here, but I don't have to be nice to him. He certainly doesn't deserve that from me.

# Chapter Four

## LAUREN

"They're asleep," Morgan says as she drops a small pill into my hand and then hands me a glass of water.

"Thank you so much." My eyes start to water as the lump rises in my throat, so I rest my head on her shoulder. I honestly don't know what I would have done without my cousin these last two weeks. It's been hell and she's walked through it with me every step of the way, even moving into the guest bedroom as she helped me manage everything.

"It's the least I could do," she says. "But I'm never going to forgive your dad for riling the twins up right before bedtime tonight."

I glance over at my dad, sitting at my kitchen table with my mom, my brothers, and my best friends' husbands. I can tell by the way his mustache is twitching and his hands are waving that Dad's entertaining them with the outlandish stories he's famous for.

"Of course he did." My lips curve up at the corner. It's as much of a smile as I can manage, despite my overwhelming affection for my dad. The way he's doted on my girls has been exactly what they needed this week. They don't understand that their dad is gone. They may not even remember him, except through pictures and stories.

I wipe away a tear, wishing my parents weren't leaving tomorrow.

Tomorrow it will be real. Everyone else will go back to their normal lives, and I will still be in this new hellscape where I'm a widow, my children are fatherless, my exciting new job offer is a distant memory, and all my friends and family—except Morgan—are across the country.

I glance around my kitchen, but no one seems to be paying attention, so I pop the Xanax in my mouth discreetly and swallow it down with the water, promising myself that this is only until I get through these first few weeks. My doctor insists that the benefits—namely me being a functioning human capable of taking care of small children while also balancing the stress and heartbreak of this situation—mean I should continue taking it daily until I'm confident I can manage without it.

"I'm going to go get you some food. You need to eat something," Morgan tells me.

"I'm really not hungry," I assure her.

"You need to eat. You can't lose any more weight." She pauses to eye me skeptically, and I know what she sees. My collarbones jut out at the edges of this V-neck dress, my shoulders are overly bony, and my face looks gaunt.

I'm not hungry, but I know she's right. "Fine."

As soon as Morgan steps away, my sister, Paige, is there by my side.

"Hey, I'm hanging out with your friends in the dining

room. Why don't you come sit with us for a bit? The girls are in bed, you can relax. I've already poured you a glass of wine."

"I'm fine with water," I say, holding up the glass in my hand. I know better than to mix alcohol and anxiety medication.

"Okay, but come relax with us. You've been circling all evening, taking care of everyone here, when you should be letting us take care of you. I know that caring for people is your love language," she says as she puts a hand on each of my shoulders and looks me straight in the eye, "but right now the person you need to take care of is *you*."

I don't bother saying that keeping busy is helping me get through this. That the simple acts of refilling people's drinks and making sure everyone's had enough to eat, listening to stories about my nieces and nephews, and loving on my girls —it all helps take my mind off the fact that I'm a thirty-year-old widow with two little kids and no idea how I'm going to move forward after this tragedy.

I don't need to say any of that—Paige already knows.

Instead, I let her lead me into the dining room where Jackson, Sierra, and Petra are sitting around the long, narrow table with the sixteen high-back wooden chairs Josh picked out for this space. It's the kind of table you'd expect to see in a medieval movie, and I've always kind of hated it, but I've softened it up with a long ivory and gold runner and several candles in hurricane vases.

The three of them have their heads tucked together and don't notice us approaching. "Maybe we can finally get her to move back to Boston," Sierra says.

"That wouldn't take much convincing," I say with a sigh

as I pull out the chair next to her and sink into it while Paige walks around the table and sits across from me, next to Petra.

"Would you really?" Jackson asks, her big green eyes lighting up with hope. It means I'd be less than two hours from her and Sierra.

I haven't told any of them how I pestered Josh relentlessly this summer to move to Boston. At first, he appeared to seriously consider the idea. I didn't want to jinx it by getting anyone else excited before I knew whether it was possible, so I kept my mouth shut. And as summer faded to fall, Josh seemed less and less interested in the discussion. When he finally vetoed the idea, I was glad I hadn't said anything to anyone else, even if it meant I had to stew in my sadness alone. At least I hadn't gotten anyone else's hopes up only to disappoint them.

I take a deep breath and tell them about the rejected idea. "I wish I could have gotten him to agree to it then."

It turns out my argument for moving—that aside from my cousin Morgan, everyone else I loved lived within three hours of Boston—wasn't as compelling as his argument for staying—that we'd just built this beautiful house in the mountains overlooking Park City, and that he needed easy access to skiing.

"What would be different if you had?" Sierra asks as she sweeps her long blond hair over her shoulder.

"Maybe he wouldn't have gone on that trip. Maybe Washington, or Idaho, would have been too far away." I know how unlikely that is. Josh has traveled the globe for skiing as long as I've known him. "But even if he had, at least I'd have Paige there with me, and you and Jackson would only be two hours away." Even though Sierra still travels all around the world with Beau for his snowboarding, they do consider New Hampshire to be their home base, and they spend a lot of time there with Jackson and Nate. "And with the rest of my family in Maine, and Petra in New York . . ." I drift off as I try not to think about what it's going to feel like tomorrow when they all leave, but the tears fill my eyes anyway. "I wouldn't be all alone."

"Okay, so how do we make this happen?" Jackson asks. She loves a good challenge, and I can already see the plan coming together in her mind. "What do you need us to do?"

"I mean, can you sell this house for me and find me a new place in Boston? Preferably something a little more . . ." I glance around at the floor-to-ceiling windows of the dining space and the lofted ceilings of the attached living room. This house is beautiful, but it's so *Josh* that sometimes I have a hard time seeing anything of myself reflected in our home. "I don't know . . ."

"A little more *you*?" Petra suggests.

"Yeah. Maybe something more modest? Something homey where the girls and I can be comfortable, and I don't have to worry about them getting lost if we play hide-and-seek."

"I'm on it," Jackson says, picking up her wineglass from the table. "Or at least, I'm going to get Nate to help with this. There's a realtor he worked with when we lived here, and she is amazing. I bet she could sell this place in two seconds." Before Jackson and Nate bought Blackstone Mountain, the ski resort in New Hampshire where they'd met and raced as teenagers, Nate had built himself what we jokingly refer to as *a small real estate empire.* "We're going to find you the perfect new place in Boston, and then we're all finally going to be close enough to see each other more frequently."

I allow myself to feel the flicker of excitement that lights in my chest at this possibility. There's nothing left for me in Park City, and the thought of starting over closer to friends and family brings the first sense of hope I've felt since Josh died.

But then, a shadow falls across the table and when I look over my shoulder, my mother-in-law is standing in the doorway between the kitchen and dining room. And she does not look pleased.

She's gone as quickly as she appeared, without saying a thing. It's par for the course—her disapproval of me weighs heaviest in her silence.

"Someone doesn't love that idea," Paige mutters under her breath.

"I can't imagine why," I say quietly enough that there's no way I could be heard from the kitchen. "It's not like she'll care if I stay or go."

"What about the girls, though?" Sierra asks. "Do you think she'll feel like you're taking her granddaughters away?"

I practically snort. "The only thing she'll miss is the opportunity for photos with them, so she can post the pictures on social media and all her friends can tell her what a great grandmother she is." In truth, she's seen the girls twice in the last six months—once in the fall for Josh's birthday, and then on Halloween because it was the first time the girls were old enough to dress up and trick-or-treat.

"So don't factor her opinion into your decision, then," Petra says. "You've got to do what's best for you, and given everything that's happened here, maybe a fresh start is the right choice."

Sierra puts her hand on my forearm where it rests on the table. "You know I want you close by. I miss you like crazy. But . . ." She takes a deep breath. "I also don't want you to do anything rash while you're grieving. I'm sure Boston is appealing right now, as a fresh start and a way to be closer to us and your family. But you and Josh had a great life here, in this home. Are you sure you want to walk away from those memories?"

My eyes meet Petra's across the table, and she raises her eyebrows and gives me a little nod. *Tell them*, the look says.

I take a deep breath, considering how freeing it could feel to finally unload the truth on my friends rather than having to hide behind a wall of lies. "Things may have appeared better than they actually were."

"What do you mean?" Paige asks, right as Morgan sits down next to me and slides a plate of food in front of me.

I pick up the fork from the plate and stab a piece of kung pao chicken.

"Things have been a little rocky between Josh and me for a while now."

There's no collective gasp or anything, but I can sense the surprise that pops up around the table as I tell them about how things started changing when we became parents. "I kept setting milestones in my mind, like 'when the girls get to X point, things will be better between us.' But Josh only traveled more. It felt like . . . like he was trying to escape. And every time I brought it up, every time I mentioned wanting and needing him to be around more . . ." I swallow as my eyes fill with tears.

"He gaslit her into thinking she was clingy and insecure," Petra fills in for me. My friends look at her, clearly surprised she's speaking ill of someone who just died, but I get it: she's the one who was there when I went through this.

"When Petra figured it out, she convinced me to go to therapy, which did help a bit. But I wanted Josh to go with me, too, and he refused."

Morgan puts her arm across the back of my chair and squeezes my shoulder.

"I should have known," she says. "I'm here all the time. I should have realized." Her voice is small, and I hate that I've made her feel like she's done anything wrong in this situation.

"No, I kept it pretty well hidden. I didn't want anyone else to worry." I wipe away the tears that are streaming down my face, and my voice cracks when I admit, "I thought maybe a big change, like moving to Boston, could be a fresh start for us as a family."

The silence in the air is tangible, like a weighted blanket that hugs you so tightly it starts to feel oppressive.

"I want you close by," Paige says, "but if Boston is where you wanted a fresh start with Josh, is it the right choice for you now?"

"That's a good question." I push the food around my plate. "I wanted to be back in Boston because it had everything I needed—career opportunities, family, and my best friends close by. All of that is still true."

"It *sounds* good," Sierra says, "but I still think you shouldn't make a big, life-changing decision so soon after . . . everything. Maybe give it a little time. I just don't want you to do anything you'll regret."

"Okay, I'll think about it. Right now, the thought of being

here in Park City once you all leave," I say as I glance around at my friends and my sister, "has me feeling a little . . . trapped."

"Lauren," Jackson says, and I brace myself for the truth bomb she sounds ready to drop. "You can't fill from an empty well, and if the last couple years have been as draining as they sound, you're empty. Please lean on us. Let us feel your pain with you and help you through it."

Her words are so similar to Paige's earlier concerns about me taking care of everyone but myself that I wonder if they've already all talked about this without me. And I also wonder if maybe they're right?

"All right," Paige says, and I can tell by the strained sound of her voice how choked up she is. "It's official. You have the best friends in the world. And also, I'm staying."

I can feel my eyes bulge. "What do you mean, you're staying?"

"I'm going to change my flight and stay for another week or so. Morgan's practically been living here for the last two weeks. I *want* to be here," she says when I start to shake my head no, "to help out too."

My first inclination, of course, is that I don't want to inconvenience her. But I do want my sister around. "You really don't mind?"

"Mind spending more time with my sister and nieces? Yeah, that's a real hardship," she says, brushing my concerns away with a sweep of her hand through the air.

My friends all offer to take turns coming out here and staying with me if I need them to, and for the first time since they all moved away, I feel like I truly have people in my corner. Maybe I'll get through this okay after all.

# Chapter Five

## JAMESON

The look of shock on Lauren's face as she cracks open the heavy wooden front door would be priceless, but I'm too focused on her bloodshot eyes and her wild red hair pulled back into a messy bun to enjoy her reaction.

"What are you doing here at"—she glances at her watch, which is big and looks exactly like something Josh would have bought for her—"seven thirty in the morning?"

I hand her the caramel latte in a take-out cup and hope it's still her favorite. A lot can change in four years. When her hands clasp around it, I reach beyond her to push open the door, stepping into her space as she backs up with a sigh.

"Thanks." Her voice is a perfect combination of grateful and annoyed. "Come on in, I guess."

"Are you doing okay?" I ask as I shut the door behind me.

She doesn't take her eyes off me as she takes a drink of her latte, then lowers it and lets out a deep sigh of pleasure, looks me up and down, and says, "Yeah, I'm just fantastic. So, what are you doing in my house, exactly?"

"I'm sorry for coming by so early. But I'm only in town for the morning, and I wanted to make sure you have a copy of the will and trust and see if you have any questions."

Her eyebrows dip in confusion. "I haven't slept more than a few hours a night since Josh—" She forces down a deep gulp that has me focusing on the smooth, creamy skin along her neck. "—died. So maybe I'm not processing what you're saying. What trust?"

I glance around, taking in the modern mountain house that looks like it could have been featured on some sort of design show. It's cold steel and warm wood. It's big and ostentatious. Just like Josh. Not at all like Lauren.

"The one Josh set up, along with the will, to protect all your assets in case anything should happen to either of you."

Confusion flickers in those deep blue eyes. I don't know what I expected after more than four years of no communication, but it wasn't this.

"Oh." She pauses. "Why are you . . . I mean, what's your role in all of this?"

"Josh asked me to be the executor. Why do you sound like you don't know what I'm talking about?"

"Because this is the first I'm hearing of it." She closes her eyes and takes a deep breath, then looks up and me. "All right, let's sit down and you can explain this to me." She turns and walks into the kitchen, and I follow her.

She rounds the huge island and pulls out a barstool, gesturing for me to take a seat. Then she walks past it and pulls one out for herself, leaving a stool between us. I set my bag on the seat she left as a barrier and glance over at her. She's wearing sage-green joggers and a matching top. She looks like she just rolled out of bed, but she's beautiful nonetheless. I hate myself a little for noticing—then again, I've never *not* noticed.

I watch as she touches her coffee cup to her lips, tilts her head back, and swallows. She catches me watching her as she lowers the cup to the counter, and her eyebrows scrunch up again in confusion or suspicion—it's impossible to tell which.

"Let's rewind for a second," she says, crossing her arms over her abdomen. But then her eyes fill with tears and she looks away.

I reach out and rest my hand on her shoulder, surprised and concerned when I discover how bony it is. "Hey." I wait for her to return my gaze, but she doesn't look at me.

Her breathing is deep and labored when she finally glances up and tells me, "I didn't know Josh was in Sun Valley. That's not where he was supposed to be. I also didn't know he had a trust." Her voice—normally light and happy—shakes with emotion, and I can tell how much it pains her to have to admit this, especially to me. "These both feel like things a husband should tell his wife."

I pull my hand back, and it takes everything I have not to react with my true feelings about Josh. There's no way I'm going to trash-talk the man to his widow, but I have no idea how I *should* respond to this revelation, so I focus on the business side of things instead. "Are you sure he never told you about the trust?"

"I don't know. He was always telling me about our finances, different investments, the endorsement contracts. . ." She pauses, like she's trying to remember. "So maybe he mentioned it, but if so, I don't remember. He always just took care of that stuff."

She glances out the large kitchen windows. Beyond them

is a bluestone patio surrounded by evergreens. String lights are hung from the house to the trees, and the way they are catching the rising sun makes them appear to glow bright orange.

"I assumed you knew about it and knew I was the executor. The fact that you didn't . . . I guess that explains why you were surprised to see me here."

"Should I be worried that my husband set up a trust and didn't tell me about it?"

"I'm sure he set it up because he *didn't* want you to worry," I say, not at all sure but wanting to put her mind at ease anyway. When Josh asked me to be the executor, I'd assumed Lauren was involved in that decision. It never occurred to me to ask, mostly because I'd spent the previous four years, since they got engaged and she left Boston, intentionally *not* asking about her.

She takes another deep breath, then lets out a little smile. "I'm being ridiculous. Setting up a trust to make sure the girls and I were taken care of is such a classic Josh move. Of course he had one. So what is it that I need to know, then?" she asks.

"It's all in here," I say, taking the binder out of my bag and sliding it along the counter until it rests in front of her.

I'm starting to feel that sense of panic I sometimes get when other people's emotions are out of my control, and sitting here knowing there's nothing I can do to take away her pain is killing me. I should never have introduced them in the first place—something I knew the instant the introduction left my mouth.

"You should take some time to read it," I tell her. "Then call me and we can discuss any questions you have, or any next steps."

I move my foot from the rung of the stool to the floor and shift my weight as I stand, torn between wanting to be near her and wanting to get as far away as possible.

"Wait!"

Her tongue glides across her lower lip, and I can't tear my eyes away from the sight until she turns away and looks out the kitchen window again.

I'm spending so much energy trying not to think about how it feels to be back in her presence—the unmistakable scent of vanilla that clings to her skin, the way her eyes change like the color of the ocean does in different lights and depth, how she always bites her lower lip when she's thinking —that my voice comes out almost strangled as I ask, "Yeah?"

She shakes her head like she's trying to clear something out of there. "Never mind."

"Okay." I lift my bag off the stool and look down at her. As much as I try to reassure myself that she's going to be okay, that Josh did the right thing here, I can't help but worry that there's something that doesn't add up.

"So, what are the next steps?" she asks.

"Now you'll become the sole owner of all assets, so there will be a shit-ton of paperwork. You'll need to see an estate lawyer about putting all the assets into a new trust, so that everything that now belongs solely to you is left to the girls, and you'll want to name a guardian in case anything were to ever happen to you. I'll help make sure that everything is set up correctly for the future. After that, you can choose a new executor for your new trust."

She opens her mouth to respond, but the doorbell rings right then, and her head snaps over to look at a video monitor I didn't notice sitting on the counter. It looks almost exactly like the one we had for Graham when he was a baby. And it appears that both little girls are still sleeping.

"I've got to get the door," she says. But before she's even out of her seat, her sister is walking into the kitchen.

"Door's unlocked," Paige says airily as she walks in, wheeling a suitcase behind her, then stops when she notices me sitting there. "Oh, hi, Jameson. I didn't know you'd be here." She sets a bag that appears to be from a local bagel shop on the counter.

Lauren's narrowed eyes glance back and forth between us. "You two know each other?"

"We met yesterday at the luncheon after the funeral," I tell her. I don't mention that her sister was flirting with me until she realized I wasn't flirting back.

"Hmm," Lauren replies, and I wish I could figure out what she means when she rolls that sound around in the back of her throat. I'd also love to know why it still has the same effect on me—like someone dragging their fingertips lightly over my bare skin—that it always has.

Actually, I know why: I'm an asshole. And I'm still coveting the person I can't have, even five years later.

"Jameson was just telling me about Josh's trust," Lauren tells Paige. "Which I didn't know existed until a few minutes ago."

"Oh." The sound is a breathy whoosh of air leaving Paige's mouth.

"Yeah," Lauren says, and the two share a look that, again, I can't interpret.

"I thought I smelled food," another voice says from the doorway. I turn and catch a glimpse of a woman whose strawberry-blond hair is in a ponytail, and she's wearing a cropped sweatshirt and a baggy pair of flannel pajama pants. "Oh," she says when we lock eyes. "I didn't realize we had company."

There are so many looks passing between the three of them, and so much estrogen in the room, that I'm ready to get the hell out of here. Plus, I need to catch a flight to St. Louis because while I was asleep last night, one of my hockey players decided to go and get himself a DUI—luckily no one else was hurt—and now I have a mess to clean up.

"This is Jameson," Lauren tells her. "He was Josh's agent." Again, those blue eyes are glassy with unshed tears, and I wonder how long it will be until she can say his name without tearing up. How long *should* it be?

"Hi," she says, "I'm Morgan. Lauren's cousin."

"Carson's daughter?" I can't hide my surprise. Lauren's uncle and our former boss, Carson, is big and bald, and she looks nothing like him except for her eyes—they are exactly the same shade and shape as his.

Morgan rolls her eyes and crosses her arms over her chest. "You know my dad?"

"I used to work for him at Kaplan." I don't mention that he was my agent back when I played in the NHL, or how he took me under his wing and taught me the ropes of agenting after my early retirement from hockey.

"I'm sorry," Morgan says, her voice tinged with sarcasm. Carson's like that—people either love him or hate him. But I don't get the sense that Morgan hates him, just that she knows what he's like.

"Don't be. I learned a lot from him and then moved on."

Lauren is quiet, and when I glance over at her, she's staring at me with an unreadable expression on her face. I have no idea if she knows that things didn't end well between me and Carson because by the time I branched out and started my own agency she had already followed Josh to Park City and married him.

"I better get going," I say as I step away from the counter, "I have a flight to catch."

Not much makes me uncomfortable, but standing between three women who are shooting each other looks I can't interpret is putting me on edge.

I turn toward Lauren. "I'll get you the name of Josh's estate lawyer and his financial adviser. You'll want to talk to both of them. Just let me know if you want me to be part of either of those conversations, and we can arrange a call."

"Thanks," she says, her voice flat and eyes lifeless.

She looks . . . haunted. I'm not prepared for how much it hurts seeing her like this. I miss the way I used to get her fired up by fighting with her—the way her cheeks would turn pink when she got angry, the way her eyes narrowed and grew darker, like the sea before a storm. Pissing her off was my favorite part of my job during the years we worked together at Kaplan.

Then, one night changed everything and the next night I introduced her to Josh.

That should have been the end of our story.

I need to get back to that place where she's a distant memory, someone I used to know rather than someone who's taking up every spare second of thought.

First, I need to execute this trust. Then there will be nothing tying me to her and I can finally walk away for good.

# Chapter Six

## LAUREN

I slink back against the padded booth seat to avoid the beer-soaked breath of the guy sitting next to me. I'm pretty sure his name is Brad, and while his friend is flirting with my sister, Brad does not seem to be taking the hint that I'm not interested.

Telling him I was recently widowed elicited an "I'm so sorry," but didn't deter him at all. So I rub at the side of my face with my left hand, making sure my ring catches the light. Maybe if I blind him with it, he'll back off.

I kick Paige under the table and she glances over at me, giving me a small smile, and I try not to be aggravated in return. She's been helping me all week—caring for my girls, catching up on her own work during their nap times, playing with them while I make phone calls, schedule appointments, and run errands as I navigate the part of death no one tells you about: the paperwork nightmare.

I get it. Paige is single, and a cute guy is paying attention to her. But this was supposed to be our last dinner together before she goes back to Boston.

My phone lights up on the table, and I snatch it up like it's an emergency.

"I'm so sorry," I say to Brad as I scoot out of my seat and stand. All three sets of eyes look up at me. "I've got to take this call."

I answer the phone on the second ring, even though my mother-in-law is the last person on the planet I want to speak to. I'd give anything to hear her son's voice on the other end of the phone one last time. Hers, not so much.

But I'm so desperate to get away from Brad that I don't even consider letting it go to voice mail.

"Hello?"

"Hello, Lauren." My mother-in-law's greeting is followed by silence. I treat perfect strangers with more warmth than she's ever shown me.

"Hi, Barb. How are you?" I hold the phone against my ear as I make my way through the busy restaurant, hoping the hallway that leads to the bathroom will be quieter.

"Are you . . . out?"

"It's my sister's last night here, so I've taken her out to dinner."

"Oh, well, that must be nice . . . going out." There is no mistaking the judgment in her voice, and the guilt washes over me at the implication that I shouldn't be out doing something fun—or something that *should* be fun, if it weren't for the idiots that decided to just come sit at our table with us—when her son is gone and can't do the same.

I don't respond, because if four years as part of her family has taught me anything, it's that you don't disagree with Barb Emerson.

"I'm calling because I overheard you talking to your

friends the other day about the possibility of moving to Boston."

I hope she can't hear the deep gulp that resounds in my throat.

I'd honestly expected to hear from her about that immediately, and I'd started to relax when she didn't call the next day, or any day since. I can't know for certain whether it was intentional, but it certainly feels like she waited almost a week to call just so she could catch me off guard. "Um hmm."

"I'm not sure what game you're playing."

I wait for her to follow it up with more details, but she leaves it at that.

"What do you mean?" I work hard to keep my voice light and friendly, despite the fact that she's only ever treated me like I'm trash.

I'm not sure what she's mad about this time, but I'm guessing it's the idea of me moving her grandchildren across the country. She loves the idea of grandkids, but God forbid she actually show up more than once every few months and spend any time with them. Aside from the funeral, we haven't seen her once since Josh died.

"I mean that we own half that house, and I don't want you to think for a second that you are going to sell it and skip town with the money."

My back hits the wood-paneled wall as my knees almost buckle under me. It's like my body can't do anything—not even hold my own weight—while I try to make sense of her words.

"I'm sorry, what?"

"Which part of what I said requires explaining?"

I swallow down the scream that's rising in my throat. "The part about you owning half my house."

"Well, of course," she says, and I can just picture her blond bob swinging as she juts her chin out. "Obviously, since you and Josh didn't want a mortgage and we loaned you half the cost of the property and the house you built on it, we therefore own half the house."

Is she making this up? "What do you mean, we didn't *want* a mortgage? Josh said we didn't *need* one."

"Well, with you not working and Josh having to support you and a growing family," she says, doing nothing to hide her snide tone, "we needed to help out so you could have the house of your dreams."

The house of my dreams, my ass. I was perfectly happy with our condo downtown and loved living in the same building as Jackson and Sierra. Josh was the one who wanted the big house in the mountains.

I hesitate for a moment, trying to collect my thoughts, before asking, "So how much *did* you loan him, exactly?"

"A million dollars. He was able to come up with the rest from what he'd earned skiing, and since then from sponsorships. It's too bad you had no income and couldn't have helped out . . ."

I'd had a very successful career before I met Josh, and I gave it up and moved to Park City to marry him. She has always acted like I was some sort of gold digger. I wanted to start working when I moved here, but Josh always had a reason I should wait to get a job.

First, it was that I was too busy planning the wedding. Then he wanted to extend our honeymoon phase and have me travel with him throughout Europe during ski season. It was a wonderfully romantic notion, but it would also have been quite isolating if Jackson hadn't been his physical therapist and we hadn't formed a quick and close friendship traveling together that winter. Then, it was that we wanted kids, and it didn't make sense to get a job that I'd just have to quit when a child came along, because we both wanted me to be able to stay home with the baby. I didn't know it was going to take us so long to get pregnant. It wasn't like I ever planned to be a stay-at-home wife.

". . . then we wouldn't have to be involved in this now," she finally continues.

I'm afraid to ask—*afraid to know*—what my mother-in-law thinks "being involved" looks like.

I stand up from where I was half-slumped against the wall and take a fortifying breath. "Can you please send me any paperwork you and Josh signed when you gave him the money? This is the first I'm hearing about it."

She scoffs.

"I assume you didn't just hand over a million dollars without some sort of paperwork in place," I say, straightening to my full height. I've never before stood up to her. She's spent the last several years picking apart every single thing about me, and I've held my tongue through it all because she's Josh's mother.

That stops now.

"Of course our lawyer drew up paperwork," she says.

"Great, I look forward to seeing it. You have my email. Have a good evening," I tell her. And when I end the call, I don't even feel a little bit bad about hanging up on her.

I find our waitress on my way back to the table, and ask her to bring me the bill immediately. When I make it back to the table, the cute guy is still there talking to Paige, but thank-fully Brad is gone.

"Paige, we've got to go," I tell her. She looks up, ready to object, but when she sees my face she just nods and turns toward the guy, giving him her number.

"What happened?" she asks as soon as he's gone.

I slide into the booth across the table from her chair. "That was Barb."

"Josh's mom?" she asks, as if there could be any other Barb calling me. But given how much my mother-in-law dislikes me, Paige's surprise at the impromptu call isn't unwarranted.

"Yeah," I say as the waitress arrives with the check. I pull out my card and hand it to her without even looking at the bill. I don't care what it says; I just want to get out of here.

"What did she want?" Paige asks once the waitress is gone.

"To tell me that she owns half my house."

"The fuck?" The words are practically silent, expelled on an exhale that never seems to end—it's like this news deflates Paige as much as it deflates me.

"I guess it's a good thing I'm meeting with the financial adviser tomorrow. I need to see if I can afford to buy her out. . ." I consider the alternative. "Or whether I have to sell my house to pay her back."

"You were thinking about selling your house anyway, weren't you?" Paige asks.

"Yeah, but I thought that money would be used to buy us a new house, and maybe that we could live off the rest of it for a while."

"Even if you only walk away with half the value of your

house," Paige says, as she reaches across the table and squeezes my hand in hers, "you're going to be okay. That's still an awful lot of money."

"I know. And I still need to figure out the life insurance, and all that." I sigh. "We're going to be fine. I just . . . I wasn't expecting this."

"And somehow," Paige says, "I bet you're still not surprised."

"Oh, I'm surprised. And confused. Why would Josh want to build this huge house that we couldn't afford? And now that I think about it, why couldn't we afford it? I know what our investment portfolios looked like, especially after we sold the condo. He should have already paid his parents back, and I don't understand why he didn't . . . or why I didn't know about any of this."

"I meant that you probably weren't surprised that less than a week after burying her son, Barb's already trying to screw you over."

Even in my shocked state, that does get a chuckle out of me. "When it comes to her, nothing should surprise me."

"C'mon," Paige says as I sign the receipt the waitress has set in front of me. "Let's get you home. We can talk about this more and strategize for that meeting with the financial adviser tomorrow."

She wraps her arm around me as we walk out of the restaurant, and I rest my head on her shoulder wishing she didn't have to leave. I'm doing what my friends asked and trying to give it time before making a big decision, but moving to Boston is sounding better and better every day.

---

"Are you sure you're okay?" Paige asks, her voice so quiet she's practically speaking under her breath. I hate the way she's looking at me like I'm a fragile piece of china and someone's about to drop me.

I glance around the financial planner's office, where we're sitting as we wait for him to go get some documents off the printer. I'm not at all sure that I'm okay, and I wonder if I ever will be again.

"He just told me that my husband has had almost no income for the last few years since he retired from racing, and has been slowly selling off what's in our investment accounts to live off. What the hell happened to his endorsements?" I fume, as if Paige could answer that for me. I bite my lower lip to stop it from trembling. I will not cry in this office.

"I'm so sorry. I didn't realize he'd lied to you about anything, much less something so—" she stops speaking as Henry, the financial adviser, returns with a small stack of papers in his hand.

"I've printed out the balance on all the investment accounts," he says, "along with any transactions in the last two years, so you can see when Josh sold off investments and how much he made from each transaction."

"Thanks," I say, taking the papers Henry's holding out. I tuck them under one arm, then stand and reach out to shake his hand. "I'll let you know what we decide to do with the accounts."

I don't know if I even breathe until we're back in my car. And then all the adrenaline that's been holding me together feels like it leaves my system, and I collapse back against the passenger seat, close my eyes, and let the tears flow.

Paige pulls out of our parking spot and is driving through town when I finally open my eyes and glance down at my lap.

"What the hell?!"

"What?" she asks, slamming on the brakes way harder than necessary to stop for the red light ahead.

"Look at this," I say, holding the papers out. "Look at the address these statements are being delivered to."

"Josh Emerson, PO Box 27834," she reads.

"We don't have a PO Box."

The air leaves her with a hiss. "Shit."

"Well, this explains a thing or two about how Josh kept all of this from me. No wonder I didn't come across any of the financial stuff in the mail."

"Do you want to go check it out?"

"Do we have time? Don't you need to head to Salt Lake City in like an hour to catch your flight home?"

She looks at me like I suggested she run naked through the streets. "Like I'd leave you in this moment, right after you just discovered all this . . ."

"Okay, yeah. Let me just text Morgan and see if she can stay with the girls a little longer."

We head to the post office, and I feel like I'm on autopilot —my emotions frozen and unable to process everything I've learned—as I explain the situation and show them a copy of the trust naming me as the beneficiary of all assets, along with Josh's death certificate. I fill out the paperwork to transfer ownership, and they give me a stack of mail, which I flip through quickly as I wait for them to get me a new key for the PO Box. And the thing that catches my eye is an unmarked envelope like you'd get from a bank, with something stamped in red peeking out through the clear address window.

I somehow manage to wait until we're back in the car before I tear the envelope open. Then I look over at Paige, eyes wide in terror as I hold up the statement for a mortgage I didn't know we had on our home so she can see the big red "Past Due" stamp on it.

# Chapter Seven

## JAMESON

*Boston, MA*

> **LAUREN**
> Do you have a minute?

I flip my phone over and glance at the message for the fourth time, then set the phone back facedown on the kitchen table.

"What the hell's going on?" Jules asks as she tucks a loose strand of her blond hair behind her ear and reaches for my empty plate. "You getting another booty call? It better not be from that bitchy blonde I kicked out of here last weekend."

"Please don't remind me." I swirl my glass of scotch, watching as the amber liquid coats the edges of the glass. As I often do, I've poured myself a glass after dinner and I'll sip it slowly, never drinking the whole thing. Call it a test of my willpower, like I do, or my need to prove I'm not my father, as my therapist does—either way, there's alcohol in front of me and I've still never been drunk.

"It was 4 a.m. and you were having a full-out screaming match in the hallway. You're lucky it was me you woke up and not Audrey or Graham . . ." Jules trails off as she carries our dishes across the antique cross-and-star-patterned terracotta tiled floors to the sink, not needing to finish the sentence because we both know what Graham is like—the kid is awesome, as long as he gets enough sleep. If he doesn't, it's like he's been replaced with a demonic changeling.

"We weren't having a screaming match—*she* was the only one yelling. I was trying to calm her down."

Bringing a woman back to my place is never not a mistake. Not when my two nosy sisters live downstairs and said woman wants to spend the night. Staying over is a hard no, in my book, and something I'm always upfront about.

"Yeah," Jules says, setting the plates in the sink and turning to look at me. "Because when in the course of human history has a woman ever been calmed by having a man tell her to *calm the fuck down*?" She pads across the floor in her fuzzy socks with her leggings tucked inside. With her oversized sweatshirt hanging off one shoulder and her blond hair up in a messy bun, she looks more like a college student than the co-owner of one of Boston's most up-and-coming construction companies. "C'mon, I raised you better than that."

"You're such a smart-ass." I roll my eyes as she walks back and collapses into her chair across from me, a big smile on her face. My sisters love to throw things I once said to them, like *I raised you better than that*, back at me. But she's right. I should have known better. "Won't happen again."

And it truly won't. It's just not worth the effort. From now on, if I pick up a woman at a bar, I'm going to her place even if my place is much closer, as was the case last weekend. That way, when I'm ready to head to my bed alone and she decides to start throwing shit, she can break her own stuff and we won't risk waking up my family.

"So who is it?" Jules tilts her chin toward my phone. It's taking everything I have not to pick it up and look at it a fifth time. Seeing Lauren's name is bringing up way too many emotions.

"The wife of a client."

"How would he feel about his wife texting you?" She could be joking, but it doesn't really sound like it.

"Since he's dead . . ." I shrug.

"Oh shit, Jameson." She slaps the table. "I was teasing. Are you serious?"

I nod and then rub my fingers across my forehead, hoping the pressure will relieve some of the tension that's building there.

"Why don't you seem more upset?"

"Because I like him even less now that he's dead."

"Jeez," Jules says. "What the hell happened?"

I can't possibly explain my history with Lauren. How five years ago we had dinner together and everything changed between us, but the next day my whole life was flipped upside down, and then I stupidly introduced her to Josh.

How six months later they were engaged, and I cornered her at work in the middle of her going away party to tell her how disappointed I was that she was making herself small to fit into the mold of the woman Josh wanted. How I insisted she was too fucking talented to waste her energy on becoming a Stepford Wife.

And then how it felt seeing her last weekend, a hollowed

out version of herself—not because of his death, but because he'd made her that way. She'd gone from being fierce and fiery, to completely docile. And I hated myself for how I'd let him dull her spark, and even more for how I knew I'd do anything to bring it back. Even if it meant burning myself in the process.

But I can't tell Jules any of that.

"He was skiing out of bounds and got caught up in an avalanche," I tell Jules, even though I know that's not the answer to the question she was asking.

She doesn't press me to elaborate, even though I can see her curiosity written across her face. "So why is she texting you?"

"Because in addition to being his agent, I am the executor of his will and trust."

"Is that normal? Like, do you do that for all your clients?"

"No. The fact that he didn't have a family member or close friend that he'd ask to do this, instead of me, speaks volumes."

I swirl the scotch around in my glass before taking a small sip. Now in the latter half of my thirties, I'm finally—sort of—learning to not hate the taste.

Another text has my phone buzzing in my hand, and I glance down to see *her* name on my screen again.

LAUREN

It's important.

"I need to make a call," I say to Jules, but I'm already up and heading toward the living room.

I take a seat on the arm of the sofa farthest from my sister, and turn toward the wide glass doors leading out to the very small backyard behind our brownstone.

When Lauren answers the phone, it's with a breathy "Hello?" that has so many memories running through my mind it's almost hard to respond.

"You okay?" The words come out sounding rougher than I intend.

She lets out a stuttered, heaving, "No?"

The fact that her response is a question has all the alarm bells going off in my mind. I lower my voice. "What's wrong, Lauren?" God, I hate thinking of her in that huge house in the mountains, all by herself with those babies.

"I'm fine. But I'm . . . I don't even have the words." She's definitely been crying, and it's like she can't even form a complete thought.

"Would you just tell me what's going on?"

"I had a meeting with our financial adviser a few days ago, and *one* of the things I learned is that my husband had virtually no income for the past few years since he retired."

I already knew this, so I'm tempted to ask her what *other* things she learned, but it's really none of my business. "And. . .?"

"And what the fuck, Jameson? You were supposed to be managing his career. What happened to his endorsements?"

"Lauren." The way I say her name, soft but chiding, she knows. She knows what I'm going to say next. "You know this industry. What does it take for someone to carry major endorsements into retirement?"

Silence.

"Name recognition," she says softly. "Brand partnerships. Product endorsements."

Josh was a well-known skier at one point in his career, but he waited to retire until his career was dwindling. And he never had the name recognition that some US skiers achieve, so when his endorsement contracts were up, most of the brands didn't renew. He understood that's just how it goes.

"He did have a few small endorsements, still." But clearly not what he'd led her to believe.

"Okay, so along with that, I've learned a few things that don't make sense with the trust."

I'd read that thing cover to cover when Josh sent it to originally, and again on the plane on the way out to Utah for the funeral. It was straightforward and solid. "Like what?"

"Well, the short version is, Josh borrowed half the money for our home from his parents, then just a few months ago he took out a reverse mortgage on our house for the other half of the home value. Which means I pretty much have zero equity in this house."

*Well shit.*

"And apparently we now own a house in Boston," she says, then pauses, "well, Brookline, actually. But that house isn't in the trust."

"How did you figure this all out?"

She explains about finding the mortgage statement in the PO Box, then the convoluted process of reviewing their tax returns only to find out they paid property taxes on a second property, going through papers she found hidden in Josh's office closet, and eventually tracking down the deed for a house here in Massachusetts.

"I just . . . I can't imagine how he'd pull all the equity out of our house without telling me. Or how he used that money to buy a new house, also without telling me? Or how he did this while our house was in the trust?"

I stand and start pacing the living room because I can't sit still while I'm talking about my former client doing something so underhanded and dishonest.

"I don't know the ins and outs of estate law, but I'm sure it's possible to remortgage a property that's in a trust. The point of the trust is to protect the assets after death, not to prevent you from accessing those assets while still alive. But why would he buy a house in Boston?"

She sighs, but it isn't an unhappy sound. "I'd been saying I wanted to move back to Boston for months. And it seems like maybe he was planning this really big surprise to give me exactly what I wanted."

"Was Josh the type to plan a surprise this huge?"

Behind me, I hear Audrey come back from putting Graham to sleep, and she and Jules are talking in hushed tones.

"Yeah, he loved grand gestures. The bigger, the better. But this is . . . I don't know how to explain it. Like on the one hand, he was planning to give me what he knew I needed. And on the other hand, there were some enormous secrets he was keeping, and that feels wrong." She exhales, and I can picture the tears rolling down her face.

I wonder what she means that moving to Boston was what she "needed," but I don't feel like it's my place to ask, or that she'd tell me even if I did.

"It doesn't mean anything was wrong," I tell her as I slide the glass door to our backyard open and step out onto the brick landing, because I don't want my sisters eavesdropping on this call any more than they already have. We don't normally keep secrets from each other, but these are Lauren's secrets, not mine. "He probably just wanted to surprise you with the house. Maybe he was going to give this to you as an anniversary gift?"

Do I wish I didn't have their anniversary date memorized? Yes. But did I spend months looking at it stuck to my fridge with a magnet, debating whether to attend? Also yes. Ultimately, I declined, because I know a thing or two about self-preservation.

She lets out a sound I can only describe as a strangled sob. "I don't know what I'm going to do," she practically whispers. "He's left me with no assets except a house in Boston I didn't even know about."

"I'll help you figure it out," I tell her, even as I tell myself to shut the hell up. But I know I can be the support she needs, and this is what I agreed to when I said I'd be the executor of this trust, wasn't it? "Given all this new info, do you think it makes sense to move out here?"

My entire body hums, the blood rushing through my veins at a ridiculously fast pace, at the idea of having her back in my city. She's just lost her husband. She's in no place to be thinking about me the way I'm thinking about her.

"Yeah, probably. I was already seriously considering it, and this feels like the universe—or Josh, maybe—sending me a message that it's the right decision." There's the briefest pause, then she asks, "Did you really mean what you said about helping me figure all this out?"

"As a general rule, I don't say things I don't mean."

She sighs, and I know she's holding back comments she might have about our past.

"Do you think you could swing by and look at the house

for me?" she asks. "I'd ask Paige, but she's been here for over a week, and she's heading back to Boston to basically repack her suitcase and leave on a business trip. I don't think I could ask her to squeeze this in too."

"Sure. Send me the address and I'll swing by and take a look."

"Thanks," she says. "Maybe you could text some pictures of the outside? And peek in the windows to see what it's like. I'm going to see if I can find the listing so I can see more photos, and I'll start the process of getting the deed transferred into my name."

"I'll stop by this weekend and let you know what I find out."

"Jameson," she says my name quietly, almost like she's not sure what to say. "Thank you. I don't know how you got roped into this, but I appreciate your help."

"You know . . ." I clear my throat so the words I was ready to say—that I'd do anything to help her—stay in me, where they belong. "You know I'm happy to help."

"All right." She sounds like she's stalling, but then says, "Thanks again. And, goodnight."

"'Night." I hang up the phone, and it isn't lost on me that my sisters are both sitting at the table with their chins propped on their fists, watching me intently as I step back through that door into the family room.

"We have so many questions," Audrey says.

"Too bad. I'm going upstairs."

"Hey," Jules objects, crossing her arms over her chest. "I made dinner. That means you're batting cleanup."

"That's not what that expression means," I say as I close the distance between us. "How can you possibly know so little about sports when your brother was a professional athlete?"

"How can you know so little about carpentry when you literally own a construction company?"

If I didn't love her so much, I'd probably want to strangle her.

"I own it in name only." Getting the company out of my dad's name so it could be saved for my sisters, like they'd always wanted, was the first thing I did after he finally left for good. At that point, he'd drained the business of all its cash, and I'd had to pay off a shit-ton of his subcontractors to avoid liens and lawsuits. But it's saved, and it's theirs now even if technically I still own a majority share of the company.

I head to the sink, rolling the sleeves of my dress shirt up as I go. "Alexa, play 'Bohemian Rhapsody,'" I say, and when the song fills the room and my sisters can't resist singing along like they always do, I know it means I'll be safe from any more questions about Lauren. For now.

———

The brick house sits up a hill and back from the street. The front yard is overgrown with ground ivy that's taking over the brick retaining wall on either side of the steps leading from the sidewalk to the walkway. When I reach the top of the steps, I see the small details that show me the house and the yard were once well loved—the ceramic house numbers sitting vertically on the trim of the front porch, the ornate light that hangs near the front door, and the brick trim that lines the front lawn. There's a big maple tree whose huge leafless branches loom over the front yard and the porch, and now-dilapidated planter boxes hang from the first-floor windows.

I take the steps onto the front porch two at a time and am impressed at the wide wood floorboards of the porch and the way the beadboard ceiling is painted a pale blue. This house has so much potential. The dark wooden door has a large glass panel at the top, and from what I can see through there and through the first-floor windows off the porch, the house is almost entirely gutted. Which makes sense, given the permit taped to the inside of the window and the big wooden sign staked into the grass in front of the house.

Mike Woods Contracting.

Woody, as everyone calls him, was a friend of my father's and the last time we spoke, literal punches were thrown. How is this world so small that, out of all the contractors in Boston, Josh managed to hire one who knew my father?

I pull my phone from my pocket, both wishing I didn't have to make this call and also strangely looking forward to it at the same time.

"Mike Woods," the gruff voice carries through the phone, and I'm relieved he answered. Must mean I'm not in his contacts, so he doesn't know it's me.

"Hey, Woody, it's Jameson Flynn."

"You find the trophy, you little fuck-a?" Woody's thick Boston accent and two-pack a day habit sometimes make it hard to understand him. But he's coming through loud and clear this morning.

My father and Woody were on a weirdly competitive bowling team together for nearly two decades, and their claim to fame—besides how many beers they could drink and still bowl a nearly perfect game—was that they'd won the league championships five years in a row. The winning team got their name engraved on a trophy that dated back to 1965 and got to keep it until the next year's championship. Somewhere in the chaos of my dad leaving town, that trophy disappeared.

"Jesus, Woody, was it plated in real gold or something?" He acts like my father lost the Stanley Cup. "That trophy is long gone, just like my father."

"What the hell are you calling me about, then?"

"Funny story," I say as I take another look through the windows into the house, "but I'm standing on the front porch of a property you're working on in Brookline. Nice brick house set up a hill."

"You know Josh Emerson?" His voice is distinctly hostile.

"I *knew* him. He passed away a couple weeks ago."

"Shit," Woody rasps. "That asshole owed me eight grand. I stopped work because he didn't pay his last bill."

"Hard to do from the grave," I say. "What'll it take for you to come remove this sign from the yard and the permit from the property?"

"Eight grand. Why? You gonna pay me?"

"If you walk away from this job, yeah." The money to settle this account should come from the estate, but since the house wasn't in the trust and Lauren certainly doesn't have the money right now, my life is easier if I pay him to walk away. "If you can meet me here in an hour with the house key and a copy of the contract you had with Josh, I'll have your eight grand for you."

He grunts, and I know he doesn't want to give me the satisfaction of him running over here to get his money, but he also wants to be paid. "Fine," he says, and the line goes dead.

The front porch appears to have at one time wrapped around the side of the house closest to the driveway, but that side has now been finished off with floor-to-ceiling windows. I press my face up close to the glass and notice that this room hasn't been demoed, possibly because it's newer? It looks like it might be right off the kitchen, so it could be a good playroom for the girls.

I shoot a text off to Derek with the wording of a quick agreement to terminate Woody's contract to work on this house, which I need him to draw up and send back to me; then I dial Jules's number.

She sounds distracted when she answers the call, so I say what I know will capture her attention. "Boy do I have a project for you."

"I don't have the time or capacity for another project, Jameson. I have a six-month waitlist and people asking for us to take on their projects every day."

"I'm not asking."

"Oh?" Annoyance flashes through the single word.

"Let's say I'm calling in a favor."

She scoffs. "I don't owe you a favor big enough . . ." Her voice trails off as the realization hits.

"Vegas." The one word is all I need to say.

"Well, that's the nuclear option, isn't it?" Jules's reaction is just as pissy as I'd expect it to be at my resurrecting this memory.

"It is."

"What is so important that you'd call in *that* particular favor?"

"You'll see. Can you meet me in Brookline now?"

"Really? It's Saturday morning," Jules complains, even

though I know she's been on the couch with her laptop, working on ordering supplies and invoicing customers since before I even woke up.

"Yeah."

"Can I wear my pajamas, at least?"

"Suit yourself. But bring your tool belt."

"Have I mentioned I don't have time for this?" she says, and sighs.

"How many times do I need to say 'Vegas' before you actually get your ass over here?"

I can hear her snap her laptop shut. "Say it again and you're on your own for whatever this project is. Ask nicely, and I *might* come over right now."

I take the stairs down the front porch. "*Please* get your ass over here. And check your email first. Derek's sending you some paperwork that I need you to print out and bring with you."

She mutters something about how she really doesn't want to know what's going on, then disconnects the call. Meanwhile, I follow the driveway along the side of the house. There's an older garage set back in the corner of the property and a low fence that runs between it and the house. Beyond that, there's a nice-size backyard and a deck that comes off the back of the house.

Even without going inside yet, I already know that this house is much more Lauren than the Park City house was. And I hate Josh a little less now that I know he picked a place she'd love. Maybe he was doing the right thing after all.

# Chapter Eight

## LAUREN

*Brookline, MA*

I pause on the front porch, wondering if I should wait out here. There's a slight breeze this morning, and it's blowing the fluffy snow that fell last night off the tree branches. Mid-February in the Northeast is the coldest time of year—too cold to be standing outside with little kids.

"Why isn't Jameson here yet?" Paige asks.

"Well, we *are* like ten minutes early. But I have the code, so I guess we can go in."

I reach over and punch in the six-digit code that Jameson sent me when he had new locks installed on the house. It's my anniversary date—easy to remember, but confusing as to why he knows it.

It feels like we're breaking and entering, even if all the paperwork has gone through and my name is now officially on the deed to the house.

I push the front door open tentatively, and we stand there

looking at the opening for what feels like forever, but is probably only a minute, before we step through.

"It's not"—Paige stands in the entryway with Iris in her arms—"that bad?"

When Iris squirms to get down, Paige hugs her a little closer to her body, as though she's afraid to let her go. I hold Ivy just as tight to me. Having only seen the listing photos, I'd had visions of my daughters running around empty rooms, exploring their new home this morning. Jameson had told me the house still needed some more updating before I moved in, but this is so far from what I expected to see that I don't know what to think.

The entryway is narrow, mostly taken up by a grand staircase with an ornate, rounded post at the bottom. To our right is a sitting room, and the frames of the large windows that face the street have peeling paint, but at least the windows themselves are new. The walls are open to the studs with new wiring and new pipes running between the two-by-fours.

With Ivy on my hip, I walk through the front hallway.

"I don't know what to think at the moment," I say over my shoulder to Paige as she follows me.

"Let's just see what the rest of it looks like." At the end of the hallway, we enter the kitchen. Or, what used to be the kitchen. It's been partially gutted—the cabinets and flooring are gone, and all that remains is an enormous and gorgeous soapstone sink resting on a carved soapstone pedestal under double windows overlooking the backyard.

I slide my hand along it's softly rounded time-worn edges, as I admire the beautiful white veining running through the faded gray stone. No matter what else changes in here, this sink will stay.

Josh had to have known how much I'd love a classic sink like this—that has to be why it's the only thing still in this kitchen. It feels like a gift he intentionally left me in this house he bought for us.

My throat tightens as I imagine him thinking how much I'd love this old-fashioned detail, but then Ivy pulls my hair and says, "Mama, go," as she points to the doorway where Paige—completely unaware of the significance of this sink— has moved to.

"Well, this is kind of lovely," Paige says as she stands in the arched entrance that leads from the kitchen to the dining room.

"Wow, this is more than I expected, based on what we've seen so far," I say as I trail a finger along the glass doors of a dark walnut built-in that runs the entire length of the far wall.

"This view." Paige sighs as she looks out the casement windows above the built-in.

I have to resist the urge to roll my eyes because my sister is not height challenged and can see through them, whereas when I look up all I can see, all around us, are the bare branches of trees. When I mention that, she sighs. "That *is* the view, Chicken."

The nickname grates like it always has, and I shoot a look her way, but given the way her lips turn up at the ends, it seems like my annoyance amuses her. I had knobby knees as a kid and was always craning my neck up to try to see what my taller siblings saw—so they started calling me Chicken and it stuck.

"Chick-chick?" Iris says, craning her own neck to look around the room as if a chicken might be strutting across the floor. Then Ivy leans down so quickly she almost slips out of my arms before I catch her, hugging her to me. "Where chick?" she asks, still trying to get down to go look for a chicken that doesn't exist.

Paige and I lock eyes and burst into laughter.

"No, girls," I say, smoothing my hand over Ivy's hair and smiling at Iris. "No chick-chick here."

"Auntie Paige was just being silly," Paige tells the girls as we walk out of the dining room. "Should we take a look upstairs?"

I'm trying not to be disappointed that we've already seen all there is to see on the first floor: a big front living room off the front hallway, the large but empty kitchen at the end of the hallway, and the dining room off the kitchen. The house is probably the perfect size for the girls and me, but after living in our Park City house for the past few years, it does feel a little on the small side—even though I wanted something smaller and more manageable.

I sold the Park City house fully furnished, which is the only reason I walked away from that property with any money at all. Hopefully, it'll be just enough to fix up this property and furnish it, but I was not anticipating living in a construction zone with two toddlers.

"Wait," I say, looking across the kitchen, "what's that?" I point toward an old exterior door at the opposite end of the room. It's wooden and the stain has faded in places, so it's patchy, but the top third of the door is glass and I'm not seeing trees through it, I'm seeing a ceiling.

As I turn the deadbolt and swing the door open, I'm greeted by a beautiful room that runs the length of the side of the house. It seems like at one point it may have been an exterior side porch, but it's been completely enclosed. The bead-board ceiling is painted a pale blue, and the three exterior walls are made up of enormous floor-to-ceiling windows. It overlooks the driveway, which right now is covered in so much snow it's unusable, and on the opposite side of that are several large evergreen trees blocking the view of the neighboring house.

"This room is amazing," Paige says.

"I'm starting to be able to picture us in this house," I tell her. "I can see the girls playing in this room while I make us dinner . . . you know, once we have an actual kitchen."

"How will you live here until then?" She asks the question that's been percolating in my mind since we stepped foot in the house.

"Hopefully, the contractor can give us a better idea of how long it'll be until we have walls and a kitchen. I mean, people live in their houses while renovating all the time," I say, more to reassure myself than anything.

"With two toddlers?"

"I don't know," I say, then let out a deep sigh. "We'll figure it out the same way we're figuring everything else out—as we go."

One thing I've finally managed, now three months after Josh died, is getting through a day without needing the anxiety medication that got me through the first few weeks. Many days, I can even manage a whole day without crying. His sudden death, and all the unanswered questions surrounding it, still leave me choked up sometimes—though these days it's out of frustration more than anything.

Remodeling a house, finding a job, finding childcare for

the kids . . . these are all things I'll also figure out. And I'll end up stronger for getting through this too.

"Let's go see the upstairs before the contractor gets here. How'd Jameson find him again?"

"I'm not sure. He said he'd explain once I saw the house." At the time, I was so wrapped up in selling my old house, getting this new one into my name, and arranging a cross-country move that I hadn't even thought to push him for more details. I was just grateful he was here to do things I couldn't take care of, like changing the locks and finding a contractor.

The stairs themselves are old and every tread squeaks under our feet as we make our way up. But the minute we hit the landing on the second floor, I feel like I've struck gold because the entire upstairs has already been remodeled.

All four bedrooms off the large landing area are pristine and new, plus it's warm and cozy up here in a way that's markedly different from the downstairs. And the view from the windows is all trees, everywhere you look—it feels like we're moving into a treehouse.

The full bathroom in the hallway is gutted, but the one in the primary bedroom is finished, and it's exactly my style— soft gray honed marble tiles for the walls of the shower with a gray riverstone shower floor, a white double sink vanity with a marble top, and a floor of gray slate tiles.

This couldn't be more different from the style of our bathroom in Park City. It's softer, more feminine, and I can't help but be thrilled that Josh designed this with me in mind, because this bathroom was definitely not in the listing photos.

We're just coming out of the primary bedroom when there's a solid knock on the front door. Figuring it must be the contractor, since Jameson has the code and the only keys, we head downstairs. But when I swing open the door, there's a woman standing there. And she looks as surprised to see me as I am to see her.

She's got on a thermal T-shirt under a heavy flannel, leggings, and steel-toed work boots. Her shiny blond hair is pulled back in a high ponytail, and her face is bare except for some lip gloss and mascara. She's a total knockout, and I'm confused about what she's doing on my porch.

"You must be Lauren," she says with a broad smile as she holds out her hand to me. "I'm Jules."

"Um, hi?" I have no idea how she knows who I am, or what she's doing here.

"I see my brother is late as always," she says. "So you're probably confused about who I am."

I give her a little laugh, because that's exactly how I'm feeling. "Oh, are you my contractor's sister?" I ask.

She gives a small snort and rolls her eyes. "Okay, so Jameson has clearly told you nothing?"

"Wait, you're *Jameson's sister* Jules?"

Years ago, he'd told me about his two little sisters, Audrey and Jules, who he'd raised after their father left. It had been one of the ways he'd opened up to me the night of our dinner —the one I'd thought had been a turning point for us, but in the end, hadn't meant anything to him.

"Yep," she says. "Can I come in and explain why I'm here?"

Jules steps into the entryway, and I introduce her to Paige. And that's when I notice the tool belt hanging around her hips, mostly covered by the open flannel.

"Wait a second," I say. "*You're* the contractor?"

She gives me a dazzling smile, the kind that must knock men right off their feet. She looks like someone who'd be a social media influencer, and I'm already wondering if I should search up her *Get Ready With Me* videos so I can figure out how her skin glows like that. Then again, standing here with her flannel and her tool belt, she doesn't strike me as the type that posts videos of her skincare and makeup routine.

"Yeah. My sister and I run one of the few all-female construction companies in Boston. Audrey's the architect, and I'm the structural engineer and lead contractor, and we only hire female subcontractors."

She's so young; I want to ask how she can possibly already be qualified to do this. Five years ago she was a freshman in college.

"I've been doing this since I was a kid," she says with a laugh, as though she can read my thoughts. "My dad owned this company, and I was raised doing this right alongside him since I was old enough to swing a hammer. I've had my contractor's license for years, and got my degree in structural engineering more recently. Jameson thought you might prefer to have women working on this project, so that there aren't men in and out of your house all day. I hope that's okay?"

"That's . . ." *Unbelievably thoughtful.* "Perfect."

"Great! Oh, I almost forgot," she says, reaching under her flannel and pulling two plastic hammers out of the back of her tool belt. She hands one to each of the girls, and as they scramble to get down with their new toy, Jules says "They can't do any damage with those, but it's probably safest if they play in the finished room off the kitchen. Or upstairs?"

"I can take the girls," Paige offers, "so you two can chat."

Once the girls are corralled into the only room on the first floor not in a state of construction, Jules and I head upstairs.

"I love that it's already fully finished up here," I tell her. "It's so nice to at least have this part of the house livable while the downstairs is being finished. Can you tell me about the contractor who was working on this house before you came on? Jameson only told me that the guy was problematic?"

"Woody?" Jules rolls her eyes. "Yeah, he has a history of shoddy workmanship and leaving after he gets the final payment but before the actual work is done."

We're standing in the middle of the primary bedroom, and my eyes track over to that bathroom. It's such a luxurious retreat, and exactly what I would have designed for myself. "Well, at least he did a good job bringing my husband's vision for the upstairs to life."

Jules opens her mouth to respond but is cut off by Jameson's firm voice from behind me. "Yep. Good thing he was able to bring Josh's vision to life like this."

I turn to see why Jameson's voice is borderline hostile, but I don't miss the look Jules is giving him. Behind me, he's leaning up against the frame of the bedroom door. I've never seen him in anything but a suit, so the jeans and button-up sweater that he's wearing catch me off guard. I didn't know he knew how to do casual, in any aspect of life.

He forces a smile, but a muscle in his jaw ticks. Clearly there's something I don't know about this contractor, but maybe I can get Jules to tell me more later. I feel like we're going to get along great.

"So before you move in," Jules says, and I turn my attention back to her, "we should probably address these floors. No point in moving everything in, then having to clear the space to refinish them later on. You want to stick with the hard-wood? Or did you want to carpet over them?"

We chat about the logistics, but I'm insistent on keeping the hardwood. Jules tells me she can get her floor refinisher in to take care of them this week, and Jameson insists that it's done early in the week so that even with a few days to cure, we can move in next weekend.

"Where are you staying for now?" he asks.

"We're at Paige's." It's a tight fit because she only has one spare bedroom, and between the two pack 'n plays for the girls, my bed, and our luggage, I feel like we're stacked on top of each other. "A week is probably good because I need to go get some furniture for the bedrooms and I'm sure it'll take a few days to get it delivered. Also, my car and our personal stuff from our old house are both being delivered this week," I tell Jules, and I know she hears the worry in my voice.

"We'll put everything on the finished porch when it's delivered," she tells me.

"And I'll arrange for someone to plow the driveway this winter. Want me to see about getting an automatic garage door installed too?" Jameson asks.

I glance sideways at him, trying to figure out why he's being so helpful. "You've already done so much," I tell him. "I can take care of the garage door."

"I can do it right now while you're talking to Jules about planning out the kitchen."

Jules leads me downstairs while Jameson takes her tape measure and heads outside toward the garage. She's speaking rapid-fire, telling me about how she'll get the insulation in while the electrician installs the lights, then the walls and ceilings can go up. "By the time you move in at the end of the week, all the walls will be closed up and there'll be nothing that'll pose any danger for the girls. Then it'll just be about putting the finishing touches on, and getting the kitchen done. But it'll be a while before you have a fully functioning place to cook."

"Don't worry." I laugh. "I don't do that much cooking. I'll need to get a refrigerator, but as long as I have a toaster oven and a microwave, I can make do for a long time."

She looks at me with so much sympathy it's almost amusing. "Okay. That's it. You're coming over for dinner at least once a week. I love to cook and I always make too much food."

My mouth moves, but no words come out. "I feel like that would be a huge imposition. I've got two kids!"

"And they can play with my nephew. He's four," she says, and I'm so busy trying to figure out if this means Jameson has a kid, that I almost don't notice that she keeps talking. "Audrey's always worried that he doesn't get enough time around other kids."

"No siblings?"

"No, she's a single mom. And he doesn't have any cousins or anything. But at least he's in preschool with other kids his age now. I bet he'd love hanging out with your girls and being a 'big friend' to them."

"Do you live with them?" She's talking about her family like I already know them, but aside from knowing that Jameson raised her and her sister, I'm clueless about their family.

"Oh yeah, all of us live together. When Audrey and I were in college, Jameson took our family home in the South End and converted it into a two-family. So Audrey, my nephew, Graham, and I live on the first two floors, and Jameson lives on the third."

"Hey." I hear Jameson's gravelly voice, once again from behind me, and it surprises me more than it should, because I thought he was outside. "I've got the kitchen plans from Audrey," he tells Jules. "She just dropped them off, and she's taking Graham to hockey practice, but she said she'll catch up with you later."

"Don't *you* need to be at hockey practice, since you're the coach and all?" she asks him, and her voice has a teasing quality to it.

"I'll head over when we're done here."

Jules takes the plans and lays them out on the floor, squatting down to point out how she and Audrey thought it would make the most sense to use the space. As she talks about where to add a pantry and how we can use builder-grade cabinetry and then customize it and refinish it so that I can have a kitchen in a month instead of three months, it really does feel like they've already thought of everything.

"You're just nodding," Jules says as she looks over at me. "You're not saying anything."

"That's because I agree with everything you're saying."

"Seriously? There isn't anything you want to change? You like the built-in range hood, the island, everything?"

"Yeah." I shrug. "You've obviously already studied the space and thought about the best way to fit a lot of function into it. I'm fine letting you run with that."

"Oh my God," she says as she grips my forearm, laughing. "You are my fucking dream client." Then she looks up at Jameson, where he stands against the wall watching us.

"Where in the world did you find her? And can you find me more clients like her?"

He bites his lip for a second before responding, then gives me a small nod and says, "Unlikely. She's pretty much one of a kind." Then, pushing off the wall, he adds, "I've got to head to the rink." He walks out without even bothering to say goodbye.

"If you ever want to laugh so hard you pee your pants, you should come with us to the rink on a Saturday morning. Watching Jameson coach a bunch of four-to-six-year-olds is nothing short of hysterical."

"Are you laughing because of the kids, or because of him?

"Both. Come next Saturday, you'll see."

# Chapter Nine

## JAMESON

COLT

> I need to talk to you. Drinks tomorrow after the game?

JAMESON

> Yeah, sure. Why do I get the sense you did something I'm going to need to fix?

COLT

> Uhhh . . .

I wait for my car to tell me there's a new message, but the rest of his reply doesn't come.

JAMESON

> I don't like walking blind, Colt. If this is something I might hear about or have to deal with before I see you postgame, you better tell me what the hell is going on.

By the time I park and walk through the back door, I'm

already pissed that Colt's playing these games. He's a good friend but an aggravating client because trouble has a way of finding him, and he never thinks it's his fault—especially when it is.

"What's wrong?" Audrey asks the minute I hang my coat on the hook near the door. I haven't even looked up yet, but I'm sure the rigid line of my shoulders gives me away. I can feel a tension headache coming on.

"Colt's just . . ."

"Being Colt?" she offers when I don't finish.

"Yeah." I take my wallet out of my pocket and set it with my keys in the bowl on the counter by the back door. And that's when I notice how amazing it smells in here. "What's going on?" I ask, taking in the two pitchers of drinks in the middle of the table. The kitchen is warm and smells delicious, and when I glance over at the range, both ovens are on and there are multiple pots on the stove.

"Jules had a bad day."

Because my sister cooks to de-stress, in a way we all benefit from these bad days. But this is different. "This looks like we're having company."

"About that . . ."

"Hey," Jules says, breezing into the room with a bottle of wine she must have grabbed from the cellar in one hand and her phone in the other. "Lauren says she just parked and is walking over, she'll be here in a minute."

"Lauren *WHAT*?" I know my voice was way too loud by the way my sisters look like I've slapped them and Graham comes running into the kitchen asking what's wrong.

Then Jules bursts out laughing. "You should see your face. Oh my God, relax. I invited her and the girls over for dinner because she hates cooking and Paige is away on a business trip for two nights."

"How do you even know this?"

Jules looks me up and down, then turns to Audrey in triumph. "I told you so."

"Go back and finish your show, Graham," Audrey says as she runs her hand over the top of his head affectionately. "You're going to have to turn it off when our company gets here." The minute he's out of the room, she says, "Yep, you called it."

"Called what?" I hear how terse I sound, but it doesn't stop me from narrowing my eyes at them.

Jules just laughs. "You should see yourself right now. You're so jealous."

I raise an eyebrow. "I don't get jealous."

"Welcome to this new emotion, then," Audrey says, her lips lifting into a smirk. With her medium brown hair and blue eyes, she looks the most like our father, but never more than when she smiles.

"You're so obvious," Jules says. "Mostly because you don't do favors for people—"

"Except us," Audrey adds.

"—and you're tripping all over yourself to help Lauren. Like, you paid off Woody with your own money. Don't even try to lie to me again and tell me it came from the trust, because Lauren told me how she found out about the house and how it wasn't in the trust, and what went down with her in-laws, and how she was left with almost no money. And you had me redo that whole second floor before she even saw the house, including the bathroom she was gushing over, and you let her think that her ex-husband and Woody were behind it."

"He's not her ex-husband. They weren't split up, he died."

"In any event," Jules says, "you are so gone over this girl, and you obviously have been since before she moved here. What's the deal?"

"The only deal is that I'm executing the trust I promised her husband I'd take care of. That's it." I don't mention that she's already had a new trust created and I'm really under no obligation to do anything else. I told her I'd help her get this all figured out, and that's what I'm doing.

"You keep telling yourself that if it makes you feel better," Audrey says, her voice bouncing up and down like she's mocking me.

"All right, I'm going upstairs," I say, eager to get out of here before Lauren arrives. I have no desire to have my sisters watching us and psychoanalyzing our every interaction.

I'm two steps out of the kitchen, my sisters still teasing me, when the doorbell rings. I look over just in time for my eyes to lock with Lauren's as she stares at me through the window next to the front door. *Shit.*

It's not until she lifts her eyebrows and tilts her chin toward the door that I realize I've completely stopped moving as I stand there staring at her, and I've left her out in the cold holding two toddlers.

I spring toward the door, ushering her inside. As soon as the door is closed behind her, she squats and sets her girls down, but they each grab onto one of her legs.

"They're getting way too big to carry both of them," she says with a sigh. There are about ten granite steps between the sidewalk and our brownstone that I know she had to carry them up. "And I wasn't sure what to do with the stroller, so right now it's sitting at the bottom of your front steps."

"I'll grab it and bring it in," I tell her. As I step toward the door, I catch her scent, some combination of citrus and vanilla, and it brings back so many memories that I almost recoil.

"Hey," she says, turning her head toward me and keeping her voice low. She's close enough that her warm breath moves across my cheek. "I hope it's okay that I'm here? When Jules invited me over, I was about to lose my mind with the isolation of being home alone with my girls, who were going stir-crazy in Paige's apartment. But I didn't mean to intrude on your personal space either."

"It's fine, Lauren." And because I apparently have no concern for my own emotional well-being, I add, "You're always welcome here."

The smile she gives me is the first genuine one I've seen from her since Josh died, and it cracks some of the walls I've put up around my heart. She looks like herself when she smiles like that. Hopeful and determined, instead of defeated.

I hurry down the steps because it's cold as balls out there today, collapse her stroller, and carry it back up. Everyone's in the entryway when I step back inside, and Lauren laughs and says, "I wasn't expecting you to know how to fold that thing up."

"Oh yeah," Audrey says. "Jameson's well trained. Diapers, bottles, strollers . . . he's done it all with Graham."

"Hmm," she says, a small smile playing on her lips, and I can imagine why: she's only really ever seen me in work mode.

I'm a serious guy by nature, competitive and demanding of myself and others. And when we worked together, I was at the tail end of raising two teenage girls. Work was what allowed me to keep our family home, save my dad's construction company, and put them both through college. I pushed myself as hard as I possibly could to be successful, knowing that if I wasn't, our family would fall apart.

In the early years of my career as an agent, I built on every relationship I had from my days in the NHL, bringing some of my former teammates over to my agency and recruiting new talent more easily because I knew exactly what types of players each team needed and how to negotiate with them to fill those gaps with the right person. There was no time for fun back then, only winning.

The drive and determination that helped me succeed in agenting may have had me seeming demanding or even cruel sometimes. I may have stepped on some toes and come across as ruthless, but that's what it took to get me to where I am now—my family intact and closer than ever, my sisters both happy and successful, and my own thriving sports agency.

But Lauren has only seen one side of me and has no idea who I really am or what truly matters to me. Most people don't. So the question really is: am I ready to show her?

"I'm going to go up and change," I say, nodding toward the stairs. "I'll be right back."

Because even though my original inclination was to escape to the solace of my place upstairs so I wouldn't be here when she arrived, I find that now that she's here, I want to spend more time with her, even if it means putting up with my sisters and their judgy observations all night.

———

W hen I return, everyone's already seated at the large farmhouse table that takes up the middle of our kitchen. Jules has roasted chickens, baked risotto, green beans, and roasted butternut squash laid out along the center of the table.

"Grab some margarita glasses while you're up?" Jules asks as I come in.

I take four off the open shelving along the wall and bring them over. "It's been a margarita kind of day?"

"Yeah. I swear that project in Wellesley is going to kill me. I'll be amazed if the couple gets through this build without getting divorced."

"Didn't they just get married last year?" Audrey asks.

"Yeah, and the stress of building their dream home is really getting to them. Nothing but bickering about every last detail, and every price point. Her tastes are too extravagant for their budget, and his sense of what things actually cost is deranged. It's been real fun," Jules says as she takes one of the drink pitchers and fills her glass to the brim.

I hand Audrey her glass, then take my seat across from Lauren and hand her the last glass. I've changed into jeans and a short-sleeve T-shirt, and I don't miss the way her eyes linger on the tattoos along my arms as I reach across the table.

"Jules puts the salt in the margarita, instead of on the rim of the glass. So, if you don't like salt, I can make you something else."

"I'm sure I'll love it," she says, reaching across the table and taking the glass carefully, like she's trying not to touch my hand.

Her twins are sitting on either side of her, playing with some Matchbox cars that Graham has brought to the table for them.

"Who dat?" the one with red hair like Lauren's asks as she points to me.

"This is Jameson Flynn."

"Flynn?" the other one asks, her eyes lighting up. "*Tangled*?"

Lauren's chest shakes with silent laughter, so I just give the girls my best Flynn Rider smile and their eyes widen.

"No," I tell them. "Not Flynn Rider." I point at my chest. "Jameson." The word is slow and intentional, and they look at each other, one saying "Ja-son" and the other saying "Jamesen."

"Almost," I tell them.

"You going to tell me who's who?" I ask Lauren.

She tells me the redhead is Ivy and the brunette is Iris, and then Jules says, "So before Jameson came back, you were saying that you were going to start looking for a job? What do you do for work?"

Lauren swallows, meets my eye, then looks over at Jules. "Before I got married, I was in sports marketing. I used to work at Kaplan, with Jameson." My sisters' gazes fly to me, and I just shrug. I guess I've never mentioned that we used to work together. "Before . . . everything happened . . . I had just decided to go back to work. I'd gotten a part-time job in marketing with one of the farm teams for Colorado's NHL team. But I had to turn the job down when Josh died, because I was not in a position to be starting a new job or spending an hour and a half commuting to Salt Lake City and back, three times a week."

"So, do you want to get back into sports marketing again?" Audrey asks. "Like, could you go back to Kaplan?"

"I do. And I probably could," Lauren says, then lifts her chin and glances at me. "But my uncle owns Kaplan and, I don't know, I kind of want to branch out. Prove to myself that I can get back into this industry through my own merit, not through nepotism."

God, I'd given her so much shit that first year she was at Kaplan, back when I thought she only got the job because she was Carson's niece. She proved me wrong quickly, consistently learning and growing and becoming extremely damn good at her job. So good that I started making sure she worked with my athletes, helping them land endorsement deals that sometimes doubled or tripled their income.

"You should come work for me." The words are out before I even have time to process what I'm about to say, and if the looks they're giving me are any indication, everyone's as surprised to hear me make this offer as I am. When no one says anything, I add, "I could use someone else in marketing."

Lauren flushes, then looks away. When she looks back, she says, "That's really nice of you to offer, but again, I'm not looking to get a job through nepotism."

"I'm not offering you the opportunity because you're a friend, I'm offering it because I know how good you are at what you do. I could use someone like you at my agency."

"Thank you," Lauren says, and her cheeks turn a shade of pink so deep they're almost red. "But I really think it's best if I look for a job on my own." She gives a small smile as she glances at my sisters and shrugs. "A fresh start, of sorts."

Jules and Audrey glance at each other, then at me, then at Lauren. And then as we pass the food around the table, they're peppering her with questions about where she'd want to work, and whether she's looking for full-time or part-time. But I'm only half listening, because I'm thinking about all the reasons Lauren doesn't want to work for me. And I'm more certain than ever that I want to show her I'm not the asshole she worked with five years ago.

When dinner's over, I offer to walk Lauren back to her car, which she parked about five blocks away. She insists she'll be fine.

"Walking around the city by yourself at night with your kids in a stroller is inviting danger," I say. Boston is generally a safe city, but I don't take chances with the people I care about. "Please let me make sure you get back to your car safely."

"Fine," she agrees, even though I can tell she doesn't want to. "I didn't realize that all the on-street parking in this part of the South End would be resident only," she says, "which is why I ended up parked practically in the Back Bay."

"We have parking on the side of our house. Next time . . ." I say, and she glances at me sideways in surprise. "Next time, one of us can move our car to the street and you can use one of our parking spots. I'm sorry Jules didn't think to mention it."

"She's really sweet, by the way. So's Audrey. You did a great job with them, Jameson." I can't tell her tone in the way she says this. She doesn't sound shocked that I managed to raise two teenage girls when I was so young myself. She also doesn't sound like she's being patronizing. So I can only deduce that her statement is genuine.

"Thanks. The teen years were no joke, but we got through them okay."

"I can tell how close you guys are." She clears her throat. "I'm glad they have that with you."

I glance over at her from where she walks next to me as I push the stroller, and her lips are turned down at the corners. "Why do you sound sad about it, then?"

"I'm not. I guess seeing you with your siblings is making me a bit homesick for mine, that's all."

I thought one of the reasons she wanted to move to Boston was to be closer to her own family. "Can you go home and see everyone?"

"Yeah." She sighs. "But it's an almost four-hour drive, which is really long with two toddlers, and I'm going home in a few weeks anyway for a family wedding, so I'm just going to wait and see everyone then. Plus, I have a house to move into this weekend, and I'm sure that'll keep me pretty busy for the next few weeks."

"And it sounds like you're going to be looking for a job?"

"Jameson," she says, grabbing my forearm as she stops walking. It's like electricity is running through my blood as she looks up at me. "Thank you for that offer earlier. Really. I couldn't say this in front of your sisters without them asking a lot of questions, but I don't think it's a good idea for us to work together."

I stare down at those bright blue eyes and I know that, given our history, she's right. But I push anyway. "And why not?"

"Because all we ever did when we worked together was fight."

I'm tempted to joke and say it's not *all* we did, but I also don't know if dredging up that night is a good idea right now.

"I think we're both in different places now than we were then."

She looks at the ground, then back up at me. "Maybe. But I still don't think it's a good idea."

"Just know that the offer is open, okay? If you don't find what you're looking for, maybe consider it."

"Okay," she says, and starts walking again. By the time we're back at her car, both girls are asleep in the stroller. As she gets them buckled into their car seats, I load her stroller into the back of her SUV.

"How are you going to get them both inside, asleep?" I ask, trying to picture her carrying both of them while also unlocking and opening doors.

"I'll manage," she says, and the resignation in her voice has me ready to offer to ride with her to Paige's and help her get her sleeping kids inside. "Thanks for tonight, by the way. I needed a night out so badly I didn't even think twice when Jules invited me, and I appreciate that you didn't freak out when you obviously had no idea I was coming over."

Oh, I freaked out all right. And the fact that she realized I had no idea she was coming over is evidence that she noticed.

"You're welcome at our place any time. For real."

She gives me a smile as she opens her car door and slides into her seat. I stand there watching her pull away, knowing that she's right about us not working together, and at the same time determined to see her secure in a new job and able to provide for herself and her kids.

———

"You played like an old man tonight," I say to Colt as I slide into the seat across from him in the two-person booth at the back of the bar. He's got his hat pulled low across his forehead like he always does when he's trying to go unnoticed. As the longtime star goalie of the Boston Rebels, he's one of the most recognizable faces in Boston. If people realize who he is, they'll be flocking to him.

"Felt like an old man tonight." He grimaces. "I was a fucking sieve."

It was an unusually high-scoring game, and the Rebels won by one goal in the final seconds of the third period. "Luckily, so was the other goalie."

"Goddamn Jenkins got a hat trick." Colt narrows his eyes at me. "Don't you fucking smirk like that. Just because you rep him too, doesn't mean you should be rooting against me and your former team."

"I'm always rooting for the Rebels. But Drew Jenkins has so much potential." He's been inconsistent as hell this season, so it was good to see him have a good game, even if it was against my team. "And he's looking to move back to Boston."

"Back?"

"Yeah, he went to college here." His team won the Frozen Four, and he shot straight into the NHL. "His family's in the area too." Drew spent three years in Vancouver before getting traded to Colorado, and there's a mid-season trade going on right now between Boston and Colorado that he wants in on. I'm not sure I can make it happen before the trade deadline, but I'm working on it.

"Well, for now, you aren't allowed to be happy about him doing well when he's playing us."

"You sound like a thirty-five-year-old toddler." I roll my eyes.

"I'm not thirty-five yet, asshole."

"Close enough. And speaking of toddler-like behavior, what the hell did you text me about?"

Colt sighs and pushes the brim of his hat farther down, then lifts his glass like he's toasting me. "So there's this girl in marketing . . ."

"No, you fucking didn't. You don't sleep with people you work with, Colt. What the hell is wrong with you?"

"We were at an away game in Toronto and got snowed in. We were all at the hotel bar, one thing led to another, and I chose to sleep in her room so I didn't have to share a room with three other guys."

"First of all, if you slept with her so you didn't have to share a hotel room with your teammates, you're a dick."

"Nah, she's cute. I'd have slept with her anyway."

"You're still a dick. You work with her."

"Yeah, so about that . . . not anymore."

I wait for him to continue, but he doesn't. "What happened?"

He doesn't look at me as he works on peeling off the corner of the label on the beer bottle that sits in front of him. "When I told her it was a one-time thing, she pitched a fit right in the middle of the team's offices, then marched into her boss's office and quit. Made a big stink about me leading her on, but luckily she made it clear that it was consensual."

"Oh, for fuck's sake, Colt. This is why you don't—"

"Sleep with people I work with. Got it." His voice is how I imagine a puppy would sound after getting yelled at for eating another pair of shoes.

"So what's happening now?"

"Right now, nothing. But everyone from the GM to the Director of Marketing is pissed at me. People loved her, apparently."

I flag down the waitress and order myself a scotch. I need a minute for these wheels to stop spinning so fast in my head, because what I'm hearing Colt saying is that there's a marketing position open at the Boston Rebels—and it feels almost too perfect, like the kind of thing people would say is "a sign from the universe" or some shit.

"I can't make them less mad at you about this, but I might be able to at least help them fill the position which might smooth things over a bit. I'll talk to AJ," I tell him, mentioning the team's general manager who I have a close relationship with, "because I might know just the person for that job."

Colt's eyes narrow again. "Tell me more."

"She's got years of sports marketing experience, but then took a break from working to be with her babies, and now she's looking to get back into the business. That's all I'm saying until I talk to her about it. She might not even be interested."

One of Colt's light brown eyebrows shoots up. "You like this girl?"

"I don't like anyone."

He snorts in response. "Isn't that the truth. But your voice sounds different when you talk about her."

"Stop trying to read into it. She's just someone I used to work with."

"Uh huh," Colt says, lifting his beer bottle in a mock salute. "Sure she is."

# Chapter Ten

## LAUREN

I'm two steps into the entryway of my new house, my arms loaded down with a very heavy box, when my doorbell rings and I jump in surprise, fumbling and almost dropping the box. It's not that I'm not expecting the delivery people who are bringing the new bedroom furniture, it's that I've never actually heard the doorbell's unique ringing chimes before.

I prop the box up between my bent knee and the wall to the side of the door, knowing from experience that it would be nearly impossible to pick it up from the floor again. But when I swing the door open, it's not the delivery people standing there, it's Jameson.

"Hey," I say, hating that my voice sounds as confused as I feel. What is he doing here? "What's up?"

"Can I come in for a second?" His jawline is covered in a few days' worth of stubble, and it's giving him hot guy vibes that I wish I wasn't noticing.

"Sure." I angle my body out of the way so he can walk through the doorway. As he does, he plucks the box off my knee like it weighs ten pounds and rests it on his hip, holding it with one arm. It's a relief to be able to stand up straight again now that I'm not carrying that load.

"Is this going upstairs?" he asks, eyeing the box with "Kids' Bedroom" scrawled across the top.

"Yeah."

"Want me to carry it up there for you?"

I hesitate for a moment, torn between wanting to prove that I can do this myself and knowing that me carrying a box that heavy up newly refinished stairs is a recipe for injury. "That would be great."

He slips out of his sneakers, shifts the box in front of him, and heads toward the stairs. "Which room is it going in?" he asks.

I follow behind him on the stairs and direct him to the girls' room, across the hall from mine. He sets the box in the corner I point to, out of the way of where their twin beds will be set up. "Want me to bring anything else up here for you? I don't mind."

I could do it myself. I still have a couple hours before Morgan brings the girls back, and I'd planned on moving everything. But if I let him help me, I might actually be able to start getting some things unpacked once the delivery guys arrive with the furniture.

"Okay. Thank you," I tell him as we head back downstairs. He takes off his heavy zip-up hoodie, drapes it over the post at the bottom of my banister, and stands in my entryway in his sweats, T-shirt, and socks. I hate that I notice how ripped he is. I know he was once a professional athlete, but why does he still have to have the body of one? And up close like this, it's even harder not to stare at those tattoos I noticed at dinner the other night—I want to examine them, see what he's chosen to permanently ink onto his body, figure out what it says about him as a person.

Instead, I remind myself that none of that has anything to do with me. I need to mind my own business.

I lead the way back to the finished room off the kitchen, and Jameson chuckles when he looks at the boxes packed floor to ceiling against the wall. "You were going to carry all of these upstairs by yourself?"

"I could have done it."

"Yeah, but why would you want to when you have people who could help you? You could have asked me, Jules, and Audrey to come over, and between the four of us this would have been done in half an hour."

It never occurred to me to ask them for help. "Jules and Audrey have both been here a lot this week, making sure this project," I say, nodding toward the door to the kitchen, "got far enough along that the girls and I could move in this weekend. I wouldn't have further infringed on their kindness when they were already going above and beyond, by asking them to do me a favor like this."

"Why didn't you ask me, then?" He tilts his head as he stares down at me, like he's daring me to admit just how befuddled I am any time he's around. He's a mystery—I thought I knew him, thought I knew who he was. I've spent most of the years I've known him hating him, but since Josh died, he's done nothing but try to help me. Seeing him around his sisters and nephew is like seeing a totally different version of him, and I'm left wondering who he really is.

"Why are you being so nice to me now?"

"I *am* nice, Lauren," he says as he grabs a box from the

top of one of the piles and hands it to me. I glance down to see that it says "Bedding" on it. I almost laugh because I'm sure he chose this one for me intentionally, knowing it's light enough that I could carry it easily. Then he grabs another box for himself and says, "I'm just careful who I show that side of myself to."

I follow behind him as he walks out of the room and through the kitchen. "Why?"

He pauses mid-step and looks over his shoulder, locking those dark eyes on me. "Because I've been burned too many times." He turns back toward the entryway and keeps walking, but adds, "When you're a professional athlete, and even as an agent, everyone wants something from you. Combine that with my mother leaving, my stepmother dying, and then my father leaving . . . let's just say I have trust issues."

He'd told me a little bit about his family history when we had our dinner "that night," but the trust issues part is totally new to me. I'm shocked not only that he's so in touch with his feelings but also that he's admitting it to me.

"Do you trust *me*, Jameson?" I ask, and he pauses with his foot on the first stair tread.

He looks at me over his shoulder again. "I want to."

I lift my shoulder in a small shrug. "And should I trust you?"

He lifts his shoulder, a small shrug in return. "When I've earned your trust, you should." Then he turns away from me and walks up the stairs, leaving me trying to determine his meaning.

I get the bedding box to the top of the stairs when the doorbell rings again, and this time it's the furniture delivery I've been waiting for. I show them which bedroom is mine and which is the girls', and then Jameson and I wait in the entryway, where we'll need to get the door for them each time they bring in a new piece of furniture because it's too cold to prop it open.

"I wasn't expecting to see Morgan and your girls at the rink this morning," he says when the guys head out to the truck. "I thought Morgan lived in Park City."

"She does, but she's moving back to Boston in a couple weeks. She's here this weekend looking for apartments, and she wanted to see the girls. Jules had suggested I bring them to the practice this morning," I tell him, "but obviously I needed to be here for the delivery. Plus, I wanted Morgan and your sisters to meet since they're similar ages and I think they'll get along great."

"Yeah, they all left together after practice and went out to brunch."

"You didn't want to go?"

"Three women in their twenties, and three kids under five?" His laugh is practically a grunt. "I'd rather be here."

I'm trying to figure out what to say in response, because my immediate thought is *I'd rather you be here too*, and that makes no sense. I still can't quite reconcile this version of him with how I've thought of him for the eight years I've known him. But the delivery guy is backing toward my front door, so I reach over and open it as he moves in with my new dresser, and I'm saved from having to say anything.

I close the door behind them as they move up the stairs, and Jameson hands me a business card. I glance at it, and then look back up at him, eyes wide.

"Why am I holding a business card for the general manager of the Boston Rebels?"

His dark eyes bore down as he scans my face. "Because one of the people in their marketing department left very suddenly, and they're looking for someone to fill the spot. When I mentioned that someone I worked with, who has years of experience in sports marketing, was looking for a job, she was very interested in talking to you."

*She.* Alessandra Jones is one of the few women in hockey to have made it all the way to the top and is currently the only female GM in the league. She's an icon, and working for her would be a dream.

"Jameson"—my voice is full of warning—"this feels a whole lot like nepotism, which is exactly what I told you I was trying to avoid."

After the way he, and others, treated me when I started at my uncle's agency fresh off a postgrad internship at another sports agency in New York City, I promised myself I would never accept another job acquired because I "knew someone."

"This isn't nepotism. It's me, hearing about an opportunity that would be perfect for you, and telling the GM nothing more than 'I know someone you should talk to.' I didn't pull any strings or play any angles here. If you don't want to pursue this just because I'm the one who brought it to your attention"—he raises his eyebrows and gives me a one-shoulder shrug, which lifts the sleeve of his shirt and has my eyes focused on the tattoos along his bicep—"that's your choice."

My eyes shift up to his, and he's clearly smirking at me. No doubt he noticed me staring at his carved arms and the ink decorating them.

"That's really all you said? Because I know how people

view you in this industry, and if you put even the slightest amount of pressure on her . . ."

He lifts his eyebrow again. "And how do people view me?" His voice is a balance between curious and teasing.

He's been called "the most powerful man in hockey" and a whole host of other titles, all reflective of how influential he's been in representing players and even helping coaches and GMs build just the right team. The Boston Rebels practically owe him both their Stanley Cup titles in the last decade because of how he's helped build that team postretirement.

I could go on and on about what's been written about him and his sway over this industry, but I'd never give him the satisfaction of knowing that I've followed his career that closely.

"I think you know. Tell me you didn't pressure Alessandra Jones into meeting with me?"

He looks up the stairs as the delivery guys trudge down and waits until they're out the door before he takes a step closer and says, "I didn't pressure her in any way. I vouched for your experience, but nothing else."

I gulp, both because of his proximity and because this opportunity might be too good to pass up. "All right, I'll send her an email as soon as I have a chance."

———

I've been in enough meetings at the headquarters of various sports teams' facilities that I figured I knew what I was walking into for today's meeting with Alessandra Jones.

I could not have been more wrong.

When I'm shown to her office, it's not full of the standard

high-end office furniture. Instead, her office has a high ceiling with a beautiful light fixture hanging from it, an antique pale wood desk with nothing on it but a closed laptop and clear acrylic organizers with pastel folders, and behind the desk are lovely built-ins full of books and awards and picture frames.

One wall is glass and overlooks the practice rink. An off-white couch sits along the glass, two matching chairs opposite it, and a long tufted ottoman in between. There are throw pillows on the couch and a blanket draped over one chair, and the whole space feels unimaginably cozy for an office space in a hockey rink.

The woman herself is standing behind her desk, feet crossed at the ankles and brows scrunched in concentration or displeasure as she looks at a copy of a local Boston newspaper.

"AJ?" her assistant says quietly and Alessandra looks up, startled, as if her assistant hadn't just knocked on the door before opening it.

"Why hello," she says, a broad smile replacing her scowl. "You must be Lauren."

She steps around her desk, so I take a few steps across the room and shake her outstretched hand. "It's so nice to meet you, Ms. Jones."

She laughs and says, "Please call me AJ. Everyone does." I wonder if this is something left over from childhood, or if she's chosen to use her initials instead of her first name so as to not draw focus to her gender in such a male-dominated industry.

"It's nice to meet you, AJ."

"Much better." She gestures toward the couch. "Here, have a seat."

We chat for a few minutes about the people we know in common and why I'm interested in working in hockey specifically before there's a knock on the door. She introduces me to Patrick Patrona, the Director of Marketing for the Boston Rebels, and he takes a seat in the chair next to hers.

They both ask me questions about hockey, checking not just that I understand the game, but also that I understand the unique needs and goals of the Rebels as an organization. They ask questions that touch on my previous experience in sports marketing, and I'm about to pull out some samples of my best work, when Patrick says, "So, when could you start?"

I cough to cover my gasp. "Are you offering me the job?"

"Yes," AJ says, "we are."

"But . . ." I pause, willing my heart to stop racing as my eyes dart back and forth between the two of them. "At the risk of sounding like I don't want this, don't you at least want to interview me first?"

AJ quirks her head, looking at me like she's trying to figure out if I'm okay. "That's what we just did."

"But . . ." *Just stop speaking, now!* I yell at myself inside my head. "I guess what I'm really asking is: you're not hiring me just because Jameson Flynn recommended me, are you?"

AJ's smile is the small, closed-mouth type. "He's never led me astray before, and he highly recommended your work."

"But, no," Patrick says, "we're not hiring you *because* of him. We were really impressed by your resume and the samples of work you did with athletes while you were at Kaplan. We've already seen what you can do. This interview was more about making sure you'd be a good fit for our organization."

"And we do think you'd be a good fit," AJ says, as though she can see I'm still having trouble making sense of this all.

They give me the logistics, like hours and salary, and it feels like enough pieces are lining up that this could actually work out.

"This is just happening more quickly than I anticipated." It's not totally unlike what happened in Salt Lake City, which might mean that I'm a more desirable employee than I'm giving myself credit for. "I have twins who aren't quite two yet. Since I just moved back to Boston, it might take me a bit of time to find childcare for them."

"We can be flexible on the start date," AJ says, "just let Patrick know what you need."

"I have to run to another meeting," he says, "but I'll be in touch with more details and to discuss your contract. You should hear from me by the end of the week."

I thank them both and stand to walk out with him when AJ says, "Lauren? A word?"

My stomach drops in the same way it would if a teacher had said this while my whole class was on the way out the door.

I turn to face her, and she's closer than I expect.

She's got her arms folded lightly across her ribs and her eyes crinkle as she gazes at me. "Being a woman in sports is hard enough without getting in your own way."

I can feel the groove between my eyebrows deepen as I try to make sense of what she's telling me. "Getting in my own way?"

"Yes. You came to us highly recommended by one of the most well-respected men in this industry and then suggested we shouldn't hire you based on his recommendation. You think any man in your position would do that?"

I shake my head. "I really wanted to be hired based on my own merit, not on someone else's recommendation."

"Was he coerced into recommending you?"

"What? No, I didn't even know about the position until after he had talked to you about it."

"Is your work as good as he says it is?"

I swallow down my self-doubt and remind myself that before Josh, I was a badass at my job. My work spoke for itself, enough so that Jameson was recommending me to other agents at Kaplan after I'd only been there a year or two.

"Yes."

"So why, when Patrick offered you the job, did you try to talk yourself out of having earned that?"

I wonder how much to tell her, and then figure that she's right. Being a woman in sports is hard enough—so I guess having someone else to confide in can only help.

"When I got my first job at Kaplan, most of my colleagues assumed it was because Carson is my uncle."

I watch a laugh roll around in AJ's throat, and her chest shakes with it. "I've known Carson for probably close to two decades, and one thing I can say for sure is that he wouldn't have hired you if he didn't think you deserved it. Even if you are his niece."

I think about the time, years ago, when I finally got the nerve up to ask my uncle about his decision. By that point, I'd proven myself at Kaplan over and over again, but part of me wondered if other people I worked with still harbored the belief that I hadn't earned my position there.

Carson asked, "Do you think I'd have hired you if I

wasn't one hundred percent confident that you could do the job?"

"No. But that doesn't mean there weren't more qualified candidates."

"I knew you'd be good at this, could manage the stress, and make it look easy," he said. "So who the fuck cares if there were other qualified candidates? I. Wanted. You."

I glance over at AJ as the memory flashes through my head, and she says, "And I think you know you deserved that job too."

"I do. And I did then. But I'm also a realist and getting that job through a family connection made it that much harder to prove myself at work."

"Yet you did prove yourself. Which means you worked harder and smarter than a lot of other people."

I laugh a little at that. It feels like this woman knows me because she's been me, earlier in her career when she had to overcome similar obstacles. "That's true too."

"You're probably asking yourself why I'm even involved in this hiring process when I'm the GM?"

I give her a little nod with my eyebrows raised. That question has been percolating in the back of my mind. I would think she would only be involved in hiring that related to roles that affect the team—the players, coaches, athletic trainers, that type of thing.

"Managing this team means not only recruiting the best players and coaches but also shaping the way information is communicated about the team. I didn't get involved because Jameson recommended you. I got involved because the last person in this job slept with one of my players, and that's not the type of organization I'm trying to build here. I'm already dealing with that player, but I need to make sure I can trust whoever takes this position." She drums her fingers against her elbows as she looks at me. "With you, I see another female who loves the sport, not just the players. I see someone who's early enough in their career to still have a lot of growth potential but experienced enough to add value immediately. Plus, Patrick was pretty much sold on you before he even met you too."

"I'm really excited about the opportunity to work with you both," I tell her. "I've been a Rebels fan since I was a kid. I think my dad taught me the Rebel Chant before I could even speak in full sentences."

"Don't worry," she says with a smile, "that's not a prerequisite for working here. We save that for the fans."

"Oh . . ." My smile reflects my enthusiasm. "I already have so many ideas for how to leverage that for some great marketing content."

"And this," she says definitively, "is why the job is already yours."

# Chapter Eleven

## JAMESON

I finish the skills sequence I'm leading the boys through, turn my skates to come to a stop, and glance over at the stands in time to see Lauren sitting down with one of those disposable trays of take-out hot chocolates. I tear my eyes away before anyone can notice me watching her, and focus on five-year-old Caleb, who's at the front of the line. Unlike the majority of my team of mini hockey players, Caleb shows a ton of potential.

"All right, Caleb. Go!"

He speeds off the goal line, jumps over the stick laid across the ice, and angles himself right as I pass the puck toward him. It makes contact with his stick, and he begins to roll the wrist of his top hand back and forth, showing quality stick handling and puck control as he moves toward the wide-open net, and easily taps it in. Not bad for a five-year-old.

"Nice job, Caleb! Hey, Tommy," I shout toward the next kid in line, our oldest player who's goofing off with his friend and isn't ready to go. "You going to practice some hockey, or what?"

He turns toward me right as I yell, "Go!" but he's slower getting off the line than he should be. "Gotta speed up if you're going to make it over the stick," I say, and he digs his inside edges in a bit harder, but his legs are wider than they should be. "Feet closer together!"

"I know how to skate," he grunts, but as he takes the small jump, he barely leaves the ice and catches a blade on the stick. He lands face-first, spinning off toward center ice.

I push off, and when I stop in front of him, he looks up at me with tears of frustration and embarrassment in his eyes. I sink to my knees at his side. "So here's how this is going to go. You're going to get up, skate back to that start line, and do it again. But this time you're coming off that line with some power. Keep your skates in a more neutral stance when you go to jump over the stick, get in position, and I'll have the puck waiting for you."

I can tell he wants to say something, but he's holding back. He pushes up to his hands and knees, grunts out "Fine," and pops up onto his skates. I'm not sure what the chip on his shoulder is all about, but he acts like he doesn't need a coach and then makes mistakes that could have been avoided if he'd just listened. He'll get it eventually, but he's making it harder on himself. I make a mental note to chat with his mom about what's going on.

When we're done, I skate over to the boards and step through the door, then walk over to where my family sits with Lauren and her kids. It feels so natural to see her here, and I have to remind myself that she's here to hang out with my sisters, not because of me.

Lauren's sitting a few rows up, in the seat on the end, and she leans down toward where I stand on the mats next to the seats, her voice teasing when she says, "Looking a little rusty out there, Flynn."

I grab the railing next to her seat as I look up at her. "Compared to?"

"Compared to when you used to wear the Rebels jersey."

"Why don't you throw on your figure skates and show me your triple axel," I tease right back, but there's a look that crosses over her face—part pain and part longing.

"Never going to happen," she says quietly, still looking down at me. And that's when I remember that her competitive skating career ended at US Nationals, back when she was still in high school, with a botched landing on a triple axel and a concussion that lasted for months. She's never talked to me about it, but I've seen the video.

"How about a double, instead?" I give her a little wink so that she knows I'm teasing, but she looks away, her eyes drifting over the ice. Now that our hockey practice is over, the learn-to-skate classes are starting. When she looks back at me, her face is unreadable—which never happens.

"You'll have to do some digging into old videos if you want to see me on the ice."

There's no way she can mean what it sounds like she means.

"You haven't been on the ice since you stopped competing?"

Her eyes are focused somewhere beyond me. A small shake of her head back and forth, lips held together between her teeth, is her only response.

"Lauren," I say, because I want her to look at me. I keep my voice low so no one else will overhear our conversation, though her girls are between her and Jules, and Audrey is helping Graham get his gear off, so there's no one actually listening. "Why not?"

She glances at me, then back at the ice. "I . . . I just never could quite force myself to put my skates back on."

"Not even for fun?"

"Nope." She looks back at me, her smile falsely bright, and says, "By the way, I took the job with the Rebels."

"I heard."

"Word travels fast."

"So, when do you start?"

"I'm going in for two days at the end of next week for orientation and some training, and then I'm starting part-time the following week."

"What are you doing with the girls while you're at work?"

"I'm still figuring that out, hence the part-time status to begin with. Morgan's going to help me out—she's moving back a bit ahead of schedule so she can watch the girls for me on the days I'm at work, just until I can find full-time care."

"I thought she was Petra's personal assistant? That sounds like it would be a full-time job."

"It is. But it's flexible. Petra's great like that."

"Hey," Jules says as she stands and leans over toward us. "Are you guys talking about Morgan? When's she coming back?"

Lauren looks over her shoulder, and I focus on my sister so Jules doesn't comment on me being too focused on Lauren. "She'll be back next week. She's going to nanny for my girls until I find something full-time for them."

"Good! Will you give her my number? I know she's from Boston and probably knows plenty of people, but in case she ever wants to hang out, I'm around."

"I'm sure she'd love that," Lauren says to Jules. "Especially since the last time she lived here, she was in high school."

They start chatting about where Morgan went to high school and college, and as they do, I walk around to the front row of seats, where Audrey's finishing packing up all of Graham's gear.

She gives me the side-eye as I approach, right as Graham runs up the row between the seats toward Lauren's girls. I watch as he slips into the row and gives Iris and Ivy big hugs, tickling them, then kissing them on their heads.

"You said you'd be responsible for all this if I let him play," Audrey says, the distinct tone of annoyance hanging from every word as she drops his sweaty hockey gear into the bag one piece at a time, accounting for each thing separately as I taught her.

"Sorry, I got sidetracked."

"You're always sidetracked when she's around," Audrey says, and smiles up at me. "It seems like she makes you happy."

I almost blurt out *She does, but it only matters if she reciprocates my feelings. And she made her choice a long time ago.* I catch myself just before I admit how much it still bothers me that she chose Josh. Instead, I say, "She just lost her husband. There's nothing going on between us. Just drop it, Audrey."

"If you say so." She reaches over and pokes me between the ribs trying to get a smile—or probably any kind of reaction—out of me.

"I'm headed to the locker room," I tell her. "I have to change and catch a flight."

"Remind me where you're going this time?"

"Denver. Trying to get one of my players into a mid-season trade that's in the works."

"Oh yeah? Which one?" Audrey asks. She's almost as disinterested in hockey as Jules, but at least she's trying to learn more about it because of how much Graham loves it.

"A guy named Drew Jenkins."

Graham's skate slips out of Audrey's hand and clatters against the black plastic seat below. "All right," she says, picking the skate up. "You'll be home in time for Graham's school concert Tuesday night?"

"Yep. Wouldn't miss it." I mean, twenty four-year-olds singing for half an hour . . . it's bound to be amusing. "Oh, and I need a favor."

Audrey raises an eyebrow. Normally, she's the one asking for favors.

"Lauren is looking for someone to watch the girls so she can go back to work. You heard about the job with the Rebels?"

Audrey nods.

"Is Tammy doing anything now that Graham's in preschool?"

"She's *retired* Jameson." After retiring from being a preschool teacher for thirty years, Tammy was Graham's nanny. She was the savior who stepped in and watched Graham while Audrey finished the fifth year of her architecture program and then the three-year internship that was required before she could get licensed. She stayed on last year when Audrey and Jules officially launched their all-female construction company, rebranding our father's company and calling it "Our House." So this is Tammy's first actual year of retirement.

"Yeah, but do you think she'd be interested in watching Lauren's girls? They're so easy compared to Graham."

"You make him sound like he's a maniac or something." Audrey grits her teeth together. She's doing a great job as a single mom, but Graham has so much energy that some days it takes all three of the adults living in our house to parent him.

"He's just energetic. But Lauren's girls are pretty calm. They still nap. Maybe she'd be interested, even if just until they're old enough for preschool?"

"I can ask," Audrey says. Even though I'm the one who initially found and hired Tammy, she and Audrey grew pretty close. She's practically family now, as she's essentially Graham's stand-in grandmother.

"If she's interested, would you suggest her to Lauren? Don't let her know it was my idea."

"And why not?"

"She doesn't want my help. She wants to do everything on her own, but she'd probably take your help if you offered it."

Audrey's skin is creamy, but her cheeks are always rosy, and they push up toward her eyes when she can't contain her smile. "You really like her, don't you?"

"I'm just trying to help her get her feet under her and start over," I say, hoping that once I know she's settled and can take care of herself, I'll be able to walk away knowing I did what I promised I'd do.

"Mm hmm," Audrey says, nodding vigorously just to show me how full of shit she thinks I am. "You better get going so you don't miss your flight."

I wave goodbye to my family and call up to Graham that

I'll see him at his concert in a few nights. I don't make eye contact with Lauren on my way out, because I don't want her face etched in my mind any more than it already is.

———

I'm finally walking into my hotel in Denver after a tense day of negotiation. Boston's looking to trade one of its better players for two newer guys from Colorado, and even though Drew Jenkins wants in on the deal, it's not going to happen.

I tried. But he's asking for more than what Boston can give and they're going with different players. I don't often lose, but in the end it's a money game and Boston's salary cap won't allow them to pay Drew what he's worth. I have about thirty minutes to figure out how to break this news before I meet him for dinner.

I check in with the concierge and ask them to arrange a car to take me to the restaurant after I go upstairs and grab a quick shower, but as I'm walking toward the elevators, my phone rings. When I see Lauren's name flash on my screen, I detour back to the couches in the lobby.

"Hey, what's going on?"

In the background, it sounds like she's at a construction site. "Our range got delivered today, so I just opened a box of pots and pans, and of course since they're out on open shelving right now, the girls are using wooden spoons to bang on them like they're drums."

"How long until your cabinets go in?" I ask. I told Jules to expedite everything and I'd pay the extra rush fees, but it's only been two weeks.

"I think they're getting delivered this week. Right now I have a refrigerator, toaster oven, and sink, and now I have a range too. And Jules set up a workbench for me with a wooden countertop, so at least it's possible to actually cook now."

"I thought you hated cooking."

"I do, but I also have kids to feed and I finally have my appetite back. But anyway," she says, and lets out a sigh., "that's not why I'm calling."

"You just missed me? Ahh, that's sweet." Why am I trying to put ideas into her head?

"No, I'm pissed at you."

"Really? How unusual." I hope my tone conveys my sarcasm. Pissed at me used to be her natural state.

"I need you to stop interfering, Jameson."

"And how am I interfering?"

"First the job at the Rebels—"

"Oh, you didn't want that job?" I ask and I swear I can see her rolling her eyes even from two thousand miles away.

Another sigh. "Of course I wanted it, but I wouldn't have known about it if it weren't for you. And now Tammy too?"

"What about Tammy?"

"Don't try to play like you didn't set this up. A second too-good-to-be-true opportunity in two weeks? That has Jameson Flynn written all over it."

"Are you saying," I ask, my voice dropping so low it's practically a rumble, "that *I'm* too good to be true?"

"I asked you not to interfere. You know that I want to do this on my own. And . . . I don't know. I don't want to feel like I owe you anything, but you keep getting involved."

"Good, because you *don't* owe me anything. If you need

something and I can help you, I'm going to help. Not because it's quid pro quo, but because that's just who I am."

"Since when?"

"This is how I've always been—" *with people I care about.*

"Then why am I just seeing this side of you now?"

"Maybe you weren't looking hard enough before."

I think back to the conversation we had at dinner the night before I introduced her to Josh, where I told her about my father's decline into alcoholism after my stepmom's death and how, when he finally left, I stepped in to raise my little sisters. I admitted that, despite my initial reservations about her because she was Carson's niece, she'd proven me wrong and I'd been recommending her work to other agents at Kaplan.

Then again, did I ever *show* her who I was, or did I just open up about a few things in a half-hearted attempt to prove I wasn't the asshole I'd shown her the first few years we'd known each other?

"Or maybe," I add before she can respond, "I didn't do a good enough job showing you."

"It feels like you're . . . a whole different person now than you were back then." Her voice is cautious, and I wish I knew why. Is she cautious about changing her opinion of me? Afraid that I might go and prove that I actually am the asshole she thought all along? Or is this about Josh in some way?

"I'm not a different person, Lauren." I run my hand through my hair and lean my head back against the couch in the nearly empty lobby, wishing I'd just gone up to my room and called her back. I don't want to be having this conversation in public. In fact, I don't want to be having this conversation over the phone. I want to see her in person and fucking look her in the eyes when I say these things to her. "I'm just in a different place in my life now. When you started working at Kaplan, I was only a few years into this career. I needed to be successful, and I needed to be there for my sisters. I poured one hundred percent of myself into those two things, and anyone and anything that fell outside of that . . . well, I probably wasn't the best version of myself in those cases."

I hear her breathing on the other end of the phone, but she doesn't say anything. And then one of her kids lets out a blood-curdling scream, and she says, "Oh, shit. Sorry, I'll call you back." And the line goes dead.

———

"So here's the thing," Drew says as he sets his beer back on the table. "I get why it's not going to work out right now. But I need you to get me back to Boston for next season."

"I'm going to be honest with you," I tell him, because he's two contracts into this career and he needs to hear it. "If you want to play for the Rebels, you're going to have to play better than you've been playing. When Colorado signed you, you'd had a great three years with Vancouver. But they're paying you based on how you were playing in Vancouver, and I don't know what's changed, but you're not consistently playing like you used to."

Drew looks down at his empty plate and back up at me. "I'm just not vibing with this team."

"You're not *vibing* with them? What are you, sixteen?"

What happened to good old-fashioned hard work? Put

your head down and do your fucking job. It's not about how you "feel," it's about how you play.

"I got off to a rocky start with one of the guys," Drew says, then proceeds to tell me a little about the situation, where he pissed off a much more established and respected player. No two ways about it, Drew fucked up and it sounds like it soured the whole team on him.

"It happens. So apologize," I say. "Or go out there and play like you used to play and *earn* their respect. But right now Colorado's spending a lot of money on you and you aren't delivering consistently. No way Boston is going to make you an offer unless you show them that you're still the player they've seen in the past."

Drew bites his lower lip in frustration, and his nostrils flare. "If I do turn it around this season, what are the chances you can get me to Boston?"

"They'd have to need another center. It looks like there's a chance Piatza might retire at the end of this season, which is why I thought this trade had a chance, but he hasn't announced anything yet. Why are you so anxious to get to Boston?"

"Not ready to talk about that. But if there's an opportunity, keep me posted."

"I will," I tell him as the waiter approaches to clear the table. I hand him my credit card even though he hasn't brought the bill, because now that I've straightened things out with Drew, I need to figure out what the hell happened with Lauren earlier. It's close to 11:00 p.m. in Boston and I still haven't heard back from her.

As soon as Drew and I part ways, I text Lauren.

JAMESON

Everything okay? You said you'd call back and you haven't, so I just want to make sure.

Her response comes through about fifteen minutes later, when I'm in the elevator on the way up to my hotel room.

LAUREN

Yeah, sorry about that. Quick trip to urgent care because Ivy got a bit too excited with the pans, and she dropped one on Iris's hand.

JAMESON

Is Iris okay?

LAUREN

Yeah, her hand's just bruised, nothing is broken. I'm more shook up about it than either of the girls. I guess that's what I get for talking on the phone and not paying closer attention to what they were doing.

As soon as I'm back in my room, I tap on her name at the top of our chat and hit the screen to call her, except I accidentally video call her instead. Or maybe it was a subconscious choice because I want to see her and make sure she's doing okay.

"Hey." She's lying on her side, her head on the pillow, and everything around her is black except for her face, which is lit up by the light of her phone screen. Her eyes are swollen and her face is red and wet.

"Hey. I didn't mean to make this a video call . . . but I'm glad I did."

"Why?" She lets out a laugh that's practically a snort. "You wanted to see me looking like this?"

"I wanted to make sure you know this isn't your fault. Accidents happen." I shrug off my jacket and pull on the knot at my throat to loosen my tie.

She wipes the sleeve of her sweatshirt across her face, clearing away some of the tears. "How could I not blame myself? If I wasn't so distracted talking to you, maybe Iris wouldn't have gotten hurt."

"Or maybe she would have. You could have been sitting right there next to them, and Ivy still could have picked up that pan and dropped it on Iris's hand. Right?"

She heaves out a defeated sigh. "Yeah, I guess."

"So, what are you really this upset about?"

She looks at the phone screen—at me—with the stunned look of someone who's been caught in a trap. Then she looks away. "It's just been one of those nights."

"What kind of night is that?"

I set the phone down on the dresser so it's propped up where I can see her, and then I unbutton the cuffs of my dress shirt and start unbuttoning the front.

"The kind where I remember how lonely it is doing this all by myself." She wipes at her eyes with the cuff of her sweatshirt, which she's balled around her fist. "But then again, I've been doing this alone all along."

"What do you mean?" I ask as I slip the dress shirt off.

She catches sight of me there in my tightly fitted undershirt and lifts an eyebrow. "Nothing. Sorry, these are my problems to deal with, not yours."

"Hold on a sec," I say as I step out of the view from my phone, grab my sweats off the desk chair where I'd left them this morning, and quickly change. Then I pick my phone up and head to the bed. "Okay," I say, once I'm sitting back against the headboard. "Tell me what you meant about doing this alone all along."

"I shouldn't have said anything," she says, and I think she rolls her eyes, but they are so swollen that it's impossible to tell. I hate seeing her like this, but at the same time I'm relieved and maybe even a little bit honored that she's sharing this moment with me.

"Are you sure that talking about it wouldn't help?"

She gives me a low laugh, practically an inaudible rumble. "Is talking how you work out *your* feelings?"

"Sometimes," I say, dropping my voice before I add, "Depends on what type of feelings we're talking about." A shiver runs up my spine because I know that my last comment was borderline inappropriate, and I halfway don't care.

"Really," Lauren says, her voice equally low. "And how else do you work through your feelings?"

If I didn't know she was still grieving for her husband, I'd think she was flirting with me. "You don't want to know that," I say.

"Don't pretend to know what I want, Jameson," she says, but her eyes are closed and her words are slow, like she's only half awake at this point.

"Why not?" I ask quietly as I reach over and turn out the light next to my bed so it doesn't keep her awake.

"You were always terrible . . . at understanding . . ." She pauses, almost asleep now, and I hang on to her words, hoping she'll finish that sentence so I know what it is I haven't understood. But her pouty lips are parted slightly, and her breathing is so rhythmic she has to be asleep.

I give myself a moment to watch her sleep, and then I whisper, "Good night, Lauren," before I disconnect the call.

I lie there for longer than I should, rehashing that conversation, trying to figure out why Josh wasn't the partner she needed, and what she meant when she said I've always been terrible at understanding. Did I not understand her? Or what she wanted? I'd know so much more about where I stood with her if she'd finished that sentence.

# Chapter Twelve

## LAUREN

I open the enormous box of doughnuts on the table in the office kitchen, hoping there are still some left.

When I brought them in this morning, Patrick laughed and asked, "You're bringing doughnuts to your first day of work?"

"A friend had them delivered to my house, and this is way more than my girls and I could ever eat," I'd told him. There was no way I could explain who that friend was.

For the last three days, starting the morning after our phone call, Jameson has had ridiculous amounts of food delivered to my house. First, it was a caramel latte and a dozen bagels with a note that said, "Hope Iris's hand is feeling better today." Then another caramel latte and a dozen croissants, with a note that said, "Hope your week is getting better." And this morning, my favorite latte again and a dozen specialty doughnuts, with a note wishing me good luck on my first day at the new job. Thank goodness bagels and croissants freeze well. At this rate, the girls and I will have breakfast for a month.

I've sent him thank you messages via text each time but haven't talked to him since I fell asleep during our conversation a few nights ago—partially because I'm embarrassed that he saw me crying like that, and partially because I don't remember what I said to him right before I fell asleep.

I was so tired I felt almost drunk, and it really could have been anything. I'm halfway afraid that I admitted how much he hurt me five years ago when I thought we were turning a corner—thought we'd established that we both had feelings for each other—and then he told me he couldn't "do this right now" and introduced me to Josh.

But now it's the end of the day and I'm having a major energy crash. I thought chasing toddlers around day in, day out was exhausting, but I'd honestly forgotten how draining it is using my brain like this all day.

Today has been a lot, but in a good way. However, I'm starving and tired, and I could use a little sugar pick-me-up so I have the energy to make dinner for my girls and play with them when I get home.

I've just taken a bite of the most amazing glazed old-fashioned doughnut when AJ appears in the doorway. "Hey, how was the first day?" She leans against the opening, one ankle crossed over the other. She's in heels and wide leg trousers with a skintight turtleneck, arms folded under her chest, and her dark brown hair hangs in loose waves past her shoulders.

I wonder if it's normal for the GM to stop and check on new hires, and I suspect it's probably not. I swallow my bite of doughnut, and tell her, "It was great, but also exhausting. I'm so glad to be back doing what I love, but it's an adjustment, for sure."

"Most of the things in life that are worth doing are also exhausting," she says.

I laugh out loud at that and tell her, "You sound exactly like my best friend, Petra. She hosts a TV show, and I think she said that exact thing on last week's episode."

"Wait, you're friends with Petra Ivanova?" There's true awe in her voice.

I'm taken aback for half a second at the use of Petra's new last name. It's still hard for me to adjust to, even though it's been more than six months since she took Aleksandr's name.

"Yeah. She was one of my closest friends in Park City, back before she moved to New York to be with Alex." I'm careful not to mention the circumstances around the marriage, since it's something the two of them refuse to talk about for fear the media will get ahold of the story.

"Oh my gosh," AJ sighs and leans against the doorframe. "That's so cool."

"She's going to be at the game tomorrow night," I say. New York is in town to play the Rebels and Petra's going to come up for it. "One of our other best friends, Jackson, is driving down from New Hampshire for the game too." I wish Sierra could come as well, but she's tooling around Europe with Beau.

"So you'll be at the game?"

"Yeah, Petra got us all tickets."

"You'd better not wear an Ivanov jersey," AJ teases.

"I've been a Rebels fan since I was old enough to know what hockey is. Don't you worry."

"Where are you guys sitting?" she asks, and I pull up the ticket Petra texted me and show her. "All right, I'll try to stop by and say hi. And I promise not to fangirl too hard over Petra."

I can't quite hold in the laugh that bubbles up as I imagine this powerful woman fangirling over my best friend. "She's surprisingly down-to-earth," I assure AJ.

———

Luckily, the team's practice facility and offices are in Brighton, so it's a short drive back to Brookline. And when I pull into my driveway, I notice Jules's truck is still on the street, and so is Audrey's SUV. The lights are on in the house, and I can see people moving around inside. I just sit in my car for a moment before I pull into the garage, absorbing the fact that this place feels like home already.

After I walk through the back door into the sunroom, and slip out of my shoes and hang my coat, I stop to listen to the sound of my kids playing and my friends and cousin laughing together. I have this moment of calm, like this is what was meant to happen.

I blink back the tears that spring to my eyes at the realization that Josh made this all possible, but doesn't get to be here to enjoy this with us. Even though it's been months since he passed, the grief still comes on suddenly. It's always present, and sometimes it can feel overwhelming, or sometimes it's tempered by the reality that our marriage wasn't great for a year or two before he died. But today I'm filled with guilt that he did all of this—bought this house, started to remodel it—for us. He was working on making "us" better, and I didn't know it until after he died.

I take a deep breath as I walk into the kitchen, and I'm

amazed to find that it actually looks like a kitchen. "Oh my God!"

"Mommy!" my kids yell as they run into the kitchen and each grab on to one of my legs.

"Hey, girls," I say. "What are you doing?" I lean down and pat their heads, then take another look around the kitchen, amazed that there are cabinets in all the right places. Yesterday the boxes arrived and were piled in what will be the informal eating area, between the kitchen and the sunroom, where we're standing now.

"We play with friends," Iris tells me.

"Friends?"

"She's talking about Jules and Audrey," Morgan says, walking into the kitchen with Jameson's sisters on her heels.

"You guys, this looks amazing. I can't believe you did this all in one day."

"This part was easy," Jules says. "Installing cabinets doesn't take that long. Tomorrow the people from the stone yard will be here to measure and template the countertops, I'll finish the trim work, and next week the painters will be here to paint. You're still set on the color, right?"

I've chosen a grayish sage green for the lower cabinets and white for the upper cabinets, and I think the combination will look great with the soapstone counters and the original sink.

"Yep. I can't believe how this is all coming together," I tell them. "And I can't wait to show Petra and Jackson when they're here tomorrow."

"They're going to be so happy for you," Morgan says.

"I know. They're going to love what you ladies have done here," I tell Jules and Audrey as I glance around the space and through the opening with pocket doors that they've created between the kitchen and the living room in the front of the house. "And I know they're going to absolutely love the primary bedroom and bathroom upstairs, as much as I do."

"He knew you'd love it," Jules says, then clamps her lips together as she and Audrey share a look that raises goose bumps along my spine.

"He?" I ask. They didn't know Josh. What are they talking about? When they don't respond, I say, "What was that look you two just shared?"

Jules's cheeks turn pink, and she glances at Audrey who gives her a small nod. "When we took over this project, right after Jameson fired Woody, the upstairs looked just like the downstairs—completely gutted."

"What—" I look from one of them to the other. "What do you mean, gutted?"

"I mean it had new windows, plumbing, and electrical, like the rest of the house, but no other work had been done up there."

"But . . ." I stare at them, my eyes wide. "Does that mean you two designed and completed the upstairs before I moved in?"

"Something like that," Audrey says.

"What happened, *exactly*?"

I'm part-confused and part-furious. For the past few weeks since I've been living here, I've been torn between gratitude to Josh for making this possible and guilt that I'd doubted him and his feelings for me while he was making a home here for us. And now they're telling me the part I thought Josh had specifically designed with me in mind was not from him at all?

It feels like such a ridiculous hope to have clung to, but I believed that Josh designing that space proved that he knew me, and loved me, and was making things right.

"Design isn't really my forte," Jules says. "So Audrey worked with Jameson on redesigning the upstairs."

My mouth opens but no words come out, and Jules, Audrey, and Morgan all stare at me with looks of concern. "With . . . Jameson?"

"It was sort of," Audrey says hesitantly, "his idea."

"Define 'his idea.'" I can't even quantify the confusing emotions that are circling in my brain right now, but my body has decided to respond by flooding my system with adrenaline, and I'm pretty sure I've broken out in a full-body sweat while also feeling frozen in shock.

"He wanted to make sure that the upstairs was livable before you and the girls moved in."

"So the design?" I ask. "The bedroom and bathroom . . .?"

The sisters share another look. "It was mostly him," Audrey says. "I drew up the plans, but he was the one who knew you, so he picked out what he thought you'd like."

The bedroom's vaulted ceiling with the wooden beams, the custom walk-in closet, the bathroom of my dreams . . . it wasn't my husband's doing after all?

When Jules said "He knew you'd love it," she was talking about Jameson?

"You look . . ." Morgan says, "angry?"

"I'm"—I sink to the ground, relieved that the girls have made their way back to the living room and are chasing each other around the nearly empty room—"so fucking confused."

"I don't know why he didn't want you to know," Jules says as she sits down next to me. "He didn't originally say we weren't going to tell you, but then that first day when you saw it and you mentioned Josh, he just went with that."

Audrey adds, "But we also hated feeling like we were lying to you, so Jules and I agreed that if it ever came up again, we'd tell you the truth."

"I . . ." I stammer. "I appreciate that. But also, why would *he* lie about that?"

Audrey and Morgan sit on the ground too, so we've essentially formed a circle. I can't wait to have actual furniture in here like a grown-up, but right now the floor seems like the safest place for me to be since it's as if the ground has crumbled beneath me.

"I can't say that I understand the inner workings of Jameson's mind—" Jules says.

"No one can," Audrey adds.

"—but I think he's worried about overstepping," Jules continues. "While also, obviously, wanting to make sure your house is everything you want it to be so you can get off to a good start here."

*Why does he care?* The question bangs around in my mind at the same time as I start adding things up: helping me sort out the financial mess Josh left me in, remodeling my house, arranging to have my driveway plowed when it snows and getting me a new garage door, telling me about the job with the Rebels, having Audrey connect me to Tammy, sending me and the girls breakfast every day this week.

"Does he . . .?" I groan, unable to get the words out because it sounds so impossible, especially after all this time. I'm biting down on my lower lip so hard I'm worried I'm going to draw blood, so I relax my jaw, take a deep breath, and look away. I glance around the first floor of this house that I'm starting to love, and I realize that it's all happening because of him.

They look at me expectantly, waiting for me to finish my sentence, but I can't. My emotions are all over the place. I'm not ready to even entertain the idea that he might have feelings for me. And what does that even mean for a confirmed bachelor like him?

Jules just gives me a shrug and a small smile, and says, "Have feelings for you?"

I give a small nod.

"We think so."

———

"Are you sure you're okay?" Petra asks when she, Jackson, Morgan, and I find our seats in the club section at the front of the second level. When the players take the ice, we'll be sitting about twenty-five rows behind New York.

"Yeah," I say with a sigh. "I'm just exhausted." I don't think I slept for more than two hours last night. I lay awake in my bed, my mind spinning until the first rays of light were coming through my window. I'm not sure how I made it through my second day of work today, or how I'm going to stay awake for this game.

"You've been through a lot," Jackson says. "Between the house, the new job, and the info Jules and Audrey dropped on you, I'm not surprised you're exhausted."

At least I was able to catch my friends up on everything over dinner, and Morgan filled in the parts I couldn't, like how shocked I'd looked when Jules and Audrey divulged Jameson's role in remodeling my house.

"You still haven't told us how you feel about him," Morgan says as she eyes the jersey I'm wearing.

When I'd mentioned not having any Rebels gear, Jules had said she had tons—ironic since she apparently hates hockey—and would bring something over for me. Sure enough, the jersey was folded neatly and sitting on my bed when I got home from work today. I'd unfolded it and rolled my eyes when I saw Flynn and the number 9 on the back.

Of course she'd bring me an old jersey with Jameson's name and number—it felt like a challenge, like she was giving me a choice: I could fold it back up and leave it behind, or I could be brave and put it on.

I opted for bravery. It's just a mental exercise anyway. Even though he has season tickets, it's not like I'm going to see him amid this crowd of 15,000 people. *But if I do, how will I explain wearing his jersey?* I'm choosing to ignore that question, even though it keeps popping into my head. *I won't see him.*

"I don't know how I'm feeling, to be honest."

I'd told them earlier about the night, five years ago, when Jameson and I had unexpectedly ended up at dinner together and bonded in a way I thought meant something was happening between us. And then I told them how the next night, at an event for work, Jameson said, "I can't do this," before introducing me to one of his clients, an alpine ski racer named Josh Emerson.

"It's a lot to process," Jackson says. "You probably just need a little time to absorb all this."

"Yeah. Right now, though, I think I'm going to go get a

soda. I won't make it through this game without some caffeine. Anyone want anything?"

My friends all look at me like I'm crazy because we just rolled out of dinner after completely stuffing ourselves, each of us swearing we'd never be able to eat again. I'm actually glad this jersey is so huge on me, and I'm wearing leggings with it, because I don't think my body could handle any clothing that felt restrictive right now.

I make my way up the stairs and head toward the private club-level lounge that our seats get us access to. There's a short line at the bar, so I lean against the wall as I wait, hoping that I don't fall asleep standing. One bad night of sleep should not make me this tired, but I think Jackson is right—the emotional toll of everything I've been through and this new information I've learned is catching up with me.

I close my eyes for a brief second, and then I feel someone move in close. When I open my eyes again, Jameson has one arm propped on the wall next to me, and he's leaning into my space.

"Where in the world did you find that jersey?" he asks, his voice a low growl.

"Jules gave it to me today because I mentioned I didn't have any Rebels gear."

"That's my jersey."

"Yeah, I'm aware. It has your name across the back."

"No, I mean, that's *my* jersey"—his eyes flick through the windows to the arena where we can see the big blue "R" inside the Rebels symbol painted onto the ice—"that I wore, when I played."

My breath hitches in a way that makes it feel like all the

oxygen has been sucked out of the space. "She didn't tell me that. I'm sorry . . . I didn't mean to overstep."

He leans a little closer, his lips nearly touching my ear. "You saved me the trouble of having to rip the jersey off you if you'd had anyone else's name on your back."

My eyes flick to his. They're as dark as always, but I'd forgotten that up close like this they have flecks of amber around the pupil, like sparks of fire radiating out into his irises.

"Jameson . . ." My voice is practically a whisper, and I pause because I don't know what I want to say.

"Next!" The loud, distinctly annoyed voice of the guy behind the bar cuts into the space between us and I jump away. I hadn't noticed that in the time we were talking, the line had moved and now it's my turn. I glance apologetically behind me at the people who are waiting to order.

"I have to . . ." I tilt my chin toward the counter as I move away, and Jameson gives me an amused chuckle and tells me he'll see me later.

When I get back to my seat with my large soda in my hand, I sink down between Petra and Morgan, whispering "Holy shit" over and over.

"What happened?" Morgan asks, her eyes huge and the concern evident in her voice.

"I just ran into Jameson."

Petra looks amused, like she's watching a movie with a really good plot twist.

"And . . .?" Jackson asks, leaning around Petra to look at me.

"Apparently I'm wearing his jersey."

They all look at me like I just said *The Earth is round.*

"Like, one of his *actual* jerseys," I say, feeling like I'm about to hyperventilate, "that he used to wear when he played."

"And how did he react to *that?*" Petra asks, her lips quirking up into a sly smile.

"He said I saved him the trouble of having to rip the jersey off me if I'd had someone else's name on my back." My heart is racing so fast I'm pretty sure I'm going to have a heart attack.

"Holy shit, that's hot," Petra says. "What did you do?"

"I don't even know. I just looked at him and then had to turn back to the bar because I was holding up the line."

"So, you didn't finish the conversation?" Morgan clarifies.

"No, he just fucking smirked at me and said he'd see me later." I take in a ragged breath. "This can't be . . . what the actual hell is even happening?" I practically whisper yell the last question as I drop my head into my hands. I've only been widowed for a few months; it's way too soon for the thrill that ran through me when his breath ghosted over my earlobe. I'm not ready for this. I'm not ready for *him*.

"Oh, honey," Petra says, putting her arm around me, "it's okay to feel things. Like, if you have feelings for him, that's not a bad thing."

"I don't even know what I'm feeling." I lift my head and glance around to make sure no one is listening to us. "I mean, years ago I thought I had feelings for him, but he didn't return them—"

"Are you sure?" Morgan interrupts. "Because you told us he said he 'couldn't do this now.' Not that he didn't have feelings. Maybe something happened in those twenty-four hours between your dinner and your work event?"

"I don't know. I took him at his word, that he didn't want anything to happen between us."

"But that isn't what he said," Jackson reminds me. "He said he '*couldn't* do this,' not that he didn't want to. Did you ever ask him what he meant?"

"No. I met Josh, and he just kind of swept me off my feet. Made it easy to forget about Jameson, like I thought he forgot about me."

"Did he, though?" Morgan asks again. "Because the way he told you that you were making a mistake marrying Josh sounds like he was all kinds of crazy jealous."

"That—" I take in a deep breath. "—never actually crossed my mind. I thought that was just Jameson being an asshole, like usual."

But now that they're bringing it up, I'm having all kinds of second thoughts about what actually happened five years ago.

"I don't know what he was like back then," Jackson says, reaching over and squeezing my knee, "but he certainly doesn't sound like he's an asshole now."

I roll my head back so it's resting in the crook of Petra's elbow. "Yeah, it doesn't seem that way, does it?"

And then I have the eerie feeling of being watched. When I lift my head and look around, Jameson is one section over, and looking straight at me with the self-satisfied smirk of a man who knows he's rattled me. He knows I'm talking to my friends about him, and he's enjoying it.

———

"You're allowed to cheer for your husband when he scores," I tell Petra when she sits back down with a smug, yet sympathetic look.

There are definitely some hometown fans around us who were not too happy with her jumping up and down and yelling as Aleksandr reached his stick back while falling forward past the goal, sliding the puck between Colt's legs, directly through the five-hole. Lucky shots like that don't happen often. They also don't happen without intense focus and skill, which Aleksandr is known for demonstrating on the ice.

The buzzer sounds to end the period, and the players retreat to their locker rooms. Around us, people are headed to the lounge or the bathroom, and I'm about to do the same now that I've finished my entire soda, but then I see AJ headed right toward us.

I introduce her to my friends, and half listen as she and Petra chat about hockey and the media and Petra's show. But mostly my bladder is yelling at me that I'd better go get in line or it's going to get serious, so I excuse myself and head to the bathrooms. By the time I make it through the line and am headed back out toward our seats, I can hear the music indicating that the players are taking the ice.

My phone vibrates in my hand, so I glance down at it as I rush forward, not wanting to miss the beginning of the next period, and run right into what feels like a brick wall.

But of course, as I look up, it's not a wall at all, just two hundred pounds of solid muscle, by the feel of him.

"I'm starting to wonder if you're following me," I say as I look up at Jameson.

"Maybe I'm just getting lucky running into you so frequently tonight."

"Or maybe you're intentionally running into me."

"Would you be mad if I was?" Jameson asks.

I break eye contact and glance around, noticing that the last few people here are headed back to their seats. I look back at him. "Depends . . . on why you're here every time I'm alone."

He takes a step closer. "Why do you *think* I'm here, Lauren?"

I swallow. "Jameson." I shake my head slightly, trying to clear up the confusion that always seems to creep in when he's around. "I haven't done this in a while. I could easily be misreading these signs. So I need you to be very clear with me . . . what are you thinking right now?"

"I'm thinking a week is too fucking long to go without seeing you." He reaches over and tucks a piece of hair behind my ear, and his hand slips beneath my locks, resting on the back of my neck. I like the feel of his skin against mine maybe more than I should. "And I'm feeling like we started a conversation the other night on the phone that we still need to finish."

Somehow, his answer tells me everything and nothing all at once. I'm about to clarify and ask him how he feels about *me*, when he adds, "How are you feeling?"

"Really confused. Jules and Audrey told me yesterday that you are to thank for my perfectly designed upstairs."

He swallows, but doesn't look away or say anything in response.

"How did *you* design something that's so perfectly *me*?"

139

"Do you really think I don't know you at all?" His voice is softer, more seductive than it normally is.

*But how do you know me better than my husband ever did?* That's the question I want to ask, but I don't know if I want to show all my cards like that.

"I think maybe you know me better than I realized," I admit. "And maybe I don't really know you that well at all."

"So maybe it's time to change that," he says, and he pulls me closer, dipping his head so his mouth is next to my ear. Heat flames through my body at his proximity, and I want to step closer, press myself up against him. "But first"—his breath trails along my ear and into my hair—"go enjoy the game with your friends. We'll talk later."

# Chapter Thirteen

## LAUREN

I've just gotten home from the game, thanked Paige profusely for watching my kids, checked on my girls sleeping soundly in their new toddler beds, switched my leggings and boots out for fuzzy knee-high socks, and headed back downstairs to grab a glass of water, when the text comes through.

> **JAMESON**
>
> How do you feel about dessert?

> **LAUREN**
>
> Like as a food group? I feel pretty good about it, why?

> **JAMESON**
>
> I have an enormous piece of tiramisu and need someone to share it with.

I could think it's a coincidence he has my favorite dessert, but nothing Jameson Flynn does is a coincidence.

LAUREN

Now???

JAMESON

Well, like thirty seconds from now. i just pulled up in front of your house.

I walk through the kitchen into the living room so I can peek out the window, and sure enough, his Maserati SUV is on the street in front of my house.

LAUREN

That's awfully bold, just showing up at my house. What would you have done if I was asleep and didn't answer your text?

I watch as he gets out of the car, restaurant bag in hand, and heads up the steps to my front walkway. He glances at his phone, probably reading my text, and one corner of his lip turns up in a half smile that would probably have had twenty-five-year-old me swooning.

I meet him at the front door, and when I open it, he says, "Not answering was never an option."

I roll my eyes at how presumptuous he continues to be and gesture him inside. When I close the door and turn to face him, his breath hitches. That's when I realize that I'm standing there in nothing but his jersey and fuzzy cable-knit socks pulled up to my knees.

"Nice pajamas." He winks.

"I just hadn't finished getting undressed yet."

"I have so many thoughts about that," he says, giving me a lift of one of his eyebrows like he's letting me know he isn't going to share them.

He takes off his shoes and coat, and I lead him back to the kitchen. I don't have countertops yet, but Jules did lay a big piece of butcher block across the island so I'd have a temporary counter there. He sets the bag on top and lifts out a huge box from the most famous pastry shop in the North End.

I'm about to ask him how he managed to get there after the game and then over here so quickly, when he glances around at my kitchen, which, like the rest of the first floor, has no furniture of any kind, and asks, "Where should we eat this?"

"How about the sunroom?"

He grabs the box of dessert and I bring some forks and napkins, and when we walk in, he looks around in surprise. Last time he was in here, it was floor-to-ceiling boxes. Now, the glow of the streetlights in the front of the house and the light above the garage door in the back both reflect off the snow, illuminating the room in beautiful, glowing light.

"This is a great room."

"Especially full of toddler furniture and toys." I laugh, a little uncomfortable that the only place I can offer him to sit is on one of the two adult-size beanbags that rest on the floor nearest the wall. There's no way he'd fit at the kid-size art table where my girls eat most of their meals while the rest of the house is under construction.

We make small talk about the room and how comfortable these beanbags are while we take turns passing the box of tiramisu back and forth so we can each have bites, and all the while my anxiety grows. I know Jameson didn't stop by in the middle of the night because he needed help eating my favorite dessert, or because he wanted to chat about my house.

I look down at the box in my hand, and while normally I could scarf down this entire piece—easily four servings—by myself, I find that my stomach is in knots after only a few bites.

"Jameson," I say, resting the box on my knees and looking over at him. His eyes are focused on the bare expanse of my thigh between the hem of his jersey and where the box sits, but he glances up at me quickly. He doesn't look embarrassed that I caught him looking. "What are you really doing here?"

He shrugs both shoulders and says, "I told you we'd talk later."

"No reasonable person would suspect you meant later *tonight*."

He doesn't reply, just studies my face, then focuses on my lips. "You have . . ." he points to his own lips and instinctively I lick mine.

"Did I get it?"

"No." His eyes are so dark as he reaches toward me that I can't tell the iris from the pupil. "May I?"

I nod and he swipes his thumb near the corner of my upper lip and then brings his thumb to his own lips and sucks the mascarpone cream filling off. I swear my body combusts as if he'd licked it off me himself.

"Hey, that was mine!" I say, trying to deflect any attention from the way my body is responding to this.

"Mine now. But if you leave cream on your lips like that again, I'll definitely fight you for it."

*Holy shit.* My core clenches at his suggestion, and I literally have to cross my legs to relieve some of the pressure there. When I do, his jersey rides up higher on my thigh. He eyes my exposed thigh, and then, with his voice so low it's practically a growl, he says, "And I don't think that's a fight you'd win."

"You might be surprised how hard I fight when I really want something." Am I talking about the cream filling for the dessert? I don't even know anymore.

"What you want, and what you can handle right now, might be two very different things."

"What's that supposed to mean?"

"You said it yourself tonight, Lauren. It's been a long time since you've done this. You know what I want," he says, but do I? "And we're just going to go as slow as you need."

It's like my body and my mind are at war with themselves right now. My body is urging me to stand up, swing my leg over, straddle Jameson's lap, and show him how *not* slow I want to take this. But then my mind is also pulling the alarm, reminding me that he's been a great friend, and having sex with him would definitely ruin the friendship. In the end, it wouldn't be worth it, no matter how good the idea feels right now.

"Everything that's going through your mind right now is exactly why we're going to take this slow." He takes the dessert box out of my hand and sets it on the floor by his feet.

"How do you know what's going through my mind?"

"Because I'm watching it play out on your face. Doubt. Fear. Worry." He pauses. "It makes sense that you feel all those things right now, but you won't always. You're going to get through this, Lauren, and you're going to come out stronger on the other side."

I wish I had the faith in myself that he apparently has. I wish I was the strong, fearless girl he once knew: the one who wasn't afraid to take on any challenge, who took life by the horns and wrestled it to her will.

But for the first time in a long time, I feel like I could be her—*myself*—again.

In fact, maybe I am already on that path. Moving across the country, remodeling a house to make it perfect for me and the girls, building a new friend group in Boston, getting a full-time job in the sports world . . . these are not things that Josh's wife, Lauren Emerson, would have done. These are classic Lauren Manning moves.

The fact that Jameson recognizes that I need to do this to rebuild myself and my life . . . it's like he gets me at a core level. If only he weren't the kind of guy who avoids relationships at all costs. Because the Jameson Flynn I'm getting to know is the kind of guy I'd want to keep around.

"All right," he says, "I need to get going." He stands, then bends toward me, sliding one arm under my knees, and the other around my back, and lifts me off my beanbag. His warm hand slides against my bare thigh, and it makes me realize that it's been many months—much longer than I've been a widow—since I've had a man touch me like this.

My hand is on his chest as he cradles me in his arms.

"I can feel your heartbeat," I murmur as the rhythmic beating pounds against my palm. "It's nice to know you have one."

His chest shakes with silent laughter. "You thought I was heartless?"

"Only for the first few years I knew you."

"You're adorable," he says with an eye roll, then drops my legs so I'm standing, facing him. "Walk me out?"

He leads the way back through the kitchen and down the

hallway to the entryway, then turns to face me when we get to the door. He reaches out, his hands landing on my hips, gripping them possessively through the fabric of his jersey, and when I look up at him, I don't even attempt to hide the longing I'm feeling.

"Go to bed, Lauren." His voice is thick and low, like a warning.

"You're trying to get rid of me?"

"I'm trying not to do anything you'll regret."

"What makes you think I'd regret . . . anything?"

He gives me a half smile, brings his hands to either side of my face, then kisses my forehead lightly. "You're not ready," he says, then turns to put on his shoes and his coat.

"What if I am?" I ask, not at all certain that I'm even thinking clearly right now. But I miss his proximity, his scent, his warmth, his voice. I don't want him to go. I don't know *what* I want.

"You're not." We exchange a glance, and he reaches out and caresses my cheek. "Yet."

And then he turns and walks out the door.

———

"Hey," Morgan calls from the entryway as she lets herself and Paige in. "We're here!"

"I'm in the kitchen," I call back, but my girls are already yelling "Morgan!" and running toward the entryway to greet her. They're in their fleece zip-up pajamas with wet hair from their bath, and I pause, listening to them laughing with my sister and my cousin.

I take the salad dressings I made out of the refrigerator so they can come to room temperature, and then there's a knock on the door. I walk into the entryway in time to see Paige opening the door for Jules, Audrey, and Graham. And as they crowd into the entryway, I realize that *this* is what I hoped for when I moved here . . . family close by, real friendships.

Graham has his boots and coat off in what has to be record time, and he and the girls run to the living room with a bag of books he dumps on the new rug for them to look at together.

"It looks amazing in here," Paige says, looking around at the finished space. We had to move back into her place for two days earlier this week so the downstairs floors could get refinished, but now that that's done and the countertops went in and I got a dining table and some living room furniture, this house is truly starting to feel like home.

"I'm giving Jules and Audrey one hundred percent of the credit," I say. "They designed it and did the work."

"It was a team effort," Audrey says, and I know she's also thinking about her brother's involvement. I haven't talked to him much this week because he's been traveling for work. He was at a game in Dallas a few days ago, and then I think he was in Nashville. I saw him briefly at Graham's hockey practice this morning, but then Iris had a total meltdown, so we ended up leaving early and I didn't get a chance to talk to him.

I'm still trying to come to terms with how utterly different he seems now—though I guess what I'm seeing is the side of him that he started to show me that night at dinner five years ago, before everything went sideways the next night.

It's been hard not to dwell on his proclamation that I'm

"not ready" for anything to happen between us . . . mostly because he's right. I haven't quite let go of Josh yet. Every day I spend in this house makes me realize two things: I'm happier here than I ever was in Park City with him, and in many ways, I owe this new life to him because he bought me this house.

We head back to the kitchen. Jules sets some sort of amazing smelling casserole into the warm oven, and Morgan and Paige unload a few bottles of wine onto the counter. As I pull wineglasses out of the glass-front cabinets between the sink and the dining area, Morgan tells me she grabbed my mail on the way in.

"Can you set it over there?" I point toward the countertop on the opposite side of the kitchen, closest to the entryway, where I have a bowl for keys and a tray for mail.

"Sure. You got more mail for Sophia."

For some reason, the previous owner's mail hasn't all been forwarded. It's always house-related stuff and I don't receive it often, so when I do, I write *Wrong address—return to sender* on the envelopes and stick them back in the mailbox.

"All right," I say. "I'll take care of it."

I pour my friends some wine, and Audrey asks, "Hey, how's it going with Tammy?"

This past week was the girls' first week with her. "Iris and Ivy seem to love her. I only worked half days this past week so we could ease in, but everything went really well. I'm moving up to full-time already next week. It's been more seamless than I thought it would be."

In fact, my girls are thriving. I was so worried about how they'd do with me working, since they'd only ever known a

149

world in which I was around almost every minute. But what they say about kids is true: they are highly adaptable.

"She really is amazing with little kids," Audrey says. "I don't know what I would have done without her."

"You've done great with him," Jules says, nudging Audrey's shoulder with her own. I get the sense Audrey is constantly worried that, being the only parent Graham has, she's not enough. And I love the ways I've seen both Jules and Jameson lift her up.

"He's really the sweetest little kid," I say as I nod my chin toward where we can see the kids through the new opening between the kitchen and living room. Graham can be a little wild sometimes, but right now he's sitting on the rug with his back against the couch, and the girls are sitting on each side of him. He's "reading" them a story, but by the sounds of it, he's telling them what's happening in the pictures. It's freaking adorable.

Audrey gives a little smile and says, "I worry sometimes that he's too sweet."

"Is there such a thing?" Morgan asks before tilting her wineglass back for a sip.

"I think maybe if you're a boy there is," Audrey says. "I don't want him to get picked on next year in kindergarten."

"He's going to be just fine," Jules says. "He's a Flynn."

They share a look I can't interpret, and Paige distracts us with the sound of her rumbling stomach and a groan. "Oh my God, I'm starving."

"Let's eat then," I suggest and turn to pull two different salads—a kale quinoa salad and a spinach salad with candied nuts, berries, and feta cheese—from my new refrigerator so I can dress them.

My friends ooh and ahh, and I laugh. "Salads are about the only thing I don't hate to make. Probably because there's rarely much cooking involved in them."

"Do your kids eat salad?" Audrey asks, a little awe in her voice.

"Yeah, with a generous side of chicken nuggets or grilled cheese or something."

"Maybe Graham will eat something green if your girls are," she says hopefully.

We set the food out on the table, and call the kids over, and as we sit down to eat my first real meal in my brand new kitchen, I'm overwhelmed with gratitude that this is my life now.

---

We're just finishing dessert when there's a loud knock on the door. I lean back in my seat and glance down the entryway in surprise, and when I look back at the table, everyone is staring at me.

"You going to get that?" Paige asks.

"Why do I feel like you all know who's at the door?"

Morgan shrugs. "Because we do."

"What's going on?"

"Get the door, Lauren," Paige insists. Next to her, Jules wears the same smirk that I so often see on her brother's face.

And when I open the door, Jameson's standing there in joggers and a hoody. While most women go weak in the knees at a hot guy in a suit, that's Jameson's default. I've seen him that way a thousand times. But Jameson, casual like this?

It feels like getting to see a private piece of him he doesn't show to people—like he's taken his armor off.

And because I have no idea what you even say to an insanely hot guy who shows up at your door unexpectedly, the first thing out of my mouth is "Aren't you freezing?"

In my defense, it's late-February in New England.

He steps up over the threshold, mere inches from where I'm standing. "I run hot."

*Holy shit, do you ever,* my body screams. "What—" I stammer. "What are you doing here?"

"We're going out."

"I can't—"

"You can. Jules and Morgan are going to put your girls to bed, and then Jules will stay until we get back. We won't be gone too long."

"What if—" I'm about to say *that's not okay with me,* but my girls come barreling into the entryway yelling, "Flynn!"

He squats down to their level before they get to him. "Jame-es-son." He sounds his name out for them like he did when we were at his house for dinner, and they laugh when he boops them each on the nose. They try to pronounce his name, again with limited success.

He rests his knees on the ground and sits back on his heels, looking up at me from where my girls are now trying to climb him like he's a jungle gym. "Why don't you go put on something cozy? Leggings maybe?"

"What's wrong with what I'm wearing?" I look down at my wide leg jeans and fitted sweater, remembering how cute I thought I was a few hours ago when I put this on.

"Absolutely nothing is wrong with what you're wearing."

His lips curl into that half smile that I see so often. "But it won't be comfortable for what we're doing."

"And you're not going to tell me where we're going?"

"Nope."

"Jameson," I say, my stomach flipping over at the thought of going somewhere with him, just the two of us. "This sounds an awful lot like a date."

"If I was taking you on a date, I assure you, you'd know it. This is just one friend taking another friend out to do something . . . fun."

I'm sure my face screws up into a look of skepticism when I say, "You don't exactly sound like you believe this is going to be fun."

He stands as my girls toddle off toward Graham, who's now back in the living room, and takes a step closer to me. He sure does like to be in my personal space.

"I guess how fun it is will depend on how receptive you are to my activity of choice." He leans down so his lips practically graze my earlobe, and with a voice so quiet it doesn't even sound like him, he says, "Now run upstairs and change like a good girl."

Heat flashes through my body so quickly I'm sure my skin is a brighter red than my hair, so I turn away quickly and head up the stairs. When I'm most of the way up, I glance down over my shoulder and he's standing there, watching me walk away with that same self-satisfied smirk he wore last weekend at the Rebels game.

# Chapter Fourteen

## JAMESON

"Tell me we're not at the Rebels practice facility for the reason I think," she says as we come out of the tunnel and her eyes fly toward the ice rink. The only lights are the ones above the rink, everything else, including the stands behind us, is cast in dark shadows.

"I can't do that," I say as I drop the hockey bag from my shoulder to the ground. She jumps at the noise, and I steady her with my hand on her lower back. "Everything's going to be fine."

She takes a deep and ragged breath. "I'm not skating," she says, looking down at her feet.

I reach over and tilt her chin up so she's looking at me. "Let's just put your skates on and see how you feel about it then."

"I've done this all before, Jameson. I've tried." She looks away, then back at me again. "I can't."

I cup both sides of her face in my hands and tell her, "I know you can do this." I pause. "You've never tried with me here. I'm not going to let you fall."

She sits on the bench and I kneel at her feet. She gazes down at me with those big blue eyes, and she looks absolutely terrified.

"I can't take away the fear," I tell her. "But we can work through it. I won't let you go, I promise."

She gives me a small nod, and it feels like a Stanley Cup-level victory. I hold her heel in one hand and use my other to unlace her snow boot before sliding it off and resting her foot on my thigh. When I lean over and unzip my hockey bag, she gasps.

"Are those . . ."

"No," I say. "They're not your old skates." Morgan told me that Lauren still had them, but I didn't want her to have to wear the same skates she was wearing when she fell. Since apparently they have the same shoe size, her cousin helped me get a new pair fitted and broken in for Lauren.

"Okay." The word is hesitant, but she nods.

It only takes me a minute to get her figure skates laced; then she sits there like a statue while I sit next to her and lace up my hockey skates. When I turn toward her, she's staring straight ahead, her eyes darting around the rink in an anxious staccato pattern.

"Hey," I say, looping my arm around her lower back. "We're going to be just fine."

"I'm not worried about *you*," she lets out a nervous laugh as she looks over at me. "You could do this with your eyes closed and your feet tied together."

I laugh, and it seems to break a little of the tension. "Exactly. And I'm going to hold on to you and we'll go just as slow as you want. C'mon. You almost made the Olympic team."

155

"Yeah, well—" She clears her throat. "I didn't."

We've both had to walk away from the sport we loved, but at least for me it was a choice—her dreams were ripped away from her. "It's the big dreams that hurt the most when you have to give them up."

"Do you miss it?" Her words are a whisper in this wide-open, silent space.

"Every day."

"Did you ever want to go back to playing?" she asks.

I shake my head. "It wouldn't have been worth what it would have done to my family. Jules and Audrey needed me there after my dad left. And I needed them. We're all each other has."

"You're a good man," Lauren says quietly.

"Mostly." I give her a little wink, then stand, using my arm that's encircling her back to raise her up with me. "Let's skate."

She lets out another shaky breath. "I read somewhere that bravery is being scared, but doing it anyway."

I try to step us forward, but she stands with her skates firmly rooted in place.

"Do you trust me?" I ask.

She looks up at me, her face pale and her eyes huge. "This isn't about trust, Jameson. It's about fear."

"The reason you're still afraid," I say softly, "is because you haven't been back on the ice again since you got hurt. You're letting the what ifs consume you. But what if you *can* do this? What if everything is okay?"

"What if I don't want to?"

"I think that if you didn't want to, you wouldn't have let me put those skates on your feet. Let's just step out onto the ice. We don't have to move. And you can hold on to me the entire time."

"You'd like that," she says lightly.

"Indeed, I would. You want a helmet?"

She looks back up at me. "If you're not going to let me fall, I guess I don't need one, right?"

"I'm *not* going to let you fall."

I step through the door onto the ice, and when I turn around, she's standing there looking at the shiny white surface like it's going to eat her alive. I put one hand on either side of that doorway and leave just enough room on the ice for her.

"Step right out here and hold on to me."

I know she's terrified of falling again. And in this moment, I'm fucking terrified of falling too. Not literally, but of falling for her. Because seeing her hurting like this is killing me, and I don't know any other way to help her get to the other side of this fear except to walk through it with her. Kind of like I've been doing in the wake of Josh's death.

She moves one hand to the top of the boards and tentatively steps over the threshold. When her blade hits the ice, she grabs my sweatshirt frantically, like she's going down even though she's completely steady on one foot.

"Wrap your arm around my waist."

She does as I ask, then slowly steps her other skate onto the ice and her other arm wraps behind my back. We stand there for a moment, just breathing.

"How's it feel to be back on the ice?"

"Give me a minute to get used to the idea," she says, but she loosens her grip on me as she rests her forehead against my sternum.

I keep one arm firmly planted on top of the boards and wrap my other arm around her back, anchoring her to me. She's taking deep breaths, and I can feel her heart pounding. I'm afraid she's going to work herself up and talk herself out of this.

"Eyes on me."

She tilts her head back until she's gazing up at my face.

"What do you think about moving? I'll go backward, slowly. You just hold on."

She gives me a little nod, but the minute we move, her eyes fly shut.

"Look at me, Lauren," I say, and when she opens her eyes, they're the prettiest shade of Robin's egg blue. "Breathe with me." I take some slow, deep breaths as we move across the ice at the slowest pace I can possibly set. When we make it to the other side of the rink, she's still looking up at me, and she's breathing normally again.

"That wasn't—" She twists her mouth as she thinks. "—as bad as it could have been."

"A ringing endorsement for my skills."

She gives me a small smile. "You sure this isn't just one big plan to get me pressed up against you?"

"Trust me, Lauren. This is tame compared to the plans I have for you."

Her cheeks heat with an almost instant flush and her eyes widen in surprise. She swats at my arm, but I keep her held tightly against me. "That's not how friends talk to each other, Jameson."

I know she doesn't actually believe I just want to be her friend, but if it's what she needs to tell herself for now, I'll let it go.

"I suggest you don't squirm like that while you're pressed up against me."

She instantly stills, one hand on my arm and one at my hip. "And why not?"

I turn us so her back is against the boards, then take her hands and place them so they're resting along the top. "For exactly the reasons you'd think." And then I skate away, taking a lap around the rink, because if I don't get some distance from her my body's going to try to take over, and I've promised myself, and her, that we'll take this slow.

When I return, she looks remarkably comfortable compared to the woman who stepped out on the ice with me five minutes ago.

"So here's the thing," she says, sliding her skates backward and forward beneath her while she grips the wall. "Part of why I was so terrified to get back on the ice after my accident—beyond never wanting to experience another concussion or the lingering headaches—was because it was a perfect landing."

This feels like a big admission, but I don't understand why. "What do you mean?"

"I mean, that triple axel was textbook perfect. I landed it the same way I always did, the same way I'd landed it hundreds of times before. And in that moment at Nationals, the landing *felt* perfect. I have no idea what happened, why my skate slipped out from under me, why my head crashed into the ice. None of that should have happened."

I skate forward until there's barely any space between us.

"My skating was on fire that night," she continues. "My jump was perfect. And I still got hurt. A nick in the ice? Overly fatigued muscles? My blade slipping? Who knows what caused it. If it was entirely out of my control, how can I prevent it from ever happening again?"

"So what you're telling me is you had complete control of every part of the jump and performed it perfectly and that whatever went wrong was out of your control?"

"Yes, exactly." She wraps one arm around her ribs, hugging herself, and holds onto the wall with the other arm.

"You can't let what is impossible to control control you, or you'll never grow. It's called a freak accident because there's no way to predict or prevent it. But freak accidents don't happen over and over."

I put my hands on her hips and pull her toward me gently, then spin myself around so I'm behind her, cradling her body in mine. I keep my hands on her hips, but dip my head down and ask, "How do you feel about actually moving again?"

"I feel . . . less scared than before. But only if you don't let go of me."

As long as I've known her, she's the woman against whom all other women have been measured. And no one else has even compared. I am a goner for her, and have been since the very first moment we met. I thought I'd lost her, but now that she's back I have every intention of keeping her—no matter how slowly I have to take this until I'm certain she's ready.

"Believe me, Lauren, there's no way I'm letting you go."

---

Colt glances out the window for the third time in as many minutes. The snow is coming down fast now, and later tonight this will be a full-fledged blizzard. "Dude, if you're afraid of a little snow," I say as I nod toward the door of my office, "go ahead. The new endorsement paperwork's signed already."

The sky is darker than it has any right to be at four o'clock. Derek's already left because he wanted to catch the train before they shut down public transportation. Until now, we've had a relatively mild winter, so the media is really hyping up this storm.

"Nah, it's fine." He tilts his celebratory beer back, takes a long swallow, and then says, "So I heard you were at the rink Saturday night."

"Yeah?" I take a sip of my scotch and wonder how this information reached him.

"With a girl."

"Uh huh."

"You going to tell me why you rented out the rink for her?"

"How the fuck did you know that?" I snap. Sometimes it feels like nothing I do is private, and I'm not ready for anyone to know how I feel about Lauren—except for her.

He lets out the bellowing laugh that, among other things, he's famous for. "I guessed. They don't just let people come in and skate whenever they want. Not even when they're retired players. So, why did you need the rink to yourselves?"

It's my turn to glance out the window. Shit, the snow's going sideways now, which means the wind is picking up. There's only about an inch on the ground, but with flakes this big, it's going to start accumulating fast.

"She hasn't skated in a while."

"You don't rent out a whole rink for a woman just because she hasn't skated in a while. Who is she?"

161

"Just a friend."

"You also don't rent out the practice rink of a professional hockey team for a friend." His voice has an annoyed edge to it. "Who the hell is this woman?"

I don't mean to let the corner of my lips curve up, but the memory of Lauren's face—that huge smile, and the way the happiness just radiated off her by the time we got off the ice—has been etched into my mind for the better part of a week.

"Wait," Colt says, dragging his hand through his sandy-blond hair as he rolls the word out slowly. "Is this the same girl you were talking about a few weeks ago? The one you said would be good for that marketing job—waaait . . ." His eyes get wide, like it's all coming together in his mind. "Holy shit. The redhead?"

I take another sip of my scotch. "I don't know what you're talking about."

"The hell you don't. When AJ got done ripping me a new asshole about sleeping with that girl from marketing, she said I was lucky that the person you recommended for that position was better than the one who'd left it. And the person who has that job now is a hot redhead—"

I don't mean to slam my glass down on my desk, but it has Colt raising both his hands in surrender, which is just fine with me.

My teeth are clenched together so hard when I say, "Do not fucking look at her."

He laughs again. "Just friends, eh?"

"Yes, actually. We *are* just friends. And because she's my friend, I don't want you going anywhere near her."

"I see how it is." His chest shakes with laughter, because Colt can't take anything seriously. Everything's a fucking game with him, which makes him a lot of fun to hang out with, but not someone I'd want near anyone I actually cared about. "Don't worry—"

He stops speaking when my phone starts buzzing on the table, Lauren's name flashing across the screen.

Colt nods down where we both look at the phone. "That her?"

I reach for the phone and tell Colt, "Don't fucking say *anything*." Because he has the emotional maturity of a ten-year-old, it wouldn't be the first time he'd yelled something highly inappropriate right when I answer the phone.

"What are you doing right now?" she asks the minute the call connects. Her voice is slightly panicked.

"Just finishing up a meeting with Colt, why? Is everything okay?"

Across from me, Colt cocks an eyebrow, mouths *Just friends,* and nods with the assurance of someone who knows he's right.

"Not really. I'm kind of stuck at work. There's this delivery of marketing swag coming in for the charity game. I said I'd stay and sign for it, since I live the closest and everyone else had a longer drive home in this weather. The truck was supposed to be here an hour ago and I can't leave until it arrives, but Tammy's at my house with the twins and she needs to go home. Her husband's going to come pick her up because of the weather." Her voice goes high-pitched and speeds up when she says, "I need someone to be home with my girls until I can get there. Paige is in New York for work and Morgan went with her so she could see Petra, Jules is still out in Wellesley at the jobsite and traffic on Route 9 is apparently at a standstill, and Audrey said

163

Graham came home from school with a sore throat and a fever."

"So I'm your last resort?" I tease as I stand and walk over to my closet to grab my coat.

"My last hope, is more like it."

"That's better," I say. "I'll head straight to your house."

She breathes a sigh of relief. "You're amazing."

"You have no idea."

She lets out a laugh that's half snort, and meanwhile, Colt rolls his eyes.

"I'll let Tammy know you're coming. And—" She pauses. "—and thank you, Jameson. Really. I don't know what I'd have done if you weren't able to help me."

"I'll see you soon. Drive safely, okay?"

# Chapter Fifteen

## LAUREN

It's well past six when I pull into my driveway, and if I didn't have four-wheel drive there's no way I'd make it up the hill in the six-plus inches of snow that have fallen in the last few hours. At this point, it's coming down so hard and so fast that I can barely see five feet in front of me, and I feel lucky to have made it home at all. The roads were empty, a sure sign that I shouldn't have been out driving on them either.

When my single-wide driveway levels off at the top of the hill, it widens to accommodate two cars. Jameson's Maserati is sitting off to the side, next to the sunroom, leaving room for me to pull into my garage.

He's shoveled the path from the garage to the back door, and I pause once I'm in the sunroom, as I do almost every night I come home, appreciating how good I have it now—how supported I feel by my friends and family, how happy I am at my job, how much I love my new house, how my girls are happy and healthy and settling into our new life here with remarkable ease.

I drop my boots and coat in their spot and head into the kitchen. It smells amazing in here, and through the opening into the living area I see Jameson sitting on the couch with Ivy on one side of him, Iris on the other, and his arms looped around both girls. And they're watching *Tangled*—the movie I never used to want to watch with them because I hated how much Flynn Rider reminded me of Jameson Flynn.

The man in question is currently in his suit pants with the sleeves of his dress shirt rolled up to his elbows. The top two buttons of his shirt are open, and he looks so fucking delicious sitting here, in my space, with my girls, that I need to remind myself to breathe.

I ran off and married someone else when he turned me down, and he never wanted to settle down or have kids in the first place. And yet, I just came home to him on my couch with my kids. I have to remind myself that this is not going to be a repeated thing, even though, in this moment, I wish this was the norm.

But it makes no sense—we make no sense. Settled down with kids—this isn't the life he wants. I've known that about him for years. And I need to remember it, because even though he's made it clear he wants *me*, I come with a whole lot of additional baggage that I don't think he's ready for. Coming over and watching my kids for a couple hours while I'm stuck at work does not mean he wants to settle down like this.

But seeing him here still makes me smile. And that's when Jameson looks up, sees me grinning like a lunatic in the doorway, and sends a wink my way that has heat flashing through my body so hot, and so fast, that I turn away in embarrassment, heading back into the kitchen. I need to get a handle on this whole flushing situation if I'm going to continue spending time with him, because I can't keep picturing us having sex every time he looks at me.

I lift the lid on the pot simmering on my stove to find pasta sauce bubbling away. There's another pot next to it, full of hot water, so I turn it on to bring it back up to a boil.

Behind me, the movie pauses and Jameson says, "Mom's home."

I like the way that sounds coming out of his mouth way more than I should.

Excited squeals precede the girls' stampede, and then their bodies are plowing into mine, each of them hugging a leg like they always do. Then they sit on my feet, demanding that I walk around with each of them attached to me, which lately has felt like my daily workout. I can't believe how fast they're growing—and that thought is followed by the same one as always: that Josh is missing this. Then again, he missed most things even when he was alive.

Jameson stands on the other side of the massive island, his hands each on the back of a different barstool, watching me.

"You cooked" is all I can manage to choke out under the weight of his stare. I take a few awkward steps with my kids attached to my legs.

"I thought you might be hungry."

"I'm starving."

"Okay, how about I finish cooking this and then we can eat?"

I almost say *You don't need to get home?* But I hold my tongue because I realize I don't *want* him to go home. I want him to stay and have dinner with us.

Him, here in my house, watching a movie with my girls, cooking us dinner . . . it feels right. It feels like what I've always imagined the other half of a relationship *should* feel like. Working together, small sacrifices and little acts of service for each other.

I'm not even in a relationship with Jameson, and it makes me realize how terribly one-sided my marriage was. Except, that wasn't one-sided in the beginning either. Josh put on a really good show until he had me locked down. And I'm terrified of making the same mistake again—trusting that what someone shows me is real, only to find out later that it was all an act.

"Where'd your mind just go?" Jameson asks as he walks around the island toward me. That's when I realize I didn't answer his question.

"Sorry. I was just thinking . . ." I don't know what to say, and I'm not great at coming up with things on the spot. But there's no way that I can tell him that I was envisioning a future for us. Jameson Flynn doesn't do relationships, and I don't think I'd ever recover from a fling with this man.

I'm a single mom rebuilding my life. Things are finally going really well, and having sex with him would fuck up everything—my friendship with him, my friendship with his sisters, the sense of independence I'm rebuilding for myself.

It's not worth what I stand to lose.

He approaches me cautiously, like he's afraid I'll scare and run off—as if I could with a kid attached to each leg. He stops in front of me, reaching out to tuck a piece of my hair behind my ear. I revel in the adoring way he looks at me as the pads of his fingertips graze along the top of my cheekbone, run through the hair at my temple, and drag along the shell of my ear.

A sound escapes my throat, and I'm horrified to realize it sounds a lot like a moan. And by the way his dark eyes light up, I know he didn't miss it either. He smirks, then says, "Let me get this pasta going."

He turns and walks the few steps to the stove, where I can hear the water starting to boil.

These mixed signals—acting like he wants me, then turning and walking away—are making my brain hurt, so I take my girls upstairs with me to change out of my work clothes. Even though nothing's going to happen, I put on a sexy light pink lace bra and thong. Just in case. Then I put on joggers and a matching top, brush out my long hair, slide my feet into my slippers, and pick up my girls to bring them back downstairs where they run back into the living room to play.

As I walk around the island toward the stove, Jameson eyes me over his shoulder, and then the timer goes off. While he moves to drain the pasta, I head to the fridge because I'm fairly certain I have some Parmesan cheese in there.

"You're going to a wedding next weekend?" he asks casually as I shut the refrigerator door. I glance over and he's holding an invitation that was sitting on my counter near the sink.

"Yeah. My cousin is getting married. Paige and I are going up together."

"What about Morgan?" he asks, as he lifts the colander out of the sink.

"It's my dad's nephew getting married, and Morgan is related on my mom's side of the family. She's staying here with my girls, since it's an adult-only reception." He sets the invitation down, and I watch him move around my kitchen like he belongs here, dumping the colander full of pasta into the sauce, then reaching for the Parmesan cheese I set near the stove for him. "Paige is going to be my wingman at the wedding."

He raises an eyebrow at the same time he gives me a side-eye. "Your wingman?"

"Yeah, she's going to keep my ex-boyfriend from high school away from me."

Justin, who I dated for over two years in high school, is recently divorced from my ex-best friend. He's been texting me lately and dropping some not-so-subtle hints about how much he's looking forward to seeing me at the wedding. I could not possibly be less interested in exploring that opportunity, and am actually dreading seeing him.

His tone is dry. "That's not the point of a wingman, Lauren."

"Well, whatever you'd call it, that's Paige's role this weekend." I grab some plates out of the cabinet and carry them over to the stove.

When I set them down, he steps up behind me, planting his hands on the counter on each side of me so that I'm boxed in his arms. A thrill runs up my spine when he drops his voice low and says, "If you really want him to leave you alone, you should bring a date."

I allow myself a moment to enjoy his warmth. I allow myself to picture what it would be like to bring him with me too, but then I also imagine how people would look at me if I brought a date to a wedding only four months after Josh's death.

"I have a date. Her name is Paige."

He pushes off the counter, letting his fingertips skim up my forearms as he steps back. "Well, if you change your mind and want someone better suited for the job, all you have to do is ask."

———

Dinner has been cleaned up, the girls have been bathed and put to bed, and Jameson and I now stand at the front windows in my living room, looking out at the storm. The drifts of snow at the edges of my yard are easily a foot or two high at this point. I haven't heard a snowplow go by since I got home, and though we can hardly see to the other side of the street through the torrent of white flakes and the glare of the streetlights in the storm, the road appears to be a pristine pillow of white snow—probably about eight or nine inches of it I'd guess—which will make them completely impassable.

"I think you missed your window for driving home," I tell him.

In my peripheral vision I see him look over at me but I continue looking out the window, trying not to freak out at the thought of him spending the night here.

"Let's not pretend," he says from beside me, "that there was ever a chance of me going home tonight."

My stomach erupts into a full-out riot of butterflies. I'd been so busy enjoying having him here that I hadn't really been thinking about how he'd get home in this weather. But in the back of my mind, I must have realized that I'd barely gotten home before the roads were impassable, and that was hours ago. But neither of my guest bedrooms have furniture in them—the only bed is in my bedroom.

"There's no way," he continues, beside me, "that I'd leave you here alone to clear all this snow tomorrow. Do you even have a snowblower?"

He's staying because he knows there's no way I can deal with this much snow by myself with two kids to watch also. *This is what friends do for each other.* And someday, when he needs a friend, I hope to be able to return all these favors.

"Yeah, I bought one when I moved in." We've had a mild winter until now. It's snowed an inch or two here or there, but then it always got warm enough to melt it right away so the snowblower hasn't been needed.

"Ever used one?"

"No, but I read the manual." Back in Park City, Josh always took care of snow blowing when he was home, and if there was a storm and he wasn't home, he had a landscaping company that would come by and plow our driveway and take care of our walkway—a service I continued to use until we moved.

I suddenly feel entirely incapable. Like, how am I an adult who has always lived somewhere with snow, and I have no idea how to operate a snowblower? I'm afraid that Jameson is going to ask the same question, but all he says is "It's not that hard. I'll show you tomorrow."

I turn toward him. "Thank you—for being here with Ivy and Iris today, for cooking dinner, helping me clear the snow tomorrow. I . . . I feel like I'm taking advantage of your generosity."

He fully turns toward me, puts his hands on my hips, pulls me a step closer to him, and stares down at me with a look that's some combination of fondness and lust.

"I wouldn't be here if I didn't want to be, Lauren." He

leans down and kisses my forehead, just like he did last weekend when he told me I wasn't ready.

But ready for what? I want this man, and he wants me. Is he waiting for me to be strong enough—mentally and emotionally—that a one-night stand wouldn't absolutely wreck me? Because I'm not sure I'll ever be in that place.

I lean forward, resting my forehead on his sternum like I did this at the ice rink when he helped me overcome one of my biggest fears. He's been such a solid, steadying presence for me these past few months—I've come to depend on him, and his friendship, maybe more than is healthy.

"The only thing about you staying here tonight is that I don't have another bed to offer you—"

"I'll sleep on the couch." His voice is insistent, his words final. He's not looking to share my bed with me tonight, which is both a relief and a disappointment.

While I've certainly spent plenty of time lately thinking about Jameson in my bed, it's always been part of a fantasy—I've never allowed myself to believe that it might actually happen. It shouldn't happen. It can't.

"Why don't you take my bed and I'll sleep on the couch. I'm much smaller than you, so it'll probably be more comfortable for me."

"I'm fine with the couch. So what do you normally do once the girls go to bed?"

I pull back and look up at him. "Clean up? Read? Watch TV? Catch up with my friends?" Man, my life sounds boring.

"Well, we've already cleaned up, and it's only"—he lifts his wrist and glances at his watch—"eight o'clock. You want to watch a movie or something?"

We settle into the couch and decide on a movie, and

we're about fifteen minutes into a rom-com I can't believe I convinced him to watch when Petra's text comes through.

> **PETRA**
>
> Hey, Morgan and Paige are staying with me because all flights into Boston were canceled. How are you doing with your first big snowstorm?

I glance over at Jameson, who's still focused on the TV, and then back down at my phone. Holding it in one hand on the opposite side of my body, and hoping he can't see my screen, I type with my thumb to respond.

> **LAUREN**
>
> Doing okay. Jameson's here.

> **PETRA**
>
> ?!?!

> **LAUREN**
>
> My nanny went home early. He watched the girls and made dinner. Now we're snowed in.

> **PETRA**
>
> Morgan, Paige, and I are all jumping around right now, and Aleksandr is looking at us like we're annoying him.

I laugh out loud, imagining the scene, and Jameson's head snaps over, looking at me. "Sorry, it's just Petra texting me right now." *Go back to watching the movie so I can tell my friend about you being here.*

PETRA

Please tell me you're planning to sleep
with him?

I flip my phone facedown on the couch, praying he wasn't looking at the screen in my hand when that message came through. But his small snort is proof that he did see it. He lifts his arm, putting it around my shoulders and pulling me to his side. "Tell her it's none of her damn business."

My shoulders shake with laughter. "That's only going to rile her up more."

"Whatever," he says, and I can feel him shrug.

LAUREN

Jameson says it's none of your damn
business ;-)

PETRA

Holy shit!!! Girl . . . DO IT!

LAUREN

I'm leaving this conversation now . . .

PETRA

Which means it's going to happen.
Eeeeeeeeeeeee!

LAUREN

Good night . . .

"Now who's riling her up?" Jameson asks, letting out a chuckle. The feel of his warm breath across the top of my head has goose bumps rising all over my body, and reality sets in. *I want this man.*

But I can't have him. Or rather, I could, for a night. But how could we go back to just friends after that? We couldn't.

And I'm not willing to lose the friendship, even though I suspect the sex would be amazing.

"Put the phone down," he says.

"Now? When they're all sitting around speculating whether we're too busy having sex to respond?"

"Let them wonder," he says, and he uses the hand that's wrapped around me to grab my phone and toss it to the far end of the couch. Then he tugs me tighter against his side and says, "Now watch the damn movie and stop thinking about having sex with me."

# Chapter Sixteen

## JAMESON

I don't know if it's the shrill ringing of her phone, or the annoyed tone in which she answers it, that has me jumping off the couch from a dead sleep.

"Why are you calling me, Justin?" She makes the name sound like a curse rolling off her tongue.

*Wait? Who the fuck is Justin?* I glance at my watch and it's barely past 7:00 a.m.

"Yeah, you told me about you and Kenzie." Her voice is flat, like she's trying to sound disinterested.

I grab my phone, slip my pants on, and button them as I walk toward the stairs.

"I'm not interested—" She sounded like she had more to say, so I'm guessing she got interrupted. I want to see her face, so I know how she's feeling about this conversation. I take the stairs two at a time, trying to be quiet because it doesn't sound like the girls are up yet.

Predictably, based on how I can hear every word of this conversation, Lauren's door is only halfway shut.

I push it open, and it's dark in there, but I can see light coming from the crack in the mostly closed bathroom door.

"Justin, I'm *not interested—*"

I give two quick knocks before I push that bathroom door open, and Lauren spins toward me in surprise. She's got a short white towel wrapped around her body, and her wet hair is freshly combed and dripping around her shoulders. She mouths *My ex-boyfriend.*

I hold out my hand for the phone and she gladly hands it over. When I bring it up to my ear, he's still talking—a combination of yelling at her for being too stubborn to forgive him, and insisting he was the best thing that ever happened to her.

"I'm going to have to stop you *right there,*" I say, and the line goes silent. "She's told you multiple times she's not interested, so why the fuck are you still talking?"

"Who the hell are you?"

I'm so tempted to say *I'm her date for the wedding,* since I know he's going to be there. But she didn't seem inclined to take me up on my offer last night, and as much as I want to force her into it in this moment, I want to respect whatever she feels like she needs and can handle. Which right now, may not be having to introduce me to her family at a wedding.

"I'm the man whose name she'll be screaming long after she forgets yours."

The gratitude in Lauren's eyes is replaced by something else as she considers my words. She drops her gaze to skim across my bare chest, and then drops it lower before her head shoots up. In her eyes, I see nothing but desire.

Good, because the friend zone is fine for the short term, but we're not staying here much longer.

"We have to go now," I say to Justin. *"We're busy."*

I hit the button to end the call and Lauren deflates against the sink cabinets behind her. "Thank you," she says on an exhale. Then she shakes her head back and forth, saying, "God, I hate that asshole."

"Then why did you answer the call?" I ask as I click over to the option to block the caller. Done.

"I was fresh out of the shower and didn't want the ringer to wake the girls up, so I panicked."

At the mention of her shower, I can't help but focus on the beads of water running down her shoulders, across her chest, and pooling on the towel where it's tucked in between her breasts. Her chest is heaving, her breath coming out in sharp exhales, and without even looking back up at her, I know it means she's noticed me staring at her half naked body. She's probably also noticed how fucking hard I am right now—a normal problem when waking up, made more extreme by finding her soaking wet and wrapped in a towel.

The combination of the humidity from her shower and the fact that all my blood is currently in my dick has me feeling like it would be a good idea to make some bad decisions right now. Instead of giving into the temptation before she's ready, I turn to leave. But she reaches out and grabs my forearm, and when I turn to look at her, she's staring at her fingers where they're spread across the corded muscles.

"Maybe," she says, her voice small and tentative, "I could use a date to the wedding after all."

She's asking because she's nervous about seeing Justin, not because she wants *me* to go with her—and even though a few minutes ago I was okay with that option, now I'm realizing I don't want to go unless she actually wants me there.

I lean closer. Just slightly . . . just enough that when she looks up, it forces her to lean back over the counter. One of her arms goes back to help her balance, and as her back arches, her breasts tilt up toward me, making that towel really work to keep her covered up.

"Then maybe you should *ask* me. Nicely."

In the low light of early morning, her eyes are almost a dark blue, and goose bumps prickle her chest as my words come out slow and deep.

She raises an eyebrow in response, her chest heaves again, and then she says, "Jameson, would you please accompany me to my cousin's wedding?"

I reach past her, planting my hand on the wall between the mirrors that hang above the sinks. "Of course I will."

My lips are so close to hers I can feel when her breath hitches and she stops breathing. Then she clears her throat and starts to say something, and that's when her girls start their chorus of "Momma! Up! Momma! Up!" from the other room.

Without a second of hesitation, she slips under my arm to go get them up. Meanwhile, I pull my phone out of my pants pocket and text Derek.

JAMESON

Clear my schedule this morning, and all weekend.

DEREK

You're supposed to be in Toronto this weekend.

> JAMESON
>
> Change of plans. I have to go to a wedding in Maine.

> DEREK
>
> Who in the world is getting married in Maine?

> JAMESON
>
> Hell if I know.

———

"This place is adorable," Lauren says as we walk into the house we're staying at for the wedding. The mudroom is all slate floors and wooden benches with hooks above them for coats, along with ski racks and boot trays on the opposite wall. Beyond that, we can see into the wide-open living room, dining room, and kitchen. I set our suitcases down and shut the door behind me. "Paige is going to be bummed to have missed out on staying here."

"Why'd she decide to stay at your parents' house?"

"Since you were going to drive me up today, she ended up coming up last night so she could go to the rehearsal, and she didn't want to stay here alone."

Given the text conversation with Petra the other night, I suspect Paige wanted to give us the whole place to ourselves. But I'll let her believe this story if she wants to. She's still getting used to the idea of me in her life.

We leave our stuff in the mudroom and wander into the living room, which is light and bright, with lofted wood-planked ceilings and white walls—it looks like something straight out of a Pottery Barn catalog. The dining area has a simple farmhouse table and eight chairs, and opens to the brand new kitchen. My sisters would love this place; it's exactly the kind of ski house getaway they'd love to work on.

"How'd you find this place?" I ask Lauren.

"It's my little brother Dale's best friend's house. Lucas lives in Boston but has been remodeling this place for a while, I guess. His work schedule is really intense, so he doesn't get up here that often. He said Paige and I could stay here since it would be empty." It's sparsely furnished, and I'm not sure if that's an intentional decision, or if it's because the place has clearly been remodeled recently.

"That was nice of him."

"He and Dale have been best friends since they were in elementary school. He was practically like a fourth little brother to me."

"Do you see him at all in Boston?"

"No, I haven't seen him in years, actually. I think Paige talks to him occasionally, which is how we ended up staying here."

We double back to a small hallway off the living room, and she pushes open a bedroom door, but the room is empty. We move on to the next door, which opens to a completely new bathroom. There's only one door left off the small hallway, and when she pushes that one open, we walk into a large bedroom with a king-size bed in it. It sits atop an enormous rug that covers most of the floor. Off to the side, there's a dresser, and on the opposite wall is a big mirror leaning up against the wall.

Lauren looks around, walks to a doorway across the room, and opens it. On the other side of the door is the bathroom we saw from the hallway.

"Did we . . . miss a bedroom somewhere?" she asks.

"I don't think so."

"I . . ." She doesn't complete the sentence, just stands there looking dumbstruck. Then she pulls her phone from her back pocket and shoots off a text.

I send her a questioning look.

"Just texting Paige to ask about the sleeping arrangements," she tells me.

I take a few steps toward her and she takes a deep gulp, like she's swallowing down all her feelings and fears.

"I can sleep on the couch again, Lauren. It's not a big deal."

"I think it's my turn to sleep on the couch," she says with a nervous laugh.

"There are no turns here. If there's a bed, you're sleeping in it. End of story."

She plants her hands on her hips. "How's that fair?"

"It isn't. This isn't about fairness."

"What's it about then?"

"It's about me giving you what you need. The space and the time to figure out what you want. And when you're ready to admit that this is more than friendship, you'll know where to find me."

"On the couch?"

"Until you're ready for me to be in your bed, yes."

"Jameson," she whispers my name. "I'm not a one-night stand kind of girl. I can't do casual hookups, and I value our friendship way too much to let sex get in the way."

I take another step closer. "What in the world have I said to make you think I wanted this thing between us to be a one-night stand?"

She looks up at me, her eyes huge and her breathing erratic. "You don't . . . you don't do relationships."

Is this what she's believed all along? That all I ever wanted with her was a casual hookup? When I said I'd wait until she was ready, did she think I meant ready to sleep with me and nothing more?

"I *didn't* do relationships."

Her eyes search my face. "What changed?"

My mind wars with itself. Being honest opens me up to being hurt, but at the same time, it was my lack of openness that made me lose her in the first place. And that's not a risk I'm willing to take again.

"You showed up in my life and reminded me that you were what I'd wanted all along."

"But . . ." she stammers. "We're *friends*."

"There is no world in which I want to be your friend, Lauren. That world has never and will never exist for me."

There, now my truth is out in the open. And it's up to her to decide what she wants to do with it.

Her phone rings in her hand, and in the silence of the room, it's alarmingly loud. She glances down at it, and her finger hovers over the "decline" button, but then she looks up at me. "It's Morgan."

"You'd better take it, then." There's no way she should ignore that call when Morgan's at home with her kids.

She looks down at the phone, then back up at me, but the moment is broken. I can feel it, and so can she.

"I have work emails I need to send," I say, stepping back. "You should answer the phone."

I can see in her eyes that she's not sure she's ready for this —there was a sense of relief when the call came through. So

I'm going to respect that and make it easy for her, even though I know she's wrong. She *is* ready. But she's scared.

Her life has been flipped upside down these past few months. The one thing in this world she doesn't need is to be pressured into something she doesn't feel ready for. So I can wait as long as it takes.

# Chapter Seventeen

## LAUREN

LAUREN

Holy shit. There's only one bed here!

SIERRA

BA HA HA HA HA! You remember how Vegas turned out when Beau and I had a hotel room with one bed?

LAUREN

Yeah, SURE the one bed was why the two of you got together. Having two beds would have made a huge difference.

PETRA

She's right, Sierra. You were halfway to sleeping with him before you even left for Vegas.

JACKSON

Gah! Please stop this conversation about my brother's sex life!!!

PETRA

Sierra and Beau have sex, Jackson. This isn't news.

So . . . one bed, Lauren. How you feeling about that?

LAUREN

He offered to take the couch. Again. And then told me that he's just waiting for me to be ready for more. I think his exact words were "There's no world in which I want to be your friend. That world does not and has never existed."

SIERRA

Holy shit. That's so hot!

I glance up at Jameson where he stands in the kitchen, staring intently at his phone, a cute little scowl on his face. Why does everything this man does turn me on so much?

Resisting him was easier when I thought he just wanted a casual hookup. But now he wants more, and I'm not sure I even trust myself to decide whether that's a good idea or not. Am I ready for a new relationship? Should I be?

PETRA

She's not responding. Think she's already in that bed with him???

JACKSON

Maybe she's just too busy tearing his clothes off to pick up her damn phone?

LAUREN

You all are the worst!

SIERRA

You know what's the best? Hot sex with your hot pro-hockey player friend!

LAUREN

You sound like Petra.

PETRA

I trained her well.

LAUREN

I'm going for a run. I need to get out of here.

JACKSON

He's still going to be there when you get back, you know.

LAUREN

Yeah, but I'll be so busy getting ready for the wedding I will probably forget he's here.

PETRA

I highly doubt HE will forget YOU are there, though! Remember, we've seen the way he looks at you.

I set my phone down, determined not to respond to that comment. Suddenly it feels too warm in here. I need to get out. I need to feel the cool air on my face and burn off this sexual frustration. I need to exhaust myself with exercise so I'm not so keyed up about being in this house, with its one bed and Jameson.

I glance over at him again. He's typing something on his phone.

"I'm going to go for a run," I say, expecting a grunt of acknowledgment from him. Instead, he looks up at me and sets his phone on the kitchen counter.

"You sure? There's not a lot of room on the roads with the snowbanks."

"It's fine, I grew up running on these roads. Plus, they're clear and dry, and it's the middle of the day. There won't be a lot of traffic."

"Okay." The word is hesitant, and I can tell he's worried. "Can you . . . can you share your location with me on your phone, just in case?"

I hate the idea of anyone being able to track me. Then again, if something were to happen, and I was lying injured in a snowbank somewhere, I'd be awfully glad he could find me, right? I can always un-share my location when I get back from my run.

"Sure." I pick up my phone and tap the necessary places. "There you go. I'm going to go change," I tell him.

"All right." He sounds uneasy. "I'll shower while you're gone, so the bathroom will be all yours when you get back."

"Thanks," I say as I head into the one bedroom and shut the door behind me. I try not to think about the fact that I'm getting naked with him just on the other side of the door. As I change, I glance over at the bed taking up the majority of the room.

It's fine. I'm fine. It's not like we're going to share that bed tonight when we get back from the wedding. I ignore the tiny pang of disappointment at that thought. The guilt I feel when Josh flashes through my mind is harder to ignore.

*It's okay to move on*, I remind myself. Healthy even.

I'm less than a quarter mile into my run, and still having a mental back-and-forth about my attraction to Jameson and how much that feels like a betrayal to Josh—even though Jameson treats me better than Josh ever did—when I realize that there's something wrong with my sports bra. I think the straps are twisted around each other in the back, and it's rubbing right between my shoulder blades. I stop and reach my hand down my back, but with the multiple layers I'm wearing it's hard to make sense of what's happening back there.

I can't keep running with it like this or I'll end up rubbing the skin off and it'll look ridiculous with the open-back dress I'm wearing tonight. *Ugh.* I have no choice but to turn back and fix the problem, which means I'll have less time to get a run in. My anxiety level—a combination of sexual frustration and nerves about sharing space with Jameson—is rising. I know a run will help me manage it, and running is something I can't really do at home with two kids, so I'm trying not to be annoyed at this lost time.

I make it back to the house in record time. The door to the bedroom is cracked open and I can hear the shower running. When I knock, there's no response, so I push open the bedroom door. The door to the bathroom is closed and I figure Jameson must already be in the shower. Good, I'll just fix this bra and then get out of here. He'll never even know I came back.

I strip my fleece and my shirt off quickly, then turn to look over my shoulder in the full-length mirror so I can see what's going on. As I suspected, the back straps are wrapped around each other a few times. I reach back, trying to untangle them now that I can see what's going on, but I can't manage it. I'm going to need to take the bra off to untangle them. I wrap my arms around myself and grab the opposite sides, pull it over my head, then glance down at the offending material in my hands. I'm about to start untwisting the straps when movement in the mirror catches my attention.

I glance up, locking eyes with Jameson in the mirror. Flames flick through my entire body as I take him in, standing there in nothing but his boxer briefs. His long frame is cut with the deep grooves of hard-earned muscle that wrap around his limbs. Retirement has not diminished his physique. His skin stands out against the dark boxer briefs that are doing very little to hide his impressive size. I glance up at his face, a chiseled masterpiece with eyes of fire that reflect the desire burning through my body.

And that's when I remember I'm topless. With a gasp, my hands fly to my breasts. "I—" Where are my words? They seem to have evaporated right off my tongue as we stare at each other in the mirror, neither of us moving. "I thought you were in the shower."

"I thought you were on a run." His voice is thick and even deeper than usual.

"My sports bra was all twisted," I say, and my eyes flick to the floor where I dropped it when my hands shot up to cover my nakedness. "I came back to fix it."

I glance back up at him in the mirror, and our eyes lock again. I'm not sure what it means that neither of us looks away. And then he's crossing the room in four quick steps and stooping down to pick up my bra off the floor.

"Do you need help with this?" he asks, looking up at me through his dark lashes.

The words catch in my throat, which is so tight with need and suppressed emotion that I'm not sure I'll ever be able to talk again.

His fingers make quick work of untangling the straps, and

then he straightens up behind me. He's close enough that I can feel the heat radiating from his body, and since he's a full head taller than me, our faces reflect back in the mirror one above the other—eyes still locked on each other.

He dips his head near my ear. His voice is soft and his breath is hot when he says, "I can go back in that bathroom and leave you alone. Or I can help you take the rest of your clothes off. Your call."

My abdominal muscles contract and my hips tilt forward involuntarily as my entire core clenches. I can feel how damp my underwear is already. I clench those muscles together too, feeling an aching emptiness that I know he's willing to fill.

"Jameson," I whisper. "This is such a bad idea."

"On the contrary," he says, his head still dipped down to mine. "It's a brilliant idea."

He takes his hand and traces the curve of my neck, his palm grazing my skin, trailed by the pads of his fingers as they skim my skin and light my nerves on fire. Then his fingertips graze my collarbone as he slides his palm along my shoulder until he cups my upper arm in his hand.

Watching him in the mirror as he runs his fingers along my skin might be the most erotic thing that's ever happened to me. It's definitely better than any of the sex I've had, which says a lot—either about my attraction to him or about my lackluster past.

He reaches out to run his fingers along the back of my hand where I'm frozen, holding my own breasts. I'm suddenly aware of how hard my nipples are against my palms. I shift my hands slightly and the sensation that ricochets through me from that friction against my taut nipples has me sagging back against him—the hard planes of his chest cradling my shoulder blades.

He traces his lips along my hairline, past my ear, to my jaw. There, he opens his lips enough that he's trailing light kisses along my jawline, then down the side of my neck. A low moan escapes the back of my throat before I can stop it.

"You touching yourself like that is the sexiest thing I've ever seen." The words are mumbled against my skin, and as I watch him in the mirror, he glances up at me.

"I'm covering myself," I whisper, trying to keep my voice steady. "Not touching myself."

"If that's true, tell me to leave," he says doubtfully, and his eyes flick back to my neck where he runs his tongue along the length of it before capturing my earlobe between his teeth. His erection is pressing into my lower back, and I find myself involuntarily pushing back into him. "Or tell me to stay. You choose."

My core clenches with a contraction that shakes my whole body, and I don't even have to think about this choice. "Stay."

"Do it again." His voice is rough and demanding.

"Do what again?" I ask, my voice unsteady and thick with longing.

"Rub your hands over your nipples." His voice is so low it strums a chord deep inside me, filling me with a longing greater than any I've ever felt.

I'm not sure where the boldness comes from, but I slide my hands down so I'm cupping my breasts from the under-side, then I slide my thumbs across my nipples. I tilt my hips back into him with a groan, frustrated that the height difference means I can't run my ass along his length that I feel pressing into my lower back.

"Again." He groans as he locks eyes with me in the mirror. I do as he says, and his fingers come to my hips, where they grip me possessively. "Again."

I run my thumbs over my nipples again, and he practically growls into my hair. Then he's turning me around to face him and backing me into the wall, where he dips his head and presses his mouth to mine. His lips part and he invades my mouth unceremoniously, but it's a welcome intrusion. I meet his enthusiasm with my own, enjoying the rough thrust of his tongue as it tangles with mine and the pressure of his lips as they push against mine. What I don't enjoy is the distance between our bodies as he bends to kiss me, so I wrap my arms around his neck to pull him closer.

Without moving his mouth from mine, his hands glide from my hips over my ass and between my thighs. He lifts me up so I can wrap my legs around him.

Then his hips pin me to the wall as he thrusts against me, his hardness rubbing against my clit over and over, giving me the friction I need. He dips his head down to my breast, capturing my nipple between his lips where he circles it with his tongue.

"Yes," I hiss into his ear as I press my hips forward to meet his thrusts. "Yes!"

He rewards my enthusiasm by sucking my nipple further into his mouth, and then a hard pull sends shock waves straight through my core, which is so wet at this point I think I've soaked through not only my underwear, but my leggings as well. He brings one of his hands to my other breast, where he tweaks my nipple between his fingers gently. My head rolls back against the wall as he continues his assault on multiple erogenous zones at once. I buck my hips into him wildly, running my clit along the hard length of him until I'm panting with a need so great I can't see straight.

"I'm so close." I hiss.

He lifts his lips off me and brings them to my ear. "I know."

"Jameson, don't stop. Please," I beg, needing him to return his lips to my nipple.

Instead, a low rumble of a laugh rolls through him as he takes his hand off my other breast. "I have so many plans for your body, Lauren. And none of them involve clothes." With one arm under my ass and the other wrapped around my back, he spins and walks us to the bed where he places one knee at the end and then lowers me onto the soft fabric of the duvet.

My legs are still wrapped around his hips and I have no desire to disentangle myself, but he glances at the bathroom door and mumbles, "Shit." I glance over and see the steam billowing out of the room. I think we'd both forgotten the shower was still on. "I need to turn that off," he tells me, "and when I get back, you'd better not have pants on."

I meet his gaze and note the hunger there. "Or what?"

"Or we'll stop this right here, if that's what you want." With that, he's up and headed into the bathroom.

I spend a second reflecting on the fact that he just gave me an out, if that's what I want. But, it's not. I have no idea what it means, but this—with Jameson—is more than what I *want*. It's what I *need*.

# Chapter Eighteen

## JAMESON

When I return, Lauren is lying on the bed with no clothes on. We've been building toward this moment since she came back into my life. I'm still not sure she's one hundred percent ready to move on, but my dick is in charge now, not my brain, so those worries are pushed aside by my need to finally feel her, to taste her. I need to know if things between us will be as amazing as I always imagined they would be.

Even better than a pure lack of clothing, she's lying there with her knees bent and her feet at the edge of the bed, completely exposed. I marvel for a second at the smoothness of her skin, bare and glistening with the signs of her arousal.

"You still have clothes on," she says as I stand there gazing down at her. I prefer this confident version of her to any other iteration I've seen.

Wordlessly, I slide my boxers over my hips and down my thighs. She folds an arm behind her head, propping herself up so she can see me. "Oh." Her mouth falls open as she stares at my cock. "That's—"

"—going to give you the best orgasm you've ever had," I finish her sentence.

"We'll see," she says with a cheeky smile.

I love a challenge, so I sink to my knees at the foot of the bed, thread my arms under her knees, and put my hands around her waist, pulling her closer. I dip my head down to taste her, running my tongue along the length of her until I reach the bundle of nerves at the top, where I glide the tip of my tongue over and around her clit. Her hips jerk in response, but I keep her pinned in place with my hands splayed over her hip bones and my thumbs spreading her open in front of me.

"Oh, hell," she groans.

I run my tongue over that sensitive area again and she arches her back off the bed. Her soft pants urge me on, and I dip my tongue inside her to fully taste her. She's silky soft and delicious, and she rides my tongue as I use my thumb to lightly stroke her clit.

"More." That one word, coming from her, has one of my hands headed down to stroke myself while I watch her writhe beneath my face.

I've only managed two long strokes when she pleads, "I need more."

It's everything I can do not to get up and slam my dick into her at that moment. Instead, I slide my hand up along her belly and spread my fingers wide to graze both her nipples before sliding my hand along her neck.

When I bring two fingers to her mouth, she sucks them in greedily, twirling her tongue around them before suctioning her tongue against them repeatedly. My cock throbs with the need to feel her—my hand is woefully insufficient at the moment.

I bring my fingers down to her center, where I enter her without pretense. After having my tongue inside her, I know how ready she is. She groans as my long fingers extend into her, over and over, and when I clamp my lips over her clit, her back arches again and her hips buck wildly. I love this uninhibited version of her that chases what she wants. I want to see this version of her every day.

Her fingers are threaded in my hair, and she pulls me closer as her hips rise to meet every thrust of my fingers. I can feel her orgasm coming on, both because of her guttural moans every time I hit the right spot inside her while stroking her clit with my tongue, and also because I can feel the way her muscles start to twitch around my fingers.

"Oh, shit." She half screams, half groans, as her whole body stiffens. She rides that high for a minute, grunting repeatedly as she rocks in rhythm with my fingers and her orgasm. Then her whole body goes limp.

I kiss my way up her abdomen, across her breasts, along her sternum, and up her throat until we're face-to-face. "You okay?" I ask her.

"I've never come that hard in my life. I literally saw stars."

"Get ready for round two, then," I tell her.

"I don't have an ounce of energy left in me," she says, her eyes still closed as she exhales deeply, sinking into the mattress like she's melting.

"I bet we can dig into those reserves, but you tell me if I'm wrong."

I keep giving her an out like this—half of me praying that she pulls me to her naked body, and half of me hoping she'll bow out. We're about to cross into new territory that you can't come back from. I'm not strong enough to walk away from her again, but I'm also not positive she's ready to fully let me into her life.

Her eyes are barely slit open when she glances over at me. "I can probably find the energy somewhere."

I stand and scoop her up with one arm under her shoulders and another under her knees, then I set her at the head of the bed. She reaches over and pulls me down next to her. Then she opens those blue eyes that constantly change their shade and stares into mine. Right now, with the dim light of the gray day streaming through the windows and nothing on her body, her eyes are a deeper blue with no trace of the pale shades that frequently show through.

I reach out and cup her chin with my hand and draw her face to mine. My kiss is gentle despite the war raging in my body right now, insisting that I claim her—she needs a moment to recover, and I need her to have the energy to continue. Her tongue slides against mine, and she reaches a hand out tentatively to rest against my chest.

"Can you taste yourself on my tongue?"

"Jameson." She groans my name, and her cheeks turn pink.

"Can you?" I ask as I reach up and trail my thumb along her cheekbone. This new world, where I can touch her like I've always wanted to, is both foreign and perfect.

Her answer is a whispered, insistent "Yes."

"Do you like it?"

She doesn't look away. "I like your tongue in my mouth," she says, reaching her hand behind my neck and pulling my face back to hers. She captures my lower lip gently between her teeth, and as she slides her tongue along the tender flesh, I move my hand along the side of her body, from her knee to her armpit. Her skin is so soft and smooth—I want to touch and taste every inch of her.

The kiss turns needy and insistent, and she wraps her leg up and around my hip, pulling herself to me so that we're lying on our sides facing each other, bodies pressed together from head to toe. The feel of her along the taut skin of my cock has my hips thrusting forward, seeking friction, needing her heat. She snakes her hand between us, gripping the head of my cock in her smooth palm and sliding her hand down the length of me.

A groan erupts from my throat, and I can feel her chuckle against me. I kiss her deeply—our tongues tangling as she continues stroking her hand around my shaft—until I can't take the torment any longer. I need to have her, to possess her, to own her like she's owned me for years without even knowing it.

With a hand on her hip, I roll her onto her back beside me and rise up on my elbow. "Lauren?" I breathe out her name like it's a prayer, and in her eyes I see her need reflecting my own.

"Yes?"

"I need to be inside you." The words are raw and honest. She has no idea how long I've wanted this, but I'm sure she can tell how much I need it because my cock is achingly hard where it's pressed up against her thigh.

"Why aren't you already?"

I freeze for a moment under the weight of what this means to me, and wondering what it means to her, then I press my forehead to hers. "This is going to change every-thing." My voice is so low it's practically a whisper.

She brings a hand to my jaw and draws my face far enough from hers that we can see one another eye to eye. "I know." She gives me a small smile.

"You're sure you're okay with that?"

God, I need her to be okay with this. But I also don't want to do anything that will hurt her or potentially ruin this friendship we've built.

She closes her eyes for a moment and nods. "I'm positive. But, Jameson, it's been a long time."

"Don't worry. I'm going to take *very* good care of your body."

She lets out a sigh of contentment, a smile turning up the corners of her lips. "I always knew you would."

That reference to the past wraps around my heart painfully. "Don't think for a second that we're not going to talk about the past," I say to her. "But first I'm going to fuck you so hard you forget your last name."

"I really hope so," she says, but she sounds dubious. I push off the bed and when I'm standing, she furrows her eyebrows together in confusion.

"Condom," I say as I turn to grab one out of my suitcase.

"You brought condoms?"

"I'm very responsible like that."

"Were you planning on us having sex this weekend?" she asks as I return to the bed.

"No. But aren't you glad I brought some just in case?" As if I'd ever go anywhere without them.

"I really, really hate them. They make it hard to feel anything."

"Trust me, baby," I say as I lean over and kiss her forehead. "You're going to feel *everything*."

I kneel on the bed next to her and pick up her foot, trailing kisses from her toes, slowly up her shin. When I get to her knee, I tilt her leg sideways and kiss up the inside of her thigh. I can feel her body tensing up in anticipation, and with my eyes trained on her slick pussy, I can tell she's ready for me.

Then she reaches out, threading her fingers into my hair, gently tugging at the strands as her hips move toward me. With my other hand, I plunge my thumb into her, stroking her until I hear her gasp.

"Jameson, inside me, now."

I glance up at her, and the needy look on her face has my dick aching to be in her.

"Ask. Nicely." The words come out deeper than I intend, and I see the heat flare across her entire body in response.

"Please," she says. "I want you inside me now . . . please."

I drop her leg and tear open that foil packet, then roll the condom on in record time. I've never been this desperate to be with anyone.

I sit back on my heels and lean forward to wrap one arm under her hips, tilting them up for me. Then I plant my other arm beside her head and slide into her so slowly that she's practically mewling with longing. But I continue at this torturously slow pace because she asked me to be gentle, and I will respect that wish no matter how desperately I want to invade every inch of her hard and fast.

Her eyes are locked on mine as our bodies join together, and I can tell right when she thinks she can't take any more of me.

"Breathe," I tell her.

She exhales, then slowly inhales, and I slide farther into her. The silky glide and the intensity with which her muscles grip me has me gritting my teeth, but as her nostrils flare with another deep breath, she relaxes enough that I'm able to slide another inch or so into her.

Below me, she's laid out with her hair like flames fanning around her shoulders—a Phoenix rising from the ashes to a new life. This woman owns my heart, and I'm not certain she won't burn it to the ground. But I'm not thinking about self-preservation at the moment; the only thing I care about right now is the way I can feel her muscles tightening around my cock as she wraps her legs around my lower back.

"How gentle do you need me to be?" I ask as I begin to move inside her with slow, languid strokes.

"This is perfect," she murmurs, her lips barely moving.

I move with long, smooth strokes where I can feel every ridge of her muscles as they glide along the hard length of me. And when she relaxes a bit, I bend my knees, bringing them up under her thighs to change the angle. With my hands on her ass, I lift her to meet my thrusts. "Is this okay?"

She brings her hand to my heart, pressing against my sternum. "I trust you, Jameson. You're not going to hurt me."

I take in her tiny frame—she's physically small, but emotionally she's getting stronger. Still, I remind myself to be careful with her. She's been through so much in the last few months, but she deserves to feel good and I want to be the one to make that happen.

The first few times I glide into her, her eyes flare larger and I watch her take deep breaths. I'm filling every inch of her and I'm confident that if she could relax a little more, she'd be able to take all of me.

"Get up here with me," I say as I reach down and lift her up so she's straddling me. She wraps one hand around my neck and leans back with one arm on the bed for leverage as I seize her hips and help set the rhythm.

The view from here—watching myself enter her over and over again—is fantastic. I let my eyes wander up over the curve of her stomach, to her small but full breasts where they bounce from the impact of our bodies colliding. Her hard nipples are a rosy pink and I need them in my mouth, so I lean forward to claim one of them. As her hard, puckered peak glides against the sandpaper of my tongue, she lets out a guttural groan, and I feel the small, pulsing rhythm of her pussy as those muscles begin to convulse around me.

"Oh. My. God," she pants, and her breath ruffles my hair. "I've never . . . Oh, God."

I let myself move harder, faster, and she takes all of me with deep sighs and soft moans. "I'm going to . . ." she whispers, the words leaving her mouth in a surprised rush.

I lift my head to see her face. "I know," I tell her, right before I cover her mouth with mine. She whimpers against my lips, and I kiss her through the deep, long groans of her orgasm. When she finally comes and her throbbing muscles grip me like a vise, I tip over the edge with her.

For a minute, we stay there, me on my knees, sitting back on my heels, and her wrapped around me, her forehead resting on my shoulder, her arms wrapped around my rib cage. Eventually, I lay her back on the bed and lean down over her, my body propped up by my elbows on either side of her shoulders. I kiss her forehead, the tip of her nose, then her chin. I spend a moment memorizing every one of the light freckles across her cheekbones and the ridge of her nose, the fine lines at the edges of her closed eyelids, the swollen, pale pink of her lips. I caress her earlobe with my thumb, willing her to open her eyes, but she doesn't.

"Lauren," I say, but she only responds with a murmured "Hmmm?"

"Open your eyes, baby."

"Can't," she mumbles. "You've killed me."

My abdomen shakes against her as I silently laugh. "Open your eyes, or I'll do it again."

"So tired," she mumbles before cracking her eyes open. I can't read the look on her face, it's guarded. She's normally unable to hide her emotions, but right now I'm uneasy because I can't figure out how she's feeling.

"Do you want to nap?" I ask her.

"Mm hmm." Her eyes are closed again and she can hardly form the words. I guess that's a good sign?

There are so many things I should be doing right now, especially after canceling my work trip to be here with her. But it can all wait.

For Lauren, the whole fucking world can wait.

I go to the bathroom to clean myself up, set an hour timer on my phone in case I accidentally fall asleep, then crawl back into bed to gather her into my arms. And the second my eyes close, I'm out.

———

The sensation of someone grinding against my cock brings me back from my short sleep—this is not how I expected to wake up.

"Baby, what are you doing?" I mumble, running my hand up her arm.

Her only response is a groan, as she grinds her ass back into me again.

"Lauren," I say, dragging the backs of my fingers along the sharp line of her cheekbone, "I don't know if there's time. We have to get to the wedding."

She jolts, her entire body going rigid and then relaxing.

"What time is it?" she asks, groggily.

"Did you just wake up?"

"Mm hmm."

My chest shakes against her back with laughter.

"What are you laughing about?" she mumbles.

"Were you just dreaming about having sex with me?"

She burrows her face into the pillow. "Maybe."

"Well, now you've got me ready for another round." I slip my hand between her legs, lifting one up and over me as I sit up so I've got her legs spread on either side of me. "Look how fucking gorgeous you are," I say as I gaze down at her, "spread open for me."

"Jameson." Her tone is a warning, but then she glances down at my dick where it hovers just above her, and involuntarily arches her back and groans, I know exactly what she wants—all of me, inside of her. "Didn't you just say we had to get ready for the wedding?"

I glance at the clock on the nightstand. "How long do you need to shower and get ready, exactly?"

She follows my gaze, then literally jumps out of the bed. "Holy shit, we have to leave in an hour. I have to go shower."

"Perfect." I grin at her. "I love showers."

"Good." She looks over her shoulder at me as she walks to the bathroom. "You can make me come while you wash my body."

# Chapter Nineteen

## LAUREN

"Everything is going to be fine," Jameson says for the tenth time. I'm furiously tying the straps of my heels that lace around my ankles. These shoes are sexy as hell, and also a royal pain in the ass.

"Honestly, I'm not sure that it is."

"Are you afraid of what people will think when we walk into that wedding together?" he asks. "Or are you afraid of getting hurt again?"

I'm bringing a date to a family wedding four months after my husband died. Of course I'm concerned about what people will think. And after what I went through in my marriage, of course I'm afraid of getting hurt.

Except, the more I get to know Jameson, the more I'm seeing that he's not at all the callous asshole that I found so easy to lust after from afar when I was younger. He actually *is* the man he showed me glimpses of that night at dinner five years ago. I don't want to believe that he'd hurt me, except he's done it before. And I didn't think Josh would hurt me either. I don't know how to trust myself to know whether I should trust Jameson.

"Yes. To both questions."

"Let me prove myself to you, Lauren." He reaches over and strokes my jaw with the backs of his fingertips, and it lights me on fire. "And who gives a shit what anyone else thinks?"

"This is an important conversation," I tell him, "but we don't have time for it right now. We're already late."

"Okay, then we are coming back to it later. And just know that during this whole ceremony, I'm going to be picturing how you couldn't get out of the shower an hour ago without sinking to your knees for me first."

My breath escapes in a *whoosh* of air so loud it makes his lips twitch. "You can't say shit like that to me," I tell him as I feel my face turning red.

"Why not? It's true."

It's so true. And it was worth being late for.

"Because it makes my whole body blush, and the last thing I need is to walk into that church *looking* like we just had sex." The memories from the last couple hours have my body on high alert, already wanting him again.

He smirks at me. "Too late. It's written all over your face, and I love that about you." He reaches across me and pushes my door open. "Now let's go."

Jameson must be worried that I'll slip on the ice in these heels, because he laces his fingers through mine as we rush across the parking lot. And when we walk up to the doors of that church, his hand is on my lower back, guiding me through the entryway.

I was worried that we were so late the bride and her attendants would already be ready to walk down the aisle, but thankfully it's just the groomsmen here, still handing out programs and walking people to their seats on the correct side of the church. I stiffen when I see Justin standing there in his tux with his eyes on me, and Jameson must feel it because he leans down, presses his lips to my temple, and whispers, "Relax."

And that word pulls me right back to our shower, when he took me from behind as I was rinsing the conditioner from my hair. It was nearly impossible to accommodate him, so he bent me forward, my hands pressed to the tile of the shower wall, and cradled my back with his chest, whispering, "Relax," so he could slide into me all the way.

My core clenches as I remember how quickly he was able to make me orgasm at that angle. My first and second times ever having an orgasm from penetration both happened earlier today. And then I sank to my knees and finished him off with my mouth.

And as I look up at him, I'm not sure if I'm smiling about the amazing sex or him being here and acting as a barrier between Justin and me. Probably both.

"Here you go," Justin says, stepping forward with a program in his hand. I had been so focused on Jameson that his voice catches me off guard.

Apparently having a six foot two former professional hockey player standing next to me *isn't* enough to deter Justin—stupid idiot that he is.

"Thanks," Jameson says, grabbing the paper after I make no effort to take it from Justin's outstretched hand.

"Here, Lauren." Justin tries again, holding out his elbow toward me. "I'll show you to your seat."

Jameson steps forward, still holding my hand, and his opposite arm nudges Justin's extended elbow out of the way. "We're all set, thanks."

I tighten my grip on his hand as we walk down the aisle, my eyes scanning the rows on the groom's side, looking for my parents. "Thank you," I whisper.

He squeezes my hand in return, but doesn't say anything. From a pew near the front, I catch sight of my mom waving to us like she's stranded in the ocean and trying to flag down a passing ship that might somehow miss her. Her strawberry-blond hair is pulled back, and her smile is huge when she sees us.

"They're huggers," I say, warning Jameson as we make our way over. "Prepare yourself."

He takes my coat before we move into the pew, setting it on the far end, and I introduce him to my parents. "It's good to finally meet you," my mom says to him, making it sound like I talk about him all the time and she's just been dying to meet him.

"I think we met at the funeral," my dad says, doing a moderately good job of keeping his booming voice to a dull roar in the still-quiet church. There's a moment of awkward silence when he realizes he just mentioned my dead husband to my date, but then he continues with, "It's good to see you again." He holds out his hand, and as Jameson shakes it, Dad pulls him in for a hug. The second Dad lets go, Mom is pulling Jameson in for a hug, and I half wish I hadn't warned him, just to see what his reaction would have been.

"Lauren talks about you all the time," Mom says, her arms still wrapped around him.

"Does she, now?"

I have talked about him, in terms of him helping me with the estate. And I guess I've talked about the magic his family has worked on making my new house feel like home. And I did tell her how he was the one who told me about the job opportunity with the Rebels. But I absolutely have not talked about him in the way she's implying, not to my parents anyway. On the other side of them, I notice Paige, whose shoulders shake with laugher.

I introduce him to two of my brothers and their wives, and while we wait for the bride who is now more than fashionably late to her own wedding, Jameson talks to my dad about coaching hockey.

"Yeah," Dad says, his quintessential Maine accent making the word sound more like *ay-uhp,* "but it's feeling like it's about time for me to step down from coaching."

"Why?" Jameson asks. "You're still winning."

My dad almost single-handedly built our high school's hockey program into one of the best in the state. I've lost track of how many times they've gone to the state championship. And while I know Jameson knows about that from our dinner five years ago, I'm not sure what to make of the fact that he's still following how the team is doing.

"I'd rather go out while we're still winning. Nothing lasts forever, and it's time for me to train the next generation of coaches. I've got one assistant coach in particular, this kid Justin"—at the mention of my ex's name, Jameson's hand slips onto my bare leg, his thumb stroking the outside of my knee— "who was on my team when we won back-to-back championships over a decade ago."

Those two years cemented Justin's status as a living

legend in our small town. It's part of the reason I've never told anyone how things really ended between the two of us.

And now, I watch both my parents notice Jameson's hand on my knee at the mention of Justin's name. My mom's eyes meet mine, and she gives me a little smile. I can tell she's happy for me. I'm trying to figure out my dad's perspective when the music starts playing, and everyone turns toward the back door.

I hadn't even noticed that my cousin and his groomsmen had moved to the front of the church, and that's just fine, because for the rest of the service I intentionally look anywhere *except* at the groomsmen. And yet, I feel Justin's eyes on me the whole time, like the creep that he is.

———

Dinner is almost over when the bride and groom have their first dance. It's been a bit surreal sitting here in the clubhouse at the golf course Justin worked at in the summers while we were dating. I have so many memories of this place, and it makes me nauseous that they all revolve around being here with my ex.

Jameson's arm snakes around my waist as we stand there watching the bride and groom. He squeezes me to his side and drops a kiss on my head. I'm surprised yet relieved at how natural it feels to be here with him.

I was worried everything was going to be awkward, but my brothers have talked to him nonstop about hockey, peppering him with questions about what it was like to play for the Rebels and what it's like being an agent for some of the biggest names in the sport. He and Paige have bantered, her giving him shit about everything from his expensive suit to the way he hasn't even finished his drink, whereas most of us have had a couple.

"He's staring at you like a total stalker," Jameson says quietly enough that no one will hear him over the music. I know he's talking about Justin—I've felt his eyes on me all night.

"Yeah." I step in front him and he wraps his arms around me as he anchors my body to his. I keep my voice equally quiet when I say, "I don't know what his problem is. He wasn't like this in high school."

"What was he like?"

I give a little shrug as I look up at Jameson and quietly tell him, "Everyone loved him—teachers, parents, our peers. He was a good student, a three-sport athlete, and he worked at the kids' camp at this golf course in the summer. I don't know, he was just, like, an upstanding guy."

I'm not sure what he sees in my face when I say this, but he takes two steps backward, bringing me with him so we're farther from our table. "But?"

"But he was cheating on me with my best friend. And when I found out about it and confronted him, he . . ." I pause to think about how to explain what happened, because at the time it didn't make sense at all. "It was dark, we were outside his house because he was walking me to my car. I told him I knew about him and Kenzie, and he vehemently denied it. When it was clear that I didn't believe him, and wasn't going to give him another chance . . ." I look around to make sure no one might overhear us. ". . . I turned to get in my car and wound up face-first on the ground."

"What?" Jameson's voice is like a knife slicing through

the air, and I'm relieved we're back against the wall and not still at the table where he could be overheard.

"I don't know what happened. When I looked up from the ground, Justin was standing over me, asking if I was okay. He said I must have tripped. I don't know . . . I think I was still pretty traumatized by that fall at Nationals, because this felt the same. Like the ground had just evaporated beneath me. I couldn't help but think he'd tripped or pushed me on purpose. But I also couldn't prove it."

"If he lays another hand on you, Lauren—"

"It's fine," I say, looking up at him and giving his forearms a squeeze. "I don't know for sure that he *did* lay a hand on me. And he's certainly not going to here, with our families and friends and *you* around."

"He'd better not." I've never heard this tone from him before. He sounds intimidating as hell.

I turn in his arms so I'm facing him, and run my hands down the lapels of his suit jacket. "Hey," I say, my voice soothing because I can tell I've riled him up with this story. It's exactly why I've never told anyone from home—it's not worth the discord it would cause. "Let's go dance."

Jameson glances past me, at the dance floor, like he's just noticing that the music has changed and other couples are now dancing with the bride and groom.

"All right," he says, taking my hand and leading me out to the center of the room. Once there, he wraps one arm around my lower back, pulling me to him, and slides his other hand under my hair along the back of my neck. His touch feels possessive. "I like you in heels," he says. "It makes you a normal height."

"Hey, my height is totally average," I say with a laugh.

"It's not my fault you're so big."

His head dips closer to mine as he drops his voice low, then says, "You'll get used to how big I am. Don't worry."

The *get used to* implies so much more than just sleeping together, and I know what he said earlier, but half of me is worried that he was just trying to get me naked.

"I know you said you weren't looking for casual with me," I say, choosing my words carefully, "but what *are* you looking for?"

"Are you sure you want to know? Because once I tell you, I can't take it back." His words are quiet, his question vulnerable.

"I don't scare easily," I say, studying his face and hoping he feels comfortable being honest because we can't move forward if he isn't.

"You," he says and takes a deep breath, "are the biggest risk I never took, and I've regretted it for five years. I'm not making that mistake again."

It feels like my heart skips a beat in that moment as I stare at him, feeling like he's answered all my questions and none of them at the same time.

"Why didn't you take that risk?"

"That's a bigger conversation. It's one we need to have, but this isn't the right place to have it." He kisses my forehead as we move together on the dance floor. "Just know that the answer to your question about what I'm looking for is *everything*."

That doesn't even make sense. Jameson Flynn doesn't do relationships. He doesn't want marriage and kids—he told me so himself, and his sisters have confirmed it unintentionally with things they've said about him. So what does *everything* mean for a man like him?

"I'm"—I close my eyes for a minute as he spins us slowly around the dance floor—"still trying to wrap my brain around all of this. So you're going to have to define *everything* for me."

His arm tightens around my lower back, anchoring me to him. "Whatever you want, I want that with you. I want to be there to support you, and I want the same in return. I want you to experience what it means to be loved by someone who actually treats you well, and I want to be that person. Maybe I wasn't ready five years ago, but I'm ready now. And . . . I guess I'm hoping I'm not too late?"

This feels like such a monumental admission to be making when we've been together for a few hours. But then, the memories we've built together over the past few months flash through my head: the phone calls before I moved, the way he made sure his sisters were working on my house, the primary bedroom and bathroom he designed, our conversation at the Rebels game and how he brought me dessert afterward, the way he came over and took care of my kids during the snowstorm, how he suggested he be my date for this wedding so I didn't have to face Justin alone.

All the big and small ways he's shown up for me, supported me, helped me build myself back up . . . they're all there, coalescing themselves into a movie trailer in my mind. And the image I really can't get out of my head is the one of him sitting on my couch, watching *Tangled* with Iris and Ivy —how natural it felt picturing him as a fixture in the home he's helped me build for my family.

"I feel like I'm still trying to make the shift from thinking we're friends to understanding your true intentions. But no," I say as I reach up and rest my palm against his cheek, using my thumb to smooth the worry lines at the corner of his eyes, "you're not too late."

"We're still going to take this slow."

My laugh has my shoulders shaking. "Slow?" I drop my voice to a whisper and add, "You made me come three times before we even got to the wedding. That's not slow."

He grins. "I meant the emotional aspect of this. I know what you've gone through, and I know you're not done grieving. I'm not delusional enough to think you're ready to jump into a full-blown relationship."

I consider what he's saying and realize he's probably right. Even though I want what he's offering, and I'm mostly ready, there are pieces of me that aren't. "Maybe slow is best."

He lowers his head and says, quietly, "That's fine. But this body is *mine*, and taking this slow isn't going to change that. Okay?"

"Is this your way of saying you want to be exclusive?"

"Yes. I don't share."

"Since you walked back into my life, you're pretty much all I've thought about. First, because you kept giving me glimpses of who you were beneath this hard exterior you show the world. Then, because of the way you kept showing up for me and helping me get back on my feet. And then," I give him a little smirk as I say, "because I was so attracted to you—still—that I couldn't stop picturing myself with you."

With his arm that's behind my back, he pulls me flush up against him so I can feel how hard I make him. And all I want to do is find a private place where I can fuck him again. At thirty, I'd thought the best years of my sex life were behind me. I had no idea what I was missing, and now that I do, I feel like a horny teenager.

"You keep talking like that," he says, "and we're not going to make it back to that bed before I lift this dress and push inside you again."

Images of him sliding this tight dress up my thighs, pulling my soaking wet lace thong aside, and then filling me, are taking over my brain. I need him *now*. I'm about to suggest we go find an empty bathroom, utility closet, office—any place, really—when Dale walks up and punches Jameson in the shoulder.

"Hey," Dale says, "we're getting more drinks. You want to head to the bar?"

While I mentally curse my little brother for unintentionally being a cockblocker, I'm thrilled my siblings are welcoming him into the fold in a way that they never did with Josh. He was always a bit of an outsider with my family, as I was with his.

Jameson looks at Dale and Tim, then back at me, as if he's weighing whether it's more important to be in my brothers' good graces or finish what we just started. "Sure," he says to Dale, then asks me, "What can I get you?"

I give him my drink order and he drops another kiss on the top of my head before he turns to follow my brothers to the bar, and I return to the table where my sister and sisters-in-law have gathered.

"Holy shit, he's got it *bad*," Paige says.

"Yeah, he does!" Dale's wife, Laura, laughs and looks over at me. "I think this is the first time he's stopped touching you all night. I swear the man ate one-handed so he could have his other hand on you at all times. The way he was rubbing the back of your neck after they cleared the plates . . ." She fake swoons.

"You said you were bringing a *friend*," Tim's wife, Melissa, emphasizes.

"We *are* friends," I say cautiously.

"But also, clearly, much more," Paige adds. "You've been a 'thing' for a while." Then she proceeds to tell them about the hockey game where he threatened to rip any jersey off me unless it had his last name on it.

"You weren't even there," I complain.

"Yeah, but you told me about it in excruciating detail, so it felt like I was!"

I roll my eyes at her because she's acting as if she wasn't begging me for all the details.

"I have to go to the bathroom," I tell them. I'm not ready to admit anything about what's going on between Jameson and me, because I'm still trying to figure everything out myself. So instead, I head to the far corner of the room where I know I'll find the restrooms.

# Chapter Twenty

## JAMESON

"You are so fucking whipped," Tim says, and it has me turning toward him, taking my eyes off Lauren as she walks to the bathroom.

"We're not complaining," Dale says. "It's good to see her with someone who clearly worships her."

"Josh didn't?" I ask.

"Did he actually love anyone but himself?" Dale asks Tim.

"Nah," Tim says, "I don't think so. He was too obsessed with himself to pay much attention to Lauren, or even his kids. Every time they came to visit—"

"It was like Lauren did *everything*," Dale interrupts.

"That's just not how we were raised," Tim says. "But I guess Mr. Entitled Rich Kid from Park City thought that he married her so she could cater to his every need."

I think about the family I was raised in, where my dad was a functioning alcoholic doubling as a workaholic. It must have been bad, because my mom, who I hardly remember, left before my fourth birthday. Then my dad remarried, and he and my stepmom had Audrey and Jules. My stepmom did everything for the family. At the time, I didn't know any different. I just figured that, because she was a stay-at-home mom, it was normal.

And it pisses me off to no end that Josh, who I had convinced myself was better for Lauren than I was, didn't fucking treat her like a queen.

"So if he wanted her to cater to his every need," I say, "did that change once they had kids?" Obviously, the kids took up a lot of her time and energy, and I'm wondering how Josh handled that. I think I already know the answer based on a few clues Lauren has dropped about how she was pretty much parenting on her own even before Josh died, but I want to hear their perspective.

Dale snorts in response. "You mean, like was he jealous of the attention she gave the girls?"

"Yeah, I guess that's what I'm asking."

"Probably," Tim says. "He wasn't exactly a hands-on dad. He talked a lot about things he would do with the girls when they were older, like teaching them to ski or taking them camping, but as far as the last two years . . . nah."

I glance over at the hallway in the back to see if Lauren has come out of the bathroom yet, but she hasn't.

"Now we're just trying to figure out if you're going to treat her better."

I take a sip of my scotch and tell them the truth. "I already do."

"We're also trying to figure out if she's as into you as you clearly are to her."

"She's getting there," I say. "She's been through a lot, though, so I'm not going to rush her." I wouldn't normally share these thoughts, especially with the guys, but I respect their concern and protectiveness, so I want them to know my intentions.

"Good," they say together.

I glance over at the hallway again, and Lauren's walking out. She looks up, her eyes scanning the room, and I assume she's looking for me. But she freezes, then her eyes dart left and right. She looks panicked. And that's when I see the back of Justin's shaved head moving toward her.

"Hold this for me?" I say as I hand Dale my drink with an "I'll be right back" thrown over my shoulder.

I move around the edge of the dance floor, and when I get to the other side, Justin has Lauren backed up against a wide pillar. He says something to her, and she winces and recoils before he steps closer, wedging his knee between her legs and effectively pinning her to the pillar. I swear I see red creeping in at the edges of my vision.

"That's because I *have* been avoiding you." Lauren isn't trying to be quiet. "For the last twelve years, actually. Let's keep that streak going."

"C'mon, babe, don't be like that. You and me . . . together. It could be just like old times."

I pause because she's holding her own and I want to see how she handles this.

"Which old times, Justin?" Her normally sweet voice is acid. "You mean back when you were cheating on me with my best friend? I mean, thank you, but I am much happier without you in my life."

"You trying to make me jealous, Laur? Because I don't think you'll like what happens when I get jealous."

I take a step closer.

"I'm not trying to make you *anything*, Justin. Unless it's making you go away." She uses both hands and pushes hard against his chest, which knocks him back just enough that she starts to step away, but he's faster, reaching out and grabbing her upper arm so hard that she lets out a little squeal of pain.

I don't even think. I just grab Justin's tuxedo shirt right at his neck, my fingers crushing the bow tie. His top button goes flying from the force with which I twist that fabric in my hand. Justin sputters in surprise—without any coherent words leaving his mouth—while my fist presses up against the base of his neck. It takes every ounce of self-control that I possess to keep from slamming my other fist into his face. I never shied away from fighting on the ice, but I've always worked hard not to lose control off the ice.

"Take. Your. Fucking. Hand. Off. Her." I spit the words at him. "While you're at it, remove her number from your phone and her name from your memory. And do not ever speak to her like that again."

I push Justin away with a flick of my wrist before I wrap my arm around Lauren. She pushes me away, and I'm so shocked that I almost don't know what to do.

"I've got this," she tells me, and her voice is so strong and sure that it makes me smile. She sure as shit does.

She turns to face Justin, who's still standing there sputtering. "You ever touch me again and I will not only remove your balls from your body, I'll tell everyone that your huge ego is hiding a tiny dick. Get the fuck away from me and don't ever come back."

"You'll regret this," he says, then scurries away like the rat he is.

His threat has my spine prickling with anger and the need to protect her. She might think this is over, but it isn't.

I pull her close, and she doesn't resist me this time. I press my lips to the top of her head. "You okay?"

"Yeah." The word is shaky.

"Did he hurt you? Because I will—"

"I'm fine," she insists.

"We're leaving."

"I should say goodbye to my family first."

"If they find out what happened, they're going to go kick his ass," I warn, "and probably ruin the wedding."

"What do you propose instead?"

I just want her out of here, away from Justin. "Let's just sneak out, and then after the wedding is over, we can tell your family why we left. Hell, I'll go with your brothers to kick Justin's ass. But it shouldn't be here. It's not fair to your cousin and his wife."

"I feel like I should at least say goodbye to my parents . . ." she says, but if we go find her parents, there'll be questions and hugs goodbye. I sense she knows it'd be better to just leave than to make a production of it.

"How about if you text them instead, and we'll take them out to breakfast tomorrow before we head back to Boston?"

"All right," she says as I lead her around the dance floor and toward the entryway where the coatroom is. I keep my head down when we pass her brothers. I'm sure they were watching that interaction, and it's better if they think I lost control because I was jealous. "And what exactly should I tell them?"

"Tell them you have a headache. Or cramps. Or tell them I don't feel good. I don't care, just make an excuse that they'll believe for tonight." I'm not trying to be short with her, but I'm practically vibrating with fury from seeing Justin's hand on her. In my mind, it substantiates everything she said she thought happened when she broke up with him.

She types out a quick message while I get our coats, and then I'm leading her out the door and across the parking lot to my car.

———

"Why are we just sitting here?" she asks. I'm behind the wheel of my car, gripping it tightly with both hands.

I take a deep breath through my nose, and the sound fills the air over the quiet humming of the engine. "Because I'm trying to calm the fuck down."

I don't know how to explain it, except that when I saw Justin lay a hand on her, I wanted to rip his fucking throat out, bash his teeth in, and stomp on his fucking face—all at once. It wasn't jealousy; it was the thought that he might hurt her.

"Hey." She runs her hand along my arm over my suit coat. "I'm okay."

That's all that matters, yet it still doesn't soothe me.

I take a few more deep breaths, and then Lauren reaches over, slides her hand along the side of my neck, and pulls me toward her, murmuring, "Come here."

Her lips are gentle when they meet mine, but there's nothing gentle about the way I kiss her back. I suck her lower lip between mine, nipping at it before I invade her mouth. She gives it right back to me—tongues clash, the pressure builds, and when her seat belt restrains her, she unbuckles it and pushes up onto her knees and leans over the center console of my car.

My hands are greedy, pushing her coat off her shoulders so I can feel the bare skin of her arms, gripping her hip possessively, pulling her closer. I can't get close enough to her, can't touch her the way I need to when she's still halfway in the passenger seat.

"Get over here," I growl, hitting the button to slide my seat back and make room for her on my lap. She starts climbing over daintily, extending one leg over me like we've got all the time in the world.

I lift her hips, bringing her over the console and setting her down with one knee on either side of my lap. But her foot catches on the gear shift, and the bottom of her heel scratches across the temperature controls on the way to my seat.

"Jameson!" she chides. I love making her say my name—doesn't matter if it's from surprise, exasperation, or emotion. "I was trying to prevent my heels from scratching any part of your car—"

"Fuck the car," I say, grasping her ass, "I need you right where you are."

She clasps each side of my face in her hands, then tilts her hips so she's rubbing herself along my erection. She's exactly what I need—a way to divert my energy so I can calm down.

I graze my fingertips along her thighs, pushing the hem of her tight dress up and over her ass so it's bunched around her waist, and she grinds herself against me again, over and over in quick, pounding succession.

"Holy shit." She gasps. "I want you so bad right now."

I can't remember the last time I was constantly hard like I am around her—maybe when I was a teenager? I could be inside her every minute of the day, and it still wouldn't be enough.

"Lauren." I rasp out her name. "Unless we're going to finish what we've started, I need you to stop doing that."

She pauses for a moment, wraps her free hand around the back of my neck, and then, eyes locked on mine, grinds against me again. She leans her head down to mine and kisses me with the same sense of desperation I'm feeling.

My hands slide between us and I make quick work of my belt and zipper. Then I'm lifting her enough to push my pants and boxers down, and setting her back on my lap.

"I hope you don't care about this underwear," I say as I rip the seam over one hip, tearing it right in half. I repeat the action on the other side, then toss the remnants of her thong over onto the passenger seat.

"Those were my favorite pair."

"I'll buy you ten more," I say as she slides herself along my length. Holy shit she's wet for me. "This isn't going to be like earlier," I tell her, nearly frantic to be inside her.

Her eyebrows dip and she searches my face, looking for answers.

"I'm too angry about what just happened, and too keyed up, to keep this gentle."

"I want you to take what you need," she says, her hand on my cheek again. "However you need it."

With the steering wheel pressing at her back, we're too cramped. "I'm going to flip you around so you're facing forward," I tell her as I lift her hips and rotate her so she's facing the steering wheel. "Put your legs between mine."

And then I lower her down onto me, moving into her with no warning, and she grunts when I fill her, then hisses out a "Yes."

"Shit." I pause now that I'm inside of her. "I'm not wearing a condom. I don't even have one on me."

"It's fine," she says, "I have an IUD."

With her legs together like this, she's impossibly tight—the hot, slick walls of her pussy squeezing me so firmly I'm already ridiculously close to coming.

"I'm clean," I tell her, realizing that we should have had this conversation earlier in the shower. "And . . . I've never done this with anyone else."

"I'm clean too," she says, "I got tested at my annual exam before I left Park City." She squeezes her muscles, stroking my cock, so I put my hands on her hips to help her move.

With one of her hands on the steering wheel and the other on my upper thigh behind her, she helps set the pace, rocking her hips as I lift her and slam back into her. My movements are so wild this feels practically feral, but her soft grunts and the way she says "yes" over and over encourages me to keep going.

The slapping sound of our bodies meeting fills the car. It's dirty and wild and I fucking love that she's letting me take her like this. No, not letting me, *encouraging* me.

"You like fucking me in my car, Lauren?" I ask as she starts to move faster.

She looks over her shoulder at me, gives me a little smirk, and says, "Yes. I'd like it even more, though"—her voice is breathless, and she speaks between pants—"if you made me come."

I reach up along the back of her neck and twist my hand

229

around her hair until it's a red rope in my palm. Her back is exposed in this sexy dress she's wearing, and I sink my teeth into her skin above her shoulder blade. She lets out a hiss in response and moves her hips faster.

I pull that rope of hair, bringing her head back to my shoulder so her entire neck is exposed to my mouth as I kiss and suck a trail up to her ear. "There is nothing sexier than you riding my cock like this, taking me deep and bare," I tell her, and she responds with a strangled moan.

She's moving frantically on top of me, taking me quick and deep as I slide my hand along her bare hip and my finger meets her clit. She gasps at the first contact, then whispers, "Fuck, yes!" as I glide over that spot repeatedly.

Then I'm lost in the sensation of her slick heat sliding along my achingly hard dick until she's panting and moaning my name. I pull that rope of hair a little harder, anchoring her back against me as I continue slamming into her. "Good girl," I whisper, my lips right next to her ear, "Let's see your tight little pussy come all over my cock."

"I can't just come on command. . ." she starts to say, and then I roll her clit between two fingers and her muscles tighten around me, like she's made for me. And as she repeats "Yes, Jameson" over and over, all I can think is *we were meant for each other*. No matter what's kept us apart in the past, our future is together.

And that's the thought that has me exploding into her so hard I actually see stars. And as we sit there, rib cages heaving as we both catch our breath, I know I'll do absolutely anything for this woman.

"I'm sorry if I was too rough with you," I say, kissing the back of her neck.

"You weren't," she says, and she leans back against my chest so my chin rests on her shoulder. "That was . . . a little wild." She's silent for a beat, just long enough for me to notice how steamed up the windows are, then says, "But I liked it."

"I don't normally lose control like that."

"That's too bad," she says, turning toward me and dragging the bridge of her nose along my cheekbone. "I was into it."

"You liked fucking me like this? We can do that any time you want." I kiss her cheek. "But what I mean was earlier, when Justin grabbed you. I don't normally overreact like that."

"You were remarkably calm, actually," she says.

"I didn't feel calm. I always think things through—I don't make rash decisions like that. There's only one other time I've let my emotions, instead of logic, make a decision for me . . ."

"Oh, yeah?" she says.

"You might remember it, since you were there." I told her earlier today that we needed to talk about our past, and I meant it. But I'm not having this conversation when I'm balls deep in her. "Let's go somewhere we can talk."

———

"I'm one hundred percent confident this is better than the wedding cake would have been," Lauren says as she takes another bite of the chocolate cake, layered with tart cherry filling and chocolate frosting.

"People must come from all around just for the desserts," I say, looking around the small-town diner Lauren suggested we stop at. The walls are filled with framed vintage ski posters and old road signs, booths line the perimeter of the room with wooden tables and chairs in the middle, and the far wall is taken up with an enormous refrigerated case of cakes and pies.

"They do. You should see this place after the mountain closes. The ski crowd was already gone by the time we got here, but it's always packed around dinnertime." She runs the tines of her fork across her tongue, licking off the frosting that's stuck to it, and sure enough, that innocent motion has my body already aching to touch and taste her again.

"Why do I feel like you'd know everyone here?" I didn't realize quite how small her hometown was until we got up here yesterday. But it sounds like a lot of people pass through it to get to the ski mountain that's about fifteen minutes away.

"Nah," she says, and looks across the restaurant with the corner of her lower lip between her teeth. "I've been gone too long to know everyone. Things change, people change . . ."

I hate how sad she sounds about this. I'm about to tell her we can come up any time she wants, bring the girls up to see their grandparents, aunts and uncles, and cousins more often, when she saves me from sounding like I'm inserting myself into her family by saying, "So, you wanted to talk? About the last time you felt like you lost control?"

"Yeah." I take a sip of my water because suddenly my throat feels dry. We need to have this conversation, but I'm a little worried about how she's going to react to what I have to say. I know how epically I fucked up five years ago, and until recently I was convinced I'd only hurt myself in the process. I truly believed she was happy with Josh, and I'd made peace with my actions because she was better off with him. But now, I don't think that's true.

She looks at me expectantly, motioning with her fork that I should continue, but I don't know where to start.

"The last time I felt that angry and confused, and made a stupid and rash decision, was the night Audrey told me she was pregnant."

I can tell Lauren is doing the mental math. Graham's age plus nine months, puts us around five and a half years ago, right at the end of summer. "Was that the night . . ."

She doesn't need to finish her question because I nod. The night everything that was developing between us went to shit.

———

*Five Years Ago*
*Boston, MA*

I hate events like this, but I know they are a necessary evil. This awards night is like the who's who of the professional sports world. At least half my players are here, along with US athletes from every other professional sport, so I'm here too.

I'm standing near the corner of the bar nursing my drink, with my eyes trained on the doors leading onto this roof-deck. I want to see Lauren the minute she arrives. I won't be able to touch her—not with her uncle here too—but maybe I'll tell her she's been the only thing on my mind for the last twenty-four hours.

Then, this week, I'll talk to Carson. If he knows my intentions with Lauren are genuine, maybe he'll be okay with it? I'm sure he meant well years ago when he warned me that touching her would cost me my job. Back then, she was fresh out of college, too young and wholesome for a guy like me. I didn't deserve her, then. But I could be someone who deserves her now. And if my being with Lauren is an issue for him, well, maybe I will put my plan to start my own agency into hyperdrive.

My phone vibrates repeatedly in my pocket, and I slide it out to see who's calling. Audrey. I consider not answering so I don't miss Lauren when she walks in, but Audrey never calls —texting is more her speed—and the fact that she's reaching out on a Saturday night during her second weekend back at college is concerning.

"What's up?" I ask, holding the phone tight against my ear to hear her over the din of all the people milling about. I take a few steps away from the bar, and turn my back on the room.

"Where are you?"

The question has me on high alert. "I'm at an event for work. What's going on?" I ask, and then she's sobbing. "Audrey, what the hell is wrong?"

"Jesus, Jameson, give me a second," she chokes out. There's ragged breathing, but she doesn't say anything else.

"Are you okay?" Goose bumps have erupted down my spine and my heart is pounding. If someone hurt her, I'll fucking kill them.

"Yes. And no." She pauses. "I'm pregnant."

I swear I see black, like tunnel vision, the way they say happens before you faint. But I stand there, one hand braced against the wall and my phone in the other, willing myself to breathe.

"It's going to be okay," I tell her, despite how I'm feeling about this. "How long have you known?"

"I just took a test like five minutes ago."

"Okay," I say, then take a deep breath. "How does the dad feel about this?"

"I don't know."

"You haven't told him?"

She pauses. "Like I said, I just found out. You were my first call. But, Jameson, I don't think he's going to be interested in being a dad."

I press my lips between my teeth and talk myself out of punching the brick wall I'm leaning up against. "I'm going to kill him." I barely get the words out, but I mean them with the intensity of a thousand suns. If this jackass doesn't want his own child, I will end him.

"You probably would, which is why you'll never know who he is. Doesn't matter anyway, I'll love this baby enough to make up for his absence."

"You've already decided to keep it?"

"Of course I am! But I'm so scared, Jameson."

"You won't be doing this alone," I tell her. "You'll always have me and Jules." I'm immensely grateful in this moment that Jules is just across the river, starting her freshman year at MIT, and that she didn't choose to go far away to school.

"I know," she says. "And it's the only reason I'm not absolutely terrified right now."

I close my eyes against all the thoughts flooding into my head. This is about her and making sure she feels supported. There's no space for my selfishness here. It doesn't matter that, after dropping everything to raise my sisters and now finally having both of them off at college, I'm suddenly facing the prospect of helping raise another kid.

Me, who never wanted kids, who had a vasectomy years ago to make sure I never ended up with a child.

I will do *anything* for my sisters, just like I always have.

"You're not saying anything," Audrey says, filling the silence.

I open my eyes just in time to see Lauren walk onto this roof-deck. She's wearing a short, green dress that I already know will make her eyes look turquoise, and the sight of all that skin is doing crazy things not just to my body, but to my heart too.

Shit. Is this what it's like to actually care about someone who's not family?

Lauren glances around but doesn't see me, and she slowly walks in the opposite direction, away from me.

"I'm still processing all of this," I respond.

Maybe the reason I'm having trouble coming up with words is because I'm busy considering all the ways I've failed my sister. Was I too distracted with work, or too focused on Lauren, to see what was happening here? And if I can't even be there for them, can't protect them from things like this happening, how could I ever be the person Lauren needs?

In my head, I'm also running numbers. There will be a lot of costs—a nanny so she can still finish her undergrad degree and then go to architecture school, a car to drive the baby around in, all the supplies for the baby, not to mention the college tuition for both my sisters that I'm currently paying out of pocket.

And right now, as I'm spinning all of these huge changes in my mind, feels like the worst possible time to take any risks, no matter how much I want to. And I see what I have to do: stay at Kaplan, no matter what. It's the only safe path forward to make sure my family is taken care of.

This thing with me and Lauren . . . it just can't happen. I can't risk pissing Carson off right now. I can't risk my job and the security it provides.

Maybe in another year or two I can start my own agency —things will be more settled then. But it's too risky right now. And I can't ask Lauren to wait around for that long.

"We can talk about this more when I see you," she says. "How about I come home for dinner tomorrow night? I'll see if Jules wants to come too."

"Okay. Let me know if you need anything between now and then."

"Just cook me something delicious for dinner tomorrow. Right now, nothing sounds good except for pasta."

"I'll make your favorite pasta, then," I say. "I'll see you tomorrow."

I slide my phone back in my pocket and look up to check if I can see Lauren, when Josh Emerson approaches. "Hey, Jameson," he says, stretching out his hand. "Good to see you."

"You too," I say, willing myself not to look past him. He's a professional skier, and a good guy—if you like the all-American, preppy, golden boy vibe. He's nice enough and everyone seems to love him. He was also one of my first clients back when I was a new agent. It was actually his parents who hired me to manage their adult son's career, because he's nothing if not a mama's boy. "What's going on?"

"Just gearing up for the season. Have to head home next week to see my parents, then I've got a trip, then I report for training next month."

"How are your parents doing?" I ask, because it would be rude not to, even though I don't really give a shit about the answer.

My eyes are now scanning the room, looking for Lauren. I need to talk to her. Now that I have no choice but to stay at Kaplan, I have to call things off with her. I can't risk Carson finding out—even the fact that we had dinner together last night could set him off.

Besides, I remind myself, she wants things I'm not capable of giving: marriage and kids. That's not my path.

I got carried away last night—it was stupid and reckless of me to pretend that I could be the person she wants, or that she would want me as I am.

"Same old," Josh sighs. "Mom's pressuring me to settle down and get married. She wants grandkids."

"Oh?" That has me focusing back on him. "Who's the lucky lady?"

"Don't know." He shrugs and gives me a sheepish smile. "I haven't met her yet."

"You're thinking about marriage and you don't even have a particular person in mind?"

"Nah." He rakes his hand through his light brown hair, and his dimple appears as he looks at something or someone beyond me. "But if I met the right person, maybe."

"Hi." The sweet sound of Lauren's voice behind me has my spine stiffening.

I turn toward her and try not to let my breath catch. She looks even more phenomenal up close. Her long red hair hangs in loose waves, her lips are the shade of red every man dreams of having wrapped around his cock, and her dress hugs her body in a way that has my imagination running astray.

All I want to do is wrap my arm around her, guide her right out those doors and back to my place, then slip those tiny straps off her shoulders and let that dress fall to the ground.

But none of that can happen. Not anymore.

"Hey." I turn back toward Josh, not wanting to introduce them but seeing no other option as they're both standing here. "Josh, this is Lauren Manning. She works with me at Kaplan."

Josh gives her the same smile he always gives the camera when he finishes a race, and I don't miss the way he eyes her appreciatively.

"Nice to meet you, Josh," Lauren says, her voice professional as she stretches her hand out to shake his.

"You too, Lauren." He pauses for a moment, then says, "I'm going to grab a drink. Do you want anything?"

Lauren responds with a dismissive "I'll get something in a minute, thanks," so Josh heads over to the bar only a few feet away.

"Lauren," I say, dipping my head toward hers, because I can't risk anyone else overhearing our conversation.

"God, I missed you," she says, and the words pierce my heart because the last thing in the world I want is to hurt her, but I can't see that I have any other choice.

"I can't do this right now."

"What can't you do?" she says, her voice teasing as she looks up at me.

"Us."

Those big blue eyes widen in hurt and confusion, and finally she stammers, "What?"

"I'm sorry if I gave you mixed signals last night, but nothing can happen between us."

"But . . ." She drifts off when she sees the hard look on my face. I'm not going to change my mind.

She looks away, squares her shoulders, glances back at me, and says, "I don't know what's changed since last night, but I'm not going to beg for your attention." I hear the hurt in her voice and it guts me.

"Lauren . . ." The word is a plea, but I don't even know what I'm asking for. Forgiveness, maybe?

She holds her head up high, back ramrod straight, and tells me, "I hope you look back and regret this moment."

*I already do.* "I'm doing what's best for both of us. I'm not the right person for you, Lauren. Marriage and kids . . . those things you want are not the things I want."

Confusion haunts her eyes, then she turns and storms away, the graceful lines of her shoulders tempting me to follow her.

But I don't. I put my family first, like I always have.

"Are you into her?" Josh asks, appearing at my side with a beer.

The question is like a sucker punch in the gut. "No, why? Are you?"

"Dude, she's perfect. Hell yes, I could be into her." He watches her retreat, and I see what he sees. She's young and gorgeous, and I know she wants what he's apparently looking for. Letting him go after her would be doing her a favor.

Why is this so fucking hard? He could give her exactly

what she wants—what I can't give her. He'd be better for her than I would.

But God, the thought of her with anyone else makes me want to throat punch someone.

I realize, too late based on the way Josh is looking at me, that my jaw is clenched so tight it's making my teeth hurt.

"You sure you're not into her?" he asks.

I feel the same way a bull must feel when it's breathing hard, head lowered, pawing at the dirt. There's irrational anger, and all my instincts to charge are kicking in. But I take a deep breath and tell the lie that I'm confident I'll regret. "I'm sure."

*You're doing what's best for her,* I tell myself. *No matter how much it hurts.*

# Chapter Twenty-One

## LAUREN

"What. The. Actual. Fuck." I can barely get the words out past the huge lump in my throat, and the inside of my nose stings like it always does when I'm about to cry. "You had feelings for me and you . . . what? Couldn't handle thinking about a future for us because Audrey got pregnant, then you pawned me off on Josh because he was looking to settle down?"

What he's told me confirms my worst suspicions about why Josh wanted to get married so quickly—it wasn't because he couldn't live without me, it was because fucking Barb was hounding him to give her grandchildren. The irony of her hating me and almost never seeing her grandchildren is not lost on me.

Hot tears are now cresting my lower lids and I wipe them away with my napkin.

"You were always the one that got away, Lauren."

"I didn't get away. You *pushed* me away."

"Same difference."

"No." My voice reflects my certainty and my anger. "It's

not. The difference is enormous. It didn't have to happen that way."

"It did. You were too young. You were looking for forever, and I couldn't offer you that."

"That's total bullshit, Jameson, and you know it. Yeah, you found yourself in the position of having to help raise another kid, unexpectedly, just when you thought your sisters were grown and flown. But if you'd wanted to, you could have made room for me in your life, in your family. And you know what I would have done, if you'd let me?"

"What?"

"I'd have adored Graham then, just like I do now. He's a great kid, and he deserves to have *all* the people in his corner, not just you, Audrey, and Jules. But he can't, because you push everyone away."

Across the booth, he sits with that for a minute. "I don't push everyone away. The people I love, I hold them close and protect them. Jules and Audrey? Those two are the best thing I ever did."

I can't help but roll my eyes. "You sound like you're eighty. I'm not diminishing what you sacrificed to raise them." I think about what it must have been like to retire at the peak of his NHL career so he could be there for his sisters. "You did a really great job. But also, you're entitled to the life you want to have. You're entitled to be happy too."

He gets up and comes to my side of the booth, sliding in next to me. He puts one arm around my shoulders and pulls me close, using his other hand to wipe away the tears. I rest my head on his chest. He smells like oranges and cloves and wood—spicy and masculine.

I'm so mad that he made this decision for us five years ago

without giving me a say. But also, I feel safe in his arms. It's a confusing and conflicting place to be.

"I don't think you understand. I *never* wanted to get married. I saw what marriage can do to a person, how it absolutely destroyed my father when my stepmom died."

"I think you saw what *grief* can do to a person. But it doesn't have to be like that, Jameson. Just because that's how your dad handled his grief, it doesn't mean you have to choose that path."

"I'd convinced myself that I was happy being single," he says. "But you make me realize that I could be so much happier."

"You're saying things that twenty-five-year-old me dreamed of hearing..." I sigh.

"But not thirty-year-old you?"

"Jameson, thirty-year-old me has two kids. And you just told me that you had a vasectomy because you *never* wanted kids."

"First of all, they're reversible. And second, I was pretty certain. But you and Ivy and Iris have made me see that differently too."

I freeze, paralyzed by this admission. "I literally just figured out that you want more than a friends-with-benefits situation..." I don't even know how to finish that sentence. "Now you're talking about marriage? And kids?"

He shrugs. "I'm saying that, for the first time in my life, I can picture that for *myself*. Even though I raised my sisters and have helped with Graham, I never pictured myself as a dad. There's never been anyone else who I wanted to imagine a future with."

"I'm starting to question whether you know the meaning

of 'take it slow,' Jameson." I make a joke out of it because I'm still processing. I didn't think there was any way I would ever trust someone again after all the ways Josh lied to me, but Jameson is making me reconsider that . . . and it scares me.

"I'm taking it slow for your sake," he says, pressing his lips to the top of my hair again. "I told you earlier, I'm not making the same mistake again. I'm not going anywhere—I'll be here, waiting, until you're ready."

"Are you sure you're okay with that? Because I don't know how long it will take me to truly be ready to move on."

"I can wait as long as you need."

I hope he really means that, because I'm not sure what it would take for me to be ready to invite someone into my life in the way he's describing. But if there's anyone I can picture that with, it's him.

―――――

"W hat the hell happened to your face?" Jules asks Jameson the minute we walk in the door. "You look even more hideous than normal."

He rolls his eyes, then winces.

"Got in a little bit of an altercation last night with Lauren's ex-boyfriend from high school."

"At a wedding?" she says. "What's wrong with you?"

"Not at the wedding," he clarifies. "After."

Apparently, sometime after I fell asleep in his arms last night, exhausted from even more orgasms, he snuck out of bed and met my brothers to go have "a little chat with our friend Justin." I knew nothing about it until I woke up this morning and the outside corner of his eye was purple and swollen.

"And why was he fighting with your ex-boyfriend from high school?" Jules asks me, her voice teasing, because she obviously thinks he got jealous.

"I was righting some wrongs, and making sure it never happens again," Jameson answers before I can say anything.

"Like I told you this morning, that situation had been handled at the wedding. I don't need you going around trying to save me, you idiot."

"It wasn't finished, because he stupidly said you were going to regret it. *Now* it's finished."

"Looks like you got what you deserved for going behind Lauren's back, though," Jules says. "Want an ice pack?"

"He got a *lucky* punch in because he got loose when Lauren's brothers were supposed to be holding him. Doesn't matter, he's never pulling that shit again."

He glances over at me and I roll my eyes. I kind of love the way my brothers got along so well with him, but I'm not some helpless woman in need of defending, and I thought I'd made that clear at the wedding.

At least his bruised eye was an opening to a conversation about Justin's past actions when we met my parents for breakfast this morning. Dad was furious that I hadn't told them when it happened, Mom was disappointed that I "didn't trust them" enough to say something sooner. I tried to explain that, at the time, I just wanted to move on and forget about it, but my dad was insistent that he didn't want to have someone on his coaching staff who'd tried to attack a woman.

Jameson said that alone was worth the black eye.

"After all the fighting you've done on the ice, you should

have been able to duck a little quicker," I tease as Jules heads to the freezer for an ice pack even though Jameson didn't say he wanted one. He looks like he needs it.

"What can I say? I'm getting slow in my old age."

I almost joke that he was probably exhausted from all the sex but catch myself just in time. We'd agreed on the drive home that "taking it slow" meant we should probably keep this to ourselves for a bit while we figured out what a relationship would even look like between us.

"Where are the girls?" I ask Jules. Morgan said she was bringing them over in my car so they'd be here when I got back, but I think she just wanted to hang out with Jules and Audrey, and probably wanted someone for my girls to play with too.

"Downstairs with Morgan, Audrey, and Graham."

"There's a downstairs?" I ask.

"Yeah, we refinished the basement a few years ago. The front part is a walk-out and serves as my and Audrey's office where we sometimes meet with clients and she does all her drafting. The back half of it is a kids' playroom—you should go check out the climbing wall I built Graham while I finish getting dinner together. You are staying for dinner, right?"

"Uhh . . ." My eyes meet Jameson's and he's clearly amused that I'm flustered by this invitation. It's one thing to not tell his sisters about us, it's another to try to pretend nothing's going on while sharing a meal with them. "Sure, that sounds great. Thanks."

———

247

I have no idea how we thought we'd be able to keep this a secret. I'm sure Audrey, Jules, and Morgan were already speculating about us before we returned from the wedding, and before we even finish the meal, it's clear they know exactly what's up. There are so many sideways glances being thrown around, even with Jameson and me at nearly opposite ends of the table.

I told myself it was better that we weren't sitting next to each other, but after thirty-six hours alone with the man, I hate having him this far away. And that's probably what's tipped them off—because every time I glance over at him, our eyes meet, which means he's doing a whole lot of looking at me too.

But how could I not stare at him? He's got Graham on one side of him, and Ivy on the other, and he's handling them both like a pro—answering all of Graham's questions, and guessing the animals as Ivy makes the relative sounds.

He's . . . good with kids, supportive and sarcastic with his sisters, and incredibly patient with me. By all accounts, he's perfect. For me, anyway.

His phone must start buzzing in his pocket because he takes it out and says, "Sorry, I've got to take this," then rushes upstairs.

Audrey and Jules look at each other, then Audrey says, "Wow, it must be serious."

But then the two of them and Morgan are staring at me. "So . . ." Jules says, then glances at Graham. "You're s-l-e-e-p-i-n-g with my brother now?"

At my instantaneous, beet-red reaction, Morgan says, "Well, that's a yes."

"Guys." The word is a hiss. "I cannot have this conversation right now."

"Why not?" Audrey asks. "We're happy about this development."

"This is something for him to talk to you about, not me," I say.

But, man, do I want to go out for drinks with the three of them and spill all my secrets. It's complicated by the fact that Jules and Audrey are related to him, though. I can't tell them about the amazing sex, or how much I liked the domineering side of him I saw in the car after that interaction with Justin.

But I could tell them about how careful he's been with me, how committed he is to the idea of *us*, how he said that my girls and I have made him rethink marriage and kids. Knowing that he'd want to step into that role with my girls . . . my heart is melting just thinking about it.

"Man, I wish I was privy to that conversation," Jules laughs.

I glance toward the stairs, thinking she must mean the one Jameson is having on the phone, but we can't hear a sound. "What conversation?"

"The one you're having in your head."

"Yeah—" The laugh that escapes borders on hysterical. "—there's a lot going on in there right now."

"Want to have a girls' night and talk about it?" Jules asks. "As long as Jameson is around to watch Graham, Audrey and I could come to your place one night this week after your girls go to bed. Maybe we can see if Paige is around too?"

"Sure," I say as Jameson comes down the stairs behind me. "We'll plan something."

249

"What was that about?" Audrey asks him when he takes his seat at the table.

"I have to go to California tomorrow." His jaw is tight, and I can sense his frustration.

"And there goes girls' night." Jules sighs, leaning back in her chair.

"What's that supposed to mean?" he asks, looking around the table at the four of us.

Next to me, Iris starts asking to get down. I take her out of her booster seat so she can toddle around, and without needing to be asked, Jameson does the same for Ivy. The two of them run into the living room, and Graham follows.

"It means we were going to see if you could watch Graham one night so Audrey and I could go have a girls' night at Lauren's place."

"I only plan on being gone for a night, or two nights, max. I'll definitely be home in time for the charity game on Wednesday night," he says, looking at me. Thank goodness. The Rebels Charity game is a huge annual fundraiser for Boston's largest homeless shelter, and Jameson is one of many former Rebels scheduled to play. "And," he says, turning to Jules, "I'm sure you can still have your girls' night on Thursday or Friday."

Is it my imagination, or does he sound just a little jealous that I'll be hanging out with his sisters one night this week instead of with him?

"How about I follow you home and help you get everything from this weekend unpacked from the car," he says to me. I'm about to tell him he doesn't need to do that, since all I have is a carry-on suitcase. And I'm more than capable of taking care of that and my kids. But then I realize this is his way of spending a little more time with me before he has to fly out tomorrow.

So after Jules and Audrey assure us they don't need help cleaning up from dinner, I head out to my SUV with my girls, and Jameson follows us home.

# Chapter Twenty-Two

## JAMESON

"Do you want me to read them a story so you can get your suitcase unpacked?"

She looks at me like I've asked her if she wants a million dollars or a free vacation, rather than spending ten minutes reading to Iris and Ivy. "Ugh . . ."

"Is that a yes?" I ask as the girls run back and forth from the bookcase in their room over to their beds, carrying a new book each time. The pile on the bed is getting bigger than what we'll be able to get through tonight.

"Normally," she says with a smile, "I'd welcome a break from doing this on my own, but . . . I don't know, I was gone last night . . ."

She missed them—it's clear in the way she looks back and forth between them.

"Want some time alone with them?"

I'm not ready to leave, because I'm hoping to get some more time with her after they go to bed. I hate the thought of not seeing her for the next two days, but I have to fly out to

LA to meet with one of my newest players who just found out he got his coach's daughter pregnant. I swear, I feel like I spend as much time babysitting these younger players as I do making deals on their behalf. I don't need the money anymore, I have more than enough. Maybe I should stop taking on new players, or perhaps expand my agency by bringing in other agents to deal with these immature idiots.

Except Colt. I'll keep that immature idiot because, even though he acts like he's twenty half the time, he's a former teammate and one of my oldest friends.

"Yeah," Lauren says, "that would be great. I'll be back downstairs in a few minutes."

I say good night to the girls, who give me good night hugs and almost get my name right when they say goodbye, and head downstairs to wait for her.

I'm sitting on the couch responding to emails when she comes down about fifteen minutes later. She doesn't say anything, just walks straight toward me, straddles me where I sit on the couch, then curls into me for a full-body hug.

I wrap my arms around her, holding her to my chest. "What's wrong?"

"I don't know. Nothing's wrong, really." Her voice is muffled by my hoodie.

"You sure?" I ask after I press a kiss to the top of her head. I can't seem to keep my hands and lips off her. If she's nearby, I want to be touching her. Dinner was torture, having her three seats away from me, and I'm not sure the distance between us made what's happening here less noticeable to my sisters. The fact that I couldn't stop looking at her was probably a dead giveaway that something's going on.

"No."

"Are you upset that I'm leaving?" I ask.

She sits up so she's looking straight at me.

"No, I'm mad at myself. Here I am, doing my best to be a strong, independent woman and a good role model for my girls. I've been through some shit, but I've come out stronger on the other side. I'm kicking ass at my new job, I'm making this place a home for me and the girls, and now you're leaving for a night or two and . . . I'm sad about it?" She sounds aggravated at herself as she pauses and looks up at the ceiling. "Like, I don't want to be this clingy person who only feels complete when you're around."

"Do you only feel complete when I'm around?" I ask the rhetorical question so she'll come to the realization herself.

"No, but I prefer it when you're around. I slept with you for the first time yesterday, and already I want you here with me as much as possible."

"It's okay to want things, Lauren. It's okay to want things for yourself, just because they make you happy. It's okay to want to spend time with me. It doesn't make you clingy or unable to be a whole person when I'm not here."

"I just . . . I remember how I felt when Josh traveled. He was gone a lot, and even when he was home, he wasn't really present. I never want my happiness to depend on another person the way it did back then, because I was always fucking disappointed."

"Listen," I tell her. "I hate that I have to leave tomorrow, but I won't be gone a second longer than I have to be." I don't know how this meeting with the coach will go tomorrow afternoon, and I can't say for sure how long I'll need to stay.

"But when I am here, I will *be here.* I'll be present. Not because your happiness depends on me, but because you deserve someone who thinks about you all the time, who wants to spend every possible minute with you—"

"We're supposed to be taking this slow." She rests her forehead on mine and whispers, "I'm scared, Jameson."

"Tell me what you're scared about, so we can find a way through it."

"I'm scared that this all seems too perfect. I'm scared that something will go wrong, and I'll get hurt. I'm scared that my girls will get attached to you, and if something goes wrong, they'll be hurt and confused too. I'm worried about another heartbreak when I'm still healing from the last one."

"Honey," I say softly, "I think you're worried about the wrong heart."

I feel her eyebrows dip together in surprise. "Hmm?"

"You should be worried about mine. Because if this doesn't work out a second time, I'm not sure how I'll recover. I never got over you the first time . . ."

She tips her chin up so her lips brush against mine when she says, "I don't think I got over you the way I thought I did either."

"You were the right person at the wrong time," I say, pressing my lips to hers.

She opens for me immediately, but the kiss is slow and sensual—we're both dragging it out, because we want every moment to last. After two full days together, the thought of being without her for the next day or two is . . . difficult.

Both my hands cup the back of her head, fingers threaded through that thick red hair, with my thumbs angling her head so I can deepen the kiss. And she must like it, because there's a growl banging around in the back of her throat as her hips start to shift right over my cock.

I can't help but press up against her, and she meets me thrust for thrust as she kisses me and runs her hands across my shoulders, down my chest, along my abdomen. She teases her fingertips under the waistband of my jeans, but then her hands are gone. In frustration, I growl and press into her harder, and she laughs against my lips as she pulls back from the kiss.

My hands fall to her thighs where they sit on either side of mine as I open my eyes to see her unbuttoning her cardigan. Beneath it, she has a lacy pink bra through which I can see the stiff peaks of her nipples, and I lean forward without hesitation and capture one between my lips, sucking right through the lace fabric. She lets out an appreciative hiss, and with her hands behind her back as she takes her arms out of her sleeves, both her breasts are pushed forward. I cup the other one in my hand, running my thumb back and forth over her other nipple, and she grinds down on top of me hard, shifting her weight forward so her clit is making contact. And then her hands are at my belt, and I'm letting go of her as I pull my shirt over my head and unclasp her bra, tossing it onto the floor with the rest of our clothes.

It's a matter of seconds before all our clothes are off and she's laid back on the couch, legs spread open, that pretty pink pussy bare before me. I grab her hips, anchoring her down as I bend forward to taste her. I run my tongue along her opening, and she tries to tilt her hips so my tongue meets her clit, but I hold her in place, stroking my tongue over her but never hitting the place she's so desperate for me to lick.

"Jameson . . ." She groans out my name.

I glance up at her. "Yes, love?"

"Stop torturing me."

One thing I'm learning about her is that, after a certain point, she doesn't like it slow.

"Tell me what you want."

"I want you to make me come with your mouth before you fuck me senseless."

"How could I say no to that?" I ghost over her clit lightly with one of my thumbs and her hips buck beneath my hands.

"Don't even think about saying no." She growls, head back with pleasure as I stroke her again, smoothing the wetness from her pussy up over her clit.

I chuckle and consider making her beg for it after that comment, but I don't want to wait, either. I want to make her come, and then I want to come inside her. It's been over twelve hours since I've held her in my arms and felt her from the inside, and that's already too fucking long.

So I kneel down in front of the couch, push the ottoman that's behind me back out of the way, and pull her up to a sitting position so she's got her legs spread on either side of me. Then, pulling her hips forward to the edge of the couch cushion, I dip my head down to taste her again. As I stroke her clit with my tongue, I enter her with two fingers, curling them forward to stroke up into her. She rides my fingers with groaning pleasure as my tongue works to drive her over the edge, and when I glance up at her, she's got both her breasts cupped in her hands.

"Yes." I hiss, lifting my mouth from her but pushing my fingers into her harder and faster. "Touch yourself. I want to see you pinch those nipples as I bring you over the edge."

She groans as she pushes her head farther back into the couch cushions and does what I ask, running her thumbs across her nipples and then pinching them between her thumb and the knuckle of her first finger. She lets out another moan of pleasure when I suck her clit into my mouth and run my tongue over it, and then she's bucking wildly under me. I fuck her harder and faster with my fingers, because that's how she seems to like it best, and in no time she's arching her back and chanting *yes* over and over as she rides out her orgasm.

She collapses back against the couch but tells me, "I'm not done. I need you inside me."

And so right there, still kneeling in front of her with her legs spread open, I push inside of her, watching myself enter her inch by inch—the way she stretches to accommodate me, how wet and tight she is against my cock, the way she sighs with pleasure when I'm fully seated inside her . . . the experience is nothing short of a miracle, every single time.

She lifts her legs up, probably propping them on the ottoman behind me, and then shifts her hips as if to tell me to get going. But I feel like I'm frozen in this moment, taking in her naked body before me—the thin column of her neck, the way her breasts spread as she lies back, the fine stretch marks along the sides of her abdomen from carrying her children, and the pink skin stretched around my cock.

I want to see this sight every night for forever.

And that's what I'm thinking about as our bodies meet, over and over. It's what I'm thinking about when I drag one leg up and over my head, flipping her around so she's kneeling before me, bent over the couch and I'm pushing back into her from behind. It's what I'm thinking about when my hands smooth over her breasts and meet her clit, bringing her to orgasm again. And it's definitely at the forefront of my mind as I grip her hips, tell her to hold on to the back of the couch, and watch myself slam into her until she's squeezing me tight as she orgasms a third time, and I fall right over the edge with her. And when I pull out, watching my cum drip out of her as I bend to grab her underwear and wipe her up, the only thing I can think is: I want to be *here*, in this house, with her. Forever.

Afterward, I lift Lauren up and lay her down on the couch, then snuggle in beside her. She lifts her head, propping it up on her elbow, and uses her other hand to trace the column of Roman numerals along the side of my rib cage.

"What are they all?" she asks.

"Dates."

"Tell me about them?"

I look down at the ink and trace my finger along the first date. "The year my mom left." I move my finger down the next two rows, telling her, "When Audrey and Jules were born." Then I trace the rest of the rows, reading them off from memory. "When I was drafted into the NHL. The year my stepmom died. The year my dad left. When I retired from the NHL."

"There's a lot of loss recorded here, Jameson." Her voice is quiet and sad as she leans in and sweeps her lips across my skin over the ink.

That gentle touch is almost painful, because she *sees* me. The part of me that I keep hidden from everyone else. And she understands. "I know. There's a lot of good, too, though."

She lays her head on my shoulder, snuggling in beside me. "Yeah, I guess that's life."

I turn so I'm lying on my side, facing her, where her head now rests on my arm. "You've had a lot of loss too. But I want you to know that I'm in this for the long haul. We're going to get through all of this together."

"I know," she says, closing her eyes. She looks so content, lying here cuddled against my side.

"We're going to regret it if we fall asleep on this couch," I tell her.

"Why's that?" she asks without opening her eyes.

"Because we're two full-grown adults and we barely fit on here. Let's go upstairs. Unless you don't want me to stay, which is completely okay too." It's her house, and her kids are here, and if she's not ready for me to spend the night, that's understandable.

"I want you to stay. But also, it might be best if Ivy and Iris don't wake up to you here in the morning."

"My flight leaves at 7:30 a.m. and I still have to stop by my house and grab some stuff on my way to the airport. So I'll probably be gone by five."

She hugs me tighter, which I take as an indication that she doesn't want me to go. We head upstairs together, and as I fall asleep with her wrapped in my arms, I'm feeling the exact same way—I don't want to leave. Ever.

---

I press a kiss to her forehead, wishing again that I didn't have to leave. I'm half tempted to text Aaron and tell him to figure his shit out with his coach on his own, but that's not the kind of agent I am. Instead, I'm already making plans in my mind for bringing another agent or two into the fold so I can take a step back. There's no reason to still be pushing myself this hard when I've already accomplished everything I set out to do and more.

I don't need money, I need time. Time to focus on myself and Lauren, and nurturing what's growing between us, and doing whatever I can to help with Ivy and Iris—I want to step up like no one ever has for these girls.

"Shit," she mumbles as I stand up. "It's Monday, isn't it?"

"Yeah. But still early. You can go back to sleep."

"I forgot to put the trash on the curb last night. The trash trucks will be here soon . . . they come so early."

"I'll do it when I leave."

She tells me where to leave the trash and recycling barrels, and then I give her another kiss goodbye and head downstairs as quietly as possible. Once outside, the barrels sound impossibly loud as I roll them down the driveway in the silence of the early morning. When I get the second one to the street, I turn and find a man standing only about five feet from me, a trash bag in his hand.

"Hey," he says as he lifts the lid to the barrels already sitting at the street next to the neighbor's driveway. "I'm Greg. I live next door."

"Nice to meet you. I'm Jameson."

"Your family just move into this place?"

"Uh, no. This is my"—I don't even know what to call Lauren—"girlfriend's place."

"Ah yes," he says. "I've seen her and the kids coming and going a few times. Seems like she did a lot of work to the place."

"Yeah, it was completely gutted before she moved in," I say, resisting the temptation to check my watch. I need to get going and don't feel like I have time for this conversation. "So there was a lot of work needed."

"The previous owners were just starting to renovate when he died in a ski accident."

I'm finding it hard to breathe. *Owners?* What the hell is he talking about? A ski accident is too coincidental for Josh not to be one half of this couple.

I glance back at Lauren's house. "A couple owned this place?"

"I think so," he says, rubbing his hands together. He's dressed in flannel pajama pants, a sweatshirt, and sneakers—clearly he was planning on running a bag of trash out to the barrel, not standing around chatting in near-freezing temperatures. "Josh lived somewhere else but was moving here. Sophia lives in Boston, so she was the one here all the time meeting with the contractor. I wondered if she'd sell the place after he died. Such a tragedy."

I clear my throat to stop from choking on the idea of Sophia owning half this house. That can't be possible. I have a million questions, but none that I think this guy would know the answer to.

"I'm sorry, I have to run. I'm catching a flight this morning."

"I'm sure I'll be seeing you around."

I walk back up the driveway to my car, which is parked next to the back door. I glance at the house and think about Lauren, sleeping inside, completely oblivious to the fact that her husband did not buy this house because he knew how much she wanted to move back to Boston, but instead bought it to be closer to another woman.

I stand there, paralyzed with indecision about what I should do with this knowledge. Do I go inside and tell her the limited amount of information I know? Or do I wait until I can get more intel? I glance at my watch and realize I'm dangerously close to not making it home and to the airport in time for my flight, yet my feet are still rooted to the spot outside her door.

In the end, I get in my car, and once I'm out of the driveway and halfway down her street, I dial a number I never thought I'd have to call again.

"Da fuck you calling me at five fifteen in the morning?" Woody's grizzled voice carries through my car speakers.

"You're a contractor. It's not like you're not awake by now."

"Don't mean I want to talk to *you* at the ass crack of dawn."

"I have some questions about the work you were doing on that house in Brookline. Specifically, who were you were working for?"

---

On my second night in LA—because of course the situation with my player and the coach's now-pregnant daughter was more complicated than I was led to believe —the email I've been waiting on from Derek finally comes through.

Woody had only been able to give me a first name and a

phone number, so I set Derek to work tracking down any available details about Sophia.

*Here's everything I could find on her. Let me know if you need anything else.*

The email contains links to all her social media accounts, and pages of attachments showing where she lives and everywhere she's worked. It takes me about an hour of digging before I've pieced together what I think might constitute the story of her and Josh.

It appears that the first time they met in person was two years ago during an event in Whistler, British Columbia. She's a brand manager for an energy drink company that was one of Josh's only remaining endorsements before he died, and she's a big backcountry skier. According to the pictures on her social media account, it looks like they skied together with a big group that week, and many other times over the next couple years.

There are no pictures of the two of them together, they're always in a group, so it's impossible to tell if they were together all along or if that was something that happened more recently. But now it's clear to me why Josh never introduced Lauren to the people he traveled with, or asked her to come on those trips—something I know always bothered her. But I don't think she ever suspected that it was because he was cheating.

I don't see anything at all about the house in Brookline, and since Sophia seems to post on social media a lot, it makes me hopeful that she didn't own any part of it. I know that only Josh's name was on the deed, otherwise Lauren wouldn't have been able to get it transferred into her name after his death.

According to Woody, Sophia was the one who had met with him most often about the renovation. Josh was only there for a few of their meetings, though he was the one footing the bill. What I don't know is whether she had any money tied up in the house, and that feels like it should be an immediate concern here.

Lauren has worked so hard to build a new life for her and her girls in that house, and the thought that Sophia might have any stake in it is unbearable.

I close out of my social media app and rest my head back against the padded headboard of the hotel bed, thinking about how in November, Sophia posted a selfie saying she had the flu and was going to miss out on an epic ski trip to the Pacific Northwest.

So, she was supposed to be there—on the "epic" trip that killed the other seven skiers who went.

The rabbit hole of images and information I just went down has left me famished, and I must have been scrolling for a long time because it's already dinner time. I contemplate going out somewhere, but I don't want to be around people right now. Instead, I order room service, then sit there staring at Sophia's cell phone number that Derek sent.

And that's when a text from Lauren comes through.

LAUREN

Miss you so much, but I'm too tired for a call tonight. I'm going to bed early. I'll need all my energy for the charity game tomorrow night, and seeing you afterward. Your flight better not be late. If you miss this game, I will kill you.

It's not even 9:30 p.m. in Boston, so she *must* be

exhausted. I know she was at work late tonight making sure everything is in order for the event tomorrow. Since marketing practically runs this event every year, it's been a huge amount of work for her. But I know she's feeling really good about it, and it's great to see her back to being herself— kicking ass at her job, confident about herself, happy. I hate that I hold information that threatens that.

JAMESON

I can't control the airlines, but I'm taking the earliest flight possible. I'll be back in Boston midafternoon.

And I miss you too, and can't wait to see you. And touch you. And taste you. Go get some sleep so you're well rested tomorrow. I plan on keeping you up all night.

LAUREN

Not me, already in bed imagining you here with me . . .

JAMESON

Not me, with my thumb hovering over the icon to video call you right now so you can show me how much you miss me . . .

LAUREN

Okay, I really need to go to sleep or this is going to go in a direction that will keep me up. I will be well rested for you tomorrow. Promise. XOXO

JAMESON

Sweet dreams.

I'm torn between being sad to not hear her voice tonight, while simultaneously being relieved that I don't have to make sure I don't bring up anything about Sophia, because that is a conversation to have in person.

I wouldn't tell her any of this right before the charity game, anyway. It's her first big event at work, and I'm not going to ruin that for her by dropping this news on her before her big night.

I really hate that there's no way for me to fix this for her— not that she'd want me to. But I'm dreading the way I know it's going to break her heart, and have her questioning everything: her marriage, her home in Boston, her ability to trust her own judgment. The least I can do is go to her armed with as much information as possible so she can decide what to do with it.

I enter Sophia's phone number into a text message and hope I don't regret what I find out.

JAMESON

> Hi Sophia, my name is Jameson Flynn. I was Josh Emerson's sports agent and the executor of his will and trust.

I don't expect an instantaneous response, but I get one.

SOPHIA

> I know who you are.

JAMESON

> Okay.

> I didn't know about your relationship with Josh until a couple days ago, or I'd have reached out sooner.

SOPHIA

I was kind of hoping no one knew about that relationship, to be honest. But I'm not surprised that it's gotten out.

JAMESON

So you knew that he was married?

SOPHIA

No . . . not until this past November.

*Wait, what?* How could she have known him for two years, since before his girls were even born, and not known he was married?

JAMESON

That brings up a lot more questions.

SOPHIA

Do you want to call me? Seems like it'd be easier to talk about this over the phone?

I hit the call icon on my phone screen and then put it on speakerphone. I'm already up and pacing around my hotel room.

"Hey," I say when she answers the phone. "I'm sorry to contact you under these circumstances."

"I'm sorry that I'm involved in this at all," she says following a heavy sigh.

"The reason I'm reaching out is that when I executed Josh's will and trust, I didn't know he was involved with someone outside his marriage."

"I didn't know he was still married. I'd only been with Josh for about six months before he died," she says, "but we'd known each other for a couple years through mutual ski friends. We'd done a lot of trips together, and when he and his wife separated—or at least, that's what he told me at the time—he made his move."

"So you thought they weren't together anymore?"

"He told me they were separated and getting divorced. We kept everything between us a secret because he was still in the middle of divorce proceedings and didn't want his wife to be able to use our relationship against him in the divorce."

I don't know if this makes it better or worse? Certainly I don't think as badly of her if she was duped by Josh, but maybe it makes it even worse for Lauren—this isn't a case of her husband being lured away by another woman, this is him intentionally going out and finding someone else while lying about his relationship.

"I'm sorry he put you in that position. It sounds like he was lying to a lot of people."

She huffs out a scoff. "Yeah, you could say that. I figured it out right before his last trip in November, and I broke things off with him."

"I'm guessing you knew the other skiers on the trip?"

"Yeah." Her voice wavers. "I lost a lot of friends that day."

"I'm really sorry."

"The survivor's guilt is real," she says. "But I don't think that's what you called to talk about."

"The main reason I called is that I want to make sure I didn't make any mistakes when I executed the will and trust, especially regarding the house in Brookline." I decide not to tell her the house wasn't in the trust, because I don't want her to consider litigating this. "I know you weren't a co-owner with Josh, but did you have any money tied up in that house before he died?"

"No." She lets out another sigh. "He owned the house, and I did most of the work. I met with the contractor, picked out the cabinets and other finishes, took care of ordering everything for him—because I believed him when he said he was remodeling this house because he wanted to live closer to me. We didn't have any concrete plans for me to move in or anything."

"Why did you do all this work for him, then?" I ask. It's none of my business, but the question just slips out.

She coughs out a laugh. "Because he had me fooled. I believed the things he said, believed that he cared about me, so I wanted to help him. The reality is, Josh didn't care about anyone but himself."

Isn't that the truth?

"I've been thinking," she says hesitantly, "about reaching out to Lauren. I have a good amount of money that truthfully should go to her—refunds for all the deposits I put down for house stuff using a debit card that Josh gave me for that purpose. The money's all been refunded and is just sitting there in a bank account with his name on it. I didn't know if Lauren knew I existed. If she did, I was pretty sure she wouldn't want to hear from me. And if she didn't know I existed, well, did I want to be the one to tell her the truth about her husband after he'd already died?"

"There's no way for her to avoid knowing, now," I tell her. "I have to tell her."

"I'll send you the bank info to share with her. Would you also tell her that I'd be open to talking to her, if she wants? I'm guessing she's living at that house now, because Woody didn't know I'd broken things off with Josh, so he told me you ended his contract. Out of a morbid sense of curiosity, I drove by one night—I just wanted to see if there was a for sale sign, but instead I saw the Utah plates on the SUV in the driveway."

I shouldn't feel a pang of sympathy for the woman who was sleeping with Lauren's husband, but I do. I'd spent the last thirty-six hours thinking she was the villain. Now I know that she was just another casualty of Josh's narcissism.

"Okay, I'll let you know."

# Chapter Twenty-Three

## JAMESON & LAUREN

### JAMESON

The number of fans that turned out for a charity game with a bunch of guys who haven't played in the NHL for years is a true testament to how deep the Rebels pride runs in Boston. We took the ice to the same fanfare of music, lights, and cheering that I remember from home games. In some ways, it doesn't feel like it's been a decade since I did this for a living, in other ways, it feels like a lifetime ago.

The crowd did the Rebels chant at the end of the first two periods like they always do, and now we're tied 2-2 with only minutes left in the period. The fans are going wild. They can't decide who to cheer for when it's Boston v. Boston, so they cheer for everything anyone does. And the fact that there's nothing on the line but bragging rights means we're all having a good time on the ice.

Except Donaldson. The man is in his fifties, but he must still skate and run drills every fucking day because he's as good as or better than the rest of us. And he's trash-talking my team like we're not all on the same side here: the side where we do this for fun to raise money for a great organization. No, he's here to win.

As he brings the puck down the outside, I misjudge his trajectory, so when I cut left he goes to my right. Luckily, our goalie blocks the shot with a shoulder check, and I'm there to grab the rebound. I take it around the back of the net and Donaldson's right behind me, but I cut him off at the net and get enough separation to bring the puck straight up the middle.

By the time I hit center ice, two of my teammates have caught up to me, and I pass it off to one of them. He takes a shot on goal, but it's blocked and I'm in the perfect position to get the rebound. Right as I pull my stick back to shoot, I'm checked from behind.

It's so completely unexpected that I fly forward, face-first, and even though I manage to get one hand out to break the fall, my chin connects with the ice. It hurts like a mother-fucker and is bleeding like one too. I hear the collective gasp of the audience as I push up to my knees while holding my blood-soaked chin in one hand. I turn and look up at Donaldson right as the athletic trainer comes up with a towel to put pressure on my wound and helps me to the bench to evaluate the damage.

Both referees and a linesman are on Donaldson and he's sent to the penalty box with a five minute major, even though there's less time than that on the clock.

Back on the bench, the athletic trainer says I need to see

the team doctor, but I refuse to go to the training room because I don't want to miss our power play—honestly, my team winning on this power play in the last few minutes of the game would be justice for Donaldson's infraction.

"You're probably going to need stitches for this," the trainer tells me as he cleans the cut, "or you're going to wind up with a jagged scar."

"Can you just tape it up for tonight and I'll take care of it tomorrow?" I ask, holding the gauze he gave me against my chin and hoping the pressure will stop the bleeding.

"I can patch it up, but you're not going to get as clean of a scar as if you have the doctor stitch it."

My eyes are still on the ice. "Whatever."

"Once the bleeding stops, he can finish the stitches up in ten minutes. Why wait?" He crosses his arms, and when I glance over at him, he's annoyed. I focus back on the ice, where my team has just scored a goal I missed because I'm dealing with the pissy trainer. Why does he care if I have a scar? All I want is to celebrate on the ice with my teammates, and then go see Lauren. That said, she may not like it if I bleed all over her face, so maybe I should take care of this.

"Fine," I say, eyeing center ice where the players are lined up to shake hands, "but first I'm going back out on the ice to wrap this up." A cheer rises up from the audience when I skate out to my teammates, still pressing a bloody piece of gauze to my chin.

After my stitches, I shower and change as quickly as I can, skipping the celebration in the locker room so I can go meet Lauren.

I saw her for a brief minute before we took the ice, but since she was working, I couldn't push her up against the wall and kiss the shit out of her. She was so in her element, telling everyone what to do and where to go, and it was unbelievably hot to see her exert control as she orchestrated media coverage, sponsors, and even the players.

I can't wait to get back to her place tonight and show her how much I missed her. And then we need to have the hard conversation I've been dreading since I learned about Sophia.

I find her on the club level, exactly where she texted me she'd be. She's got her head tucked in conversation with her friends Jackson and Sierra. She'd told me they were going to be in town for the weekend, and staying at a hotel in the city. I know they all have plans together tomorrow, so hopefully they won't mind me stealing her away tonight.

I reach out and tap Lauren's shoulder once I've come up behind her, and she spins around, pressing her entire body into mine and squeezing her arms around me so tight it's hard to breathe.

"Missed you," I whisper against the top of her head as I breathe in the scent of her.

"Missed you more," she says, then tilts her chin up and gasps when she sees the stitches along my jaw. "I didn't realize it was that bad!"

"Yeah, I'm fine." The area is still numb, but I'm sure it'll hurt again once the novocaine wears off.

We chat with Lauren's friends for a few minutes, and I'm about to suggest I take Lauren home when I hear, "Jameson!" The man's voice sounds familiar, but I can't place it. When I glance up, I see Lauren's neighbor, Greg, barreling toward us.

———

## LAUREN

Jameson looks uneasy as the man approaches us. Seems like the guy's a fan, and it makes me wonder if this happens a lot, or only at games.

"When we met the other morning," he says, holding his hand out for Jameson to shake, "I didn't realize who you were. Then there you were tonight, on the jumbotron!"

"Yeah," Jameson says, pulling his hand back. "Good to see you again. Could we catch up another time?"

"Sure. Good to see you," the man says, then as he turns to leave, he catches sight of me. "Oh, you're my new neighbor. I see you and the kids coming and going, but with the weather I haven't really had a chance to introduce myself. I met Jameson the other morning when we were both taking the trash out real early."

The guy seems nice enough, so I extend my hand. "Hi, I'm Lauren."

"I'm Greg. I'm so glad you've done so much to the house. The last owners were just starting a renovation when he died in a ski accident—"

Jameson puts his hand on the guy's shoulder. "Like I said, let's catch up later."

"Wait!" My voice is surprisingly firm, given that I feel like I can't breathe. "The last owners? Plural?"

Greg looks at Jameson, who gives him a nearly infinitesimal shake of his head, so slight he was probably hoping I wouldn't notice. "You know what," Greg says, "I already told Jameson everything I know about Josh and Sophia. I'll let him share with you."

Jameson closes his eyes and his jaw ticks.

"Nice to meet you, Lauren," Greg says, and then he's walking away.

"Let me see if I got that right. Josh was renovating that house with another woman, who he presumably was having an affair with? And you knew about it?" I need to get control of myself, because I'm fuming and I'm technically at work. But I'm confused, and upset, and horrified that he could know something like this and not tell me.

Jameson's voice is low and reassuring when he says, "I only found out the other morning as I was leaving, and I planned to talk to you about it tonight."

Behind me, I feel Jackson and Sierra's hands on me—supportive and reassuring. I take a deep breath and look up at him. "So you've known for three days?"

"Not even, and I was in LA—"

"You weren't in LA when you found out!" I know my anger should be directed at Josh for his betrayal, more than at Jameson for knowing about it and not telling me immediately. But it's hard to direct your anger at someone who's dead, and Jameson is standing right here.

"I didn't want to say anything until I had more information to share with you. Which I just got last night," he says, and when I raise my eyebrows at the idea that he's had that information for twenty-four hours, he plows on with, "but I wanted to tell you in person, so I could be there for you when you were understandably upset."

He reaches out like he's going to take my hand, but I step back. Jackson and Sierra each wrap an arm around me, supporting me.

And then tears are pricking my eyes even as I will myself

to be stronger. I just helped run one of the most successful fundraising events in the history of the Rebels, and I'm standing here about to cry, instead of basking in the success of my big night. Why? Is this what happens when I let another man into my life? He hurts me just like the first one did?

"You know what?" I tell Jameson as I hold back my tears. "I can't talk about this right now. I have a few things to wrap up here for work, and then I'm leaving with Jackson and Sierra because I need a girls' night. I'll call you tomorrow and we can talk about this then."

"Lauren, no." I hate the pain that rips through his words, but he caused this—he could have told me the truth as soon as he learned it. And now I need some time to wrap my mind around all of this.

"I'll call you tomorrow, Jameson." My voice doesn't leave room for argument, and neither does the fact that I turn and walk away from him. Away from the one person who swore up and down that he wouldn't do anything to hurt me.

# Chapter Twenty-Four

## LAUREN

When Jackson, Sierra, and I walk into my house, we find Paige half asleep on the couch in the living room. The lights are off and the TV volume is very low, and she has the girls' video monitor on the ottoman in front of her, like they might escape their bedroom if she doesn't have it close by.

"What's going on?" she asks, clearly surprised that I'm coming home with my best friends and not my boyfriend, as planned. Is "boyfriend" even the right word? We've been together for, what, not even a week? It feels like so much more.

Every good thing that's happened to me since Josh died is inextricably linked to Jameson—and I don't want to unlink him, I just want to figure out how we move forward from here.

"It's been a rough night," I say, motioning my head toward the kitchen. When I walk in, I set an entire box of liquor and mixers on my counter. It was supposed to be a quick pit stop to grab the supplies for Jackson's famous margaritas, but instead we basically bought enough alcohol to stock a home bar.

"Tell me what happened," Paige says as she helps take bottles out of the box and set them on the counter.

I use my sleeve to wipe the tears from my face. They started falling the minute we left the rink, and I haven't even attempted to stop them. I was clinging to this notion that Josh was in the process of redeeming himself by buying me this house where he knew I wanted to move, and all along, it was for someone else.

"Josh was cheating on me, and he bought this house and was remodeling it with the other woman before he died."

The bottle of tequila slips out of Paige's hand, but luckily Sierra's right next to her and has great reflexes. She hands the bottle to Jackson, who is across the island getting out a cutting board for the limes.

"What? How is that possible? And how did you find out?"

"I . . ." I can't finish the sentence. I look over at Jackson. "Can you explain?"

She nods, and Sierra puts her arm around my shoulders. "After the game, we were standing around talking to Jameson. And Lauren's neighbor came up. She hadn't met him yet, but apparently Jameson had the other morning. The neighbor let it slip that a couple owned the house before, and had started the remodel, but that they guy had died in a ski accident."

Paige's gasp is loud in the otherwise quiet house. "No."

"Yes," Jackson says. She gives me a sympathetic look, and says, "And apparently Jameson's known for a few days and he didn't tell Lauren."

"He did say that he wanted to wait and tell her when he got more information, which he got last night," Sierra adds. "And that he wanted to tell her in person."

"Which would have been impossible to do until tonight," Paige says. "Right? Because he was in LA?"

I can feel her prompting me to see this from his side.

"I know you wanted him to tell you right away," Jackson says, stirring the ingredients for the margaritas in a large glass pitcher and sounding like she's choosing her words carefully. "But would it have been better if you'd known a couple days ago? Especially finding out right before the biggest night of your new career?"

"Are you suggesting it's okay that he lied to me about this?"

"Did he lie, though?" Paige asks.

"Oh my God." I groan. "Not telling me is a lie of omission, and it's wrong."

"It sounds like he was going to tell you tonight, now that he had more information. He knew how important this event was to you, and he wanted to let you get through it before dumping this on you. It's not like he wasn't planning to tell you," Sierra says.

I look around at my friends. "You have a point, but I still would have wanted him to tell me immediately. I mean, my husband was a fucking cheater, and the whole time he made me think I was imagining him becoming more distant, pulling away from our marriage. We had sex *so* infrequently after the kids were born. I chalked it up to being new parents and being exhausted. I blamed it on myself, thinking he just wasn't attracted to me post-pregnancy. And all along"—I can hear my voice rising but can't really stop it—

"he was fucking someone else? And they were going to live *here* together?"

I look around the space, wondering how I could possibly live here now that I know the truth about why I own this house. It was never meant to be mine, it was going to be *hers.*

"That's . . ." Paige says hesitantly, "a lot of information."

There's a knock at the door. Two quick wraps—loud enough to be heard, but not loud enough to wake up the kids. Classic Jameson.

"Please," I say, grabbing Paige's hand. "I'm still not ready to talk to him about this. Tell him I will call him tomorrow when I've calmed down a bit."

She heads toward the door with nothing but a nod. I hear the door open, and then nothing. He doesn't say anything. Paige doesn't say anything. In the kitchen, Jackson, Sierra, and I just look at each other, brows knit together in confusion.

I'm about to peek into the hallway when I hear multiple sets of footsteps heading toward us. What the hell? I spin around, ready for a confrontation with Jameson, and instead find Jules and Audrey headed straight toward me, both of them with outstretched arms. I let them pull me into a group hug, and when they finally let go, I pull back and ask, "What are you doing here?"

"Jameson thought you might need more friends after . . . you know . . . what happened earlier," Jules says. "Morgan's on her way too. It's not exactly the girls' night we were talking about having, but it's the one you need."

I want to be mad at him. I *am* mad at him.

But I asked for space, for a night with my girlfriends to process this, and he is not only honoring that by not showing up, but he sent in reinforcements to support me. Why does he have to be so damn supportive and thoughtful?

"I don't know what to say."

"Please say that you're going to let us look through whatever's in here with you?" Audrey says as she hands me a manilla envelope. My name is scrawled across the front in Jameson's handwriting.

"What is this?" I ask, turning the envelope over and looking at it like there might be a bomb inside. Because whatever it is, I'm pretty confident it's going to rip my life apart.

"It's everything Jameson was going to give you tonight when he told you about Josh," Audrey tells me.

So he wasn't lying that he had more information and was going to talk to me about it tonight, in person. That's a relief, but also, a ball is forming in the pit of my stomach as I consider how cold I was to him, without giving him any opportunity to explain.

"Here," Jackson says, handing me the first margarita. "I topped yours off with extra tequila."

"Why? It's a Wednesday night, I can't be hungover tomorrow. I have a job and two kids to take care of."

"I'll spend the night," all five of them say simultaneously, and then Morgan's walking into my kitchen asking if we're having a sleepover.

"I don't have enough beds for that." I laugh.

"Whatever," Jules says, "we'll be too drunk to care where we sleep."

"Someone has to stay sober," I say. "In case anything happens with the girls. What if one of them wakes up sick or something?"

"It's fine, I won't drink," Sierra says. I see Jackson eye her sister-in-law's belly and wonder if it means what I think it means. But I'm not going to ask in front of people she doesn't even know.

Paige catches Morgan up on what she missed while I introduce Jules and Audrey to Jackson and Sierra. Then we take our margaritas over to the dining room and I set the envelope in the middle of the table, where we all stare at it.

I take a deep breath, my hand hovering over the flap of the envelope. Once I open it, I'll know things I can never forget—about my marriage, my house, and the mystery woman who was a part of both. I'll have answers. And maybe, just maybe, I'll also have some sense of how to move forward.

I open the flap and slide the papers out of the envelope. "There's a printout of an email from Derek, Jameson's assistant," I tell my friends, since they don't know who he is. I still haven't met the man, just heard about his greatness. My eyes scan the page. "Sophia Lennox," I say the name out loud.

*The other woman.* I want to think she was just the woman Josh was sleeping with, but if they were remodeling this house together, it was so much more than that. It makes me wonder if his heart was actually here in Boston, not home in Utah with me and the girls.

"It's a list of all of her social media," I say, and Jackson snatches it out of my hand.

"I'm on it," she says.

Behind that paper is a thin stack of more paper. I take another gulp of my margarita and then flip through the pages quickly, passing each page to Morgan, on my right, as I go. "She lives in the Back Bay, really close to you guys," I tell Jules and Audrey as I look at the printout of the aerial view of the map, with her address starred. "Like, I may have actually parked in front of her place when I came over for dinner the first time."

I scan the next page, a printout of her profile on a popular professional networking site. "Fuuuck," I say on a sigh. "She's a brand manager for an energy drink company. Not only were they one of Josh's endorsements, they have ties to the Rebels. They were one of the sponsors for tonight's game. She might even have been there."

I pass that page to Morgan, and slowly the pages make their way around the table. All the while, I'm wondering if Sophia knows who I am.

"Jameson was probably right about not telling me before the game. If I'd known any of this, I'd have been so focused on figuring out who she is and if she was at the game, instead of focused on doing my job."

I lock eyes with Paige, who's wearing her best *I told you so* face.

"The good news," Jackson says, "is that there are no pictures of just her and Josh together on social media."

"Of course not," I say. "She probably wasn't trying to get caught red-handed with a married man."

"The bad news," she continues, her thumb hovering over her phone as she speaks, "is that she was supposed to be on the ski trip with him in November."

"Wait, *what?* How do you know?" I ask.

"A couple days before the trip, she posted a picture saying she had the flu and wasn't going to be able to go. The weird thing is, she doesn't look sick."

"Can I see?" I hold out my hand toward her.

"Do you really want to?"

I get what she's asking. Do I really want to see the woman who was in a relationship with my husband while we were still married? The one he was starting to build a life with in this house?

*Do I?* I pick up my margarita and take another huge gulp. The tequila burns going down, but it's giving me the liquid courage I need.

I close my eyes and hold out my hand, closing my fingers around Jackson's phone when she places it in my palm. I sit there with my eyes closed, preparing myself to see her face on the screen. And then I open my eyes.

"Oh." All eyes are on me, clearly waiting for me to say more. "She's . . . really normal. I don't know if that makes me feel better or worse."

I'd envisioned that the woman he cheated on me with must be some sort of a goddess who lured him away. And while this woman is cute, she's not going to stop traffic. Her light brown hair is slightly longer than shoulder length, she has rosy cheeks and some freckles. She has huge brown eyes and thick lashes, which make her look a little mysterious given her other fair features. And Jackson's right, she's makeup free in this picture, but she doesn't look sick.

I scroll through her feed, post after post of her at work events, out with friends, or skiing. It's in one of the skiing trips that I first spot Josh. Seeing him—in his ski helmet and goggles with a smile more radiant than anything I saw from him the past few years, so happy in his element on the slopes and free of the responsibilities of being a husband and father —hurts my heart.

So this is what he was doing when he wasn't home spending time with us. He was off living his best life and fucking someone else. I let the tears fall as I continue scrolling. I find Josh in a few other group pictures, but like Jackson said, there are no couple shots of them.

When I'm done, I pass the phone to Morgan, like I have with all the papers. Then I look around the table at my friends, who are all watching me. And I'm immensely grateful for these women, and the way that being in Boston has brought us all together, new friends and old friends. I am so relieved that I'm not stuck back in Park City by myself. Maybe I would never have known the truth about my marriage if I'd stayed there, but I also wouldn't be surrounded by my friends and family who showed up tonight to support me.

"How are you doing?" Sierra asks.

*Deep breaths.*

"I'm . . . surprisingly okay." I look around for a napkin, but finding none, I wipe the tears away with my sleeve, not caring about the mascara streaking across it.

Jules lets out an uncomfortable laugh. "You don't look okay."

Morgan smacks her on the arm. "She just found out her husband was cheating on her. Don't be insensitive."

"Sorry," Jules says. "But also, Jameson wanted us to pass on some more information, if we thought you could handle it."

"Smooth as always, Jules," Audrey rolls her eyes. "Apologies for my sister's directness. She spends most days swinging a hammer and bossing people around."

"Seriously?" Jackson asks. "That's so cool. I want to hear more about that . . . another time."

"What did he want you to tell me?" I ask.

"He talked to Sophia," Jules says.

"Oh my God, Jules. Stop. Talking!" Audrey gives her sister a look, then continues, "Because your neighbor mentioned her renovating the house with Josh, Jameson wanted to make sure that she didn't have any money tied up in it, or wasn't going to try to claim that she owned some part of it. He wanted to make sure you and the girls were safe in this house, so he called her."

I nod. Of course he was looking out for me; I shouldn't be the least bit surprised. But I am. I've never had anyone stand up for and support me like he has, and it's given me the push I needed to do things confidently on my own.

"She told Jameson that she didn't know Josh was still married. Apparently Josh had told her . . ." Audrey pauses.

"Just rip off the Band-Aid," I say.

"He told her you guys were in the process of getting divorced. She didn't know he was still married."

"Oh." The word squeaks out through the pain. It feels like someone's stabbed me in the heart. Morgan's hand finds mine in my lap and she gives me a supportive squeeze. "Is it okay," I mutter, "to hate a dead man?"

"In this case? Yes," Paige says. "But it's not a good use of your energy and emotions."

"You're already moving on," Morgan says. "And honestly, I've never seen you as happy as you have been since living here. Don't let Josh's ghost get in the way of your life now. Don't give him that kind of power."

"It all sounds so simple," I say with a sigh. And I wish it was that simple. I wish I didn't still wake up sometimes in the middle of the night expecting to find him in my bed, only to remember he's dead. I wish I didn't see our kids and think about how he's missing out on their lives. I wish that every time Jameson did something wonderful and supportive, I wasn't constantly comparing it to how Josh *didn't* do things like that for me.

He's not here anymore, and yet he's always here.

"There's nothing simple about grief," Jackson says. "Especially when you didn't get to say goodbye."

"There's one more thing," Audrey adds. "If you're open to it, Sophia wants to talk to you."

A hushed silence falls over the table, the only sound in my house is the white noise machine coming through the baby monitor.

"It's the only way I'm going to get the answers I want," I say. "Isn't it?"

My friends nod grimly. "If you want someone to go with you," Sierra says, "any of us would be happy to."

I take another sip of my margarita and consider the offer. Finally, I straighten up and tell them, "This feels like something I need to do by myself. And then, I can finally move on."

# Chapter Twenty-Five

## LAUREN

"I'm heading out a little early today," I tell Patrick as I gather my laptop, notebook, and phone at the end of our team meeting. Lots of people came in late today after last night's event, but not me. I was up all night, unable to shut my brain off and go to sleep. Work this morning was exactly the distraction I needed from my never-ending thoughts about this clusterfuck situation with Josh and Sophia. "I need to head downtown for an appointment."

"No problem. I'm not sure how you're not dead on your feet today," he says. "You did an awesome job last night."

"Thank you, but we all came together to make it happen."

"Yeah, but you led the team on this, and after only being here for like a month. Good work."

I thank him and say goodbye, then head to my office before I go into Boston to meet Sophia.

I only drank the one margarita last night, because I knew I had two messages to send after my friends left, and I wanted a clear head. I texted Sophia late, and she responded immediately, almost like she'd been waiting for my message. We agreed to meet up for a drink after work today.

I wonder if she found it impossible to sleep last night, worrying about this meeting, like me.

Or was I up because I was worried about fixing things with Jameson?

I pull up my texts with him from last night and read through the messages again as I walk down the long, empty hallway to my office.

LAUREN

> I'm sorry I overreacted earlier tonight. I was furious about Josh, and I took it out on you.

JAMESON

> I get it. But please know that I was trying to help. I didn't want to tell you until after the charity game because I knew how hard you were working to make it perfect, and I wanted to have more information before I said anything. I take it you opened the envelope?

LAUREN

> Yes, and I heard about your conversation with Sophia. Thank you for all that information. I'm actually meeting her for a drink tomorrow after work.

JAMESON

Do you want me to come with you?

LAUREN

> Thanks, but no. This is something I need to do on my own.

JAMESON

I'm here if you need me. Can I see you after you meet with her?

I remember reading that message at least twenty times last night, trying to figure out the subtext. He's here for me, but he's not smothering me. He wants to be supportive, but only as much as I want him to be. He wants to see me, hopefully because he wants reassurance about where things stand between us.

I don't think I've wrecked things between us. When he told me he'd wait as long as I needed, I think this was what he meant.

LAUREN

Yes. Can I come to your place when I'm done? Morgan will be at my house watching my girls after Tammy leaves.

JAMESON

I'll be here.

I wish I'd said more to him last night. I wish I'd reassured him that everything's still okay between us, or given him a chance to reassure me. I'll make sure to make up for that tonight.

But first, I have to go meet the woman who was sleeping with my husband, remodeling a house with him, and probably planning to start a life with him.

I'm throwing my scarf around my neck and slipping a light jacket on, thankful that March has brought warmer temperatures and more sunshine, when there's a knock against the open door to my office. I look up, and AJ's standing there in a navy-blue suit that makes her look absolutely fierce.

"You okay?" she asks. There's real concern in her voice, which has me worried that I've screwed something up somehow and she's been sent to fix it.

"Yeah, I'm fine. Why?"

"Well, I was stopping by to congratulate you on a job well done last night, but you just looked so sad while you were packing your bag up. Are you sure you're all right?"

Until the last five minutes, I've managed to go most of the day without dwelling on Jameson, or Josh, or Sophia—and apparently the minute I think about the situation, it shows all over my face, which is typical.

It's one of the things Jameson said he loves about me, and that realization has me tearing up as I think about all the things I love about him, but haven't told him yet.

"It's totally not work related." I laugh through the tears. "Are you sure you want to know?"

"Will it help you to talk about it, or make it worse?" she asks.

I huff out a humorless laugh. "I don't think it can make it worse."

"Okay," she says, "so what's going on?"

"I just found out my husband was cheating on me, and bought the house in Brookline where I currently live to be closer to this woman. They were just starting to remodel it together when he died."

"Well, shit," she says, and takes a few steps into my office. "If it helps at all, I've been through something similar, so I'm always happy to listen."

"*You* have been through something similar?"

"You sound surprised."

"I am. I mean, you're Alessandra Freaking Jones. You're beautiful and strong and successful—like, the perfect trifecta. A man would have to be an absolute idiot to cheat on you."

"I think a woman who is beautiful, strong, and successful —like you are, too—can also very easily be seen as a triple threat. And weak men don't like to be threatened, so they'll find any way they can to make you feel small. They'll prioritize their own needs over yours, they'll make you feel like wanting things in your relationship means you're insecure, or like you should be grateful for any scrap of their attention they'll give you. And when you aren't appropriately grateful, when you want more from them—more support, or compassion, or love—they go looking for validation elsewhere."

"That . . . sounds all too familiar," I mumble.

"That's not about you, Lauren. That's about him. Just like my husband's affair wasn't about me. Things were fine between us when we were on more equal footing. But as I became more successful at work and had to devote more time to my job, when I was less able to cater to his needs like I always had, he didn't step up, he stepped back."

What she's describing sounds exactly like Josh once we had kids—he resented that they took my time and attention from him.

"Did I hear a rumor that you're with Jameson now?"

I nod. There's no reason she can't know about us.

"Is he supportive?"

"Unbelievably so. Not only supportive of me and my career, but he's stepped in to help me on too many occasions to count." Yet in my head, I am counting them: the will, the house, the renovation, the blizzard, skating, the wedding,

Justin, the situation with Sophia. He has literally *never* not supported me.

"I think we have this expectation," she says, "as a society, that men will work as much as it takes to be successful, but women should only work hard enough and be successful enough that it doesn't inconvenience their partner or their family. But if you've found a man who encourages you, who wants to see you to succeed and shine in every aspect of life, including your career . . . hold on to him. He's a keeper."

"I plan to." I smile. "But first, I have to go meet the other woman."

"If you need help burying the body, you can call me," she says, reaching out and squeezing my shoulder.

"I don't even have your number," I say with a laugh as I pick my bag up off my chair.

"I know you need to go. I will look your number up in our system right now and text you, so you have it. Good luck."

"Thank you so much," I say, appreciating the kindness I see in her eyes. This woman is tough as nails, but supportive too. "I didn't know I needed this pep talk until I got it."

"You didn't need it, but I'm glad it helped anyway."

I'm just getting in my car when my phone buzzes.

UNKNOWN NUMBER

It's AJ. Call me if you need anything. And just in case, I have plenty of shovels.

———

I see her, sitting at the bar, the minute I walk into the restaurant on Newbury Street. She looks just like she does in her pictures on social media: wholesome and cute, total girl-next-door vibes.

Sophia picked the restaurant, and I wish I'd gotten here before her so I could at least have gotten my bearings and picked our seats—anything to feel a modicum of control in this utterly unpredictable situation.

"Hi," I say as I approach. I don't stick out my hand in greeting or smile at her—I'm afraid my hand would be shaking and my smile would falter.

"Hi, Lauren." Her voice is kind, sympathetic even. I'm sure she *does* feel bad for me—I'm the idiot who didn't know my husband was sleeping with anyone else while we were still married.

I hang my bag on the hook under the bar and take a seat next to her as I unwind my scarf.

"I appreciate that you're open to having this conversation," I tell her, "but now that I'm here, I really don't know what to say."

"Maybe I can start?" she asks.

"Please do," I say, but then the bartender comes up to take my drink order and chats with us as he fills a glass for me. Once he's handed over my drink, I gesture for Sophia to go ahead.

"I'm sure Jameson told you that I didn't know you and Josh were still married, but I just want to say how sorry I am that I believed him and didn't look into it. I really did break things off the *minute* I realized the truth—"

"Wait, *what?*"

"I broke things off with him the minute I figured out you two were still together. Jameson didn't tell you that?"

How do I admit to her that I didn't give him a chance?

That he sent his sisters over instead, and they either didn't know she broke things off with Josh, or forgot to mention it?

"We haven't been able to really debrief his conversation with you yet. I don't think I have all the details."

"Okay," she says, then hesitates. "Is it all right if I tell you?"

"Yeah, please do. But keep it, you know, surface-level, please."

Her laugh comes out almost like a snort, and it's adorable. I wish she wasn't so likable.

"So, we were friends for like a year and a half—part of a larger ski group that met up periodically at different mountains, usually when there was some sort of an event because several of us worked for companies that have partnerships with these resorts. I never thought of him as more than a friend," she says, "but then he started opening up, talking to me more, feeding me what were apparently a bunch of lies about how bad your marriage was, how difficult the decision was to get divorced, and how hard it was on him to not see the girls every day. I didn't realize, at the time, how he was conditioning me to feel special, feel like I was the only one who understood him . . . like he needed me."

I nod, because it's not that different from how he made me feel when we were first dating . . . like I was special and he couldn't live without me.

"When I started questioning where our relationship could go, given that he lived in Park City and I lived in Boston, he bought the house in Brookline. I started helping him remodel it. Actually, it felt like I was doing all the work—meeting with the contractor, picking out cabinets and stuff for him—and he didn't seem invested in the process at all.

Like, he never actually said he was moving into the house and never asked me to move in with him."

"Wait, you guys weren't remodeling that house to live in together?"

She takes a sip of her martini. "I don't actually know. That's what I originally envisioned. But he never really talked about it that way. The more I worked on that house, and the less he was involved in it, the more I started to question what was actually happening. Combine that with the fact that half the time I called him it went straight to voice mail, or I'd go days without hearing from him, and finally, I did the thing I'd been resisting doing for the six months I'd been seeing him."

"What's that?" I ask when she stops speaking.

"I looked you up on social media."

I think back to what my social media would have shown right before he died. His birthday was in September and we went away for a night. There were definitely pictures of us out to dinner, and a selfie on the balcony of our hotel room, and then of him blowing out birthday candles on his cake, with the girls in his lap, the night we got back. In October, there would have been pictures of us taking the girls to the pumpkin patch, where he pulled them around in a wagon, and then pictures of him with the girls dressed up for Halloween. We did family portraits in October too, with all the beautiful colored leaves in the background. We must have looked like quite the happy family. "Oh."

"Yeah, 'oh' was right," she says, then presses her lips between her teeth.

"Did he try to deny that we were still together when you approached him about it?"

She rolls her eyes. "Of course. Liars lie. Josh was so damn narcissistic and selfish, I think he couldn't help himself. If he wanted something, he was going to have it, no matter who he hurt in the process. I hope you realize that."

"Realize what?"

"That what he did wasn't about you. It wasn't that you weren't a good enough wife, pretty enough, loving enough—it wasn't about you at all. It was about him having no self-restraint and being completely incapable of loving anyone as much as he loved himself."

"I don't know if that makes me feel better." I'm sure she meant for it to. "I feel . . . like an idiot for not seeing that part of him as clearly as you did."

"I only saw it because I figured out his lies. You would have too, eventually. It sounds like you had no reason to suspect anything was amiss, whereas I did."

We sit there for a minute, staring into our drinks.

"When I met Josh," I tell her, "I was living in Boston. I had family here, and a great job. He kind of swept me off my feet, and we were engaged within six months and married within a year. I left everything behind for him. But before he died, I'd been talking about moving back here because I wasn't happy in our marriage and I wasn't happy living so far from my friends and family, and I thought Boston could be a fresh start for us. So after he died, and I found out about the house . . ." I take a deep breath, realizing that this isn't as hard to talk to her about as I thought it would be. We don't know each other, but we're bound together by the same man's lies. If *anyone* could understand how I feel, it's probably her. "I thought he'd bought it to surprise me."

Now it's her turn to say, "Oh."

"Yeah. Did you know I renovated it and moved in?"

"Yeah," she says. "I figured it out."

"Now I don't know how to feel about the house. At first, it felt like the last piece of him I had left. And now that I've been there a few months, it just feels like where the girls and I were meant to be."

"Maybe it is." She shrugs.

"When my neighbor told me about you and Josh—"

"Wait, Greg?" she asks, and I nod. "He's so nosy. If there's a neighborhood gossip, it's him."

I laugh. "I only met him once, but that doesn't surprise me in the least. So when he told me you two were renovating the house together, something snapped inside me. I was still holding on to the idea that the house was proof that Josh had loved me, even though—" I stop, thinking about how nothing about that house reminds me of Josh.

"Even though?" Sophia prompts.

Even though it's the house Jameson built for me.

How is it possible to feel this way? It isn't his house, but he's the one who made sure it was a house that I would love living in. And in my mind, he's everywhere in that house. He's fed me dessert in my sunroom, cooked me dinner in my kitchen, shoveled my driveway, watched movies with my kids on my couch, and slept in my bed.

He's the man I want to come home to every day.

"Even though everything about that house reminds me of Jameson, not Josh."

"Ahh," she says with a knowing smile. "I wondered."

"Wondered?"

"When he called me, he wanted to make sure I didn't own the house or have any money tied up in it. He said it was because he'd been the executor on the will and trust, and wanted to make sure he hadn't made any mistakes. But it felt like he was trying to protect *you*, not the property."

My lips turn up at one corner because that sounds exactly like Jameson.

"I wondered if you two were together," Sophia continues. "I'm happy for you. Really. I hope he treats you better than Josh did."

"You know what," I say, "it's like night and day different. Now I know what it's like to really be loved."

He hasn't said those words to me, but he doesn't need to. He shows me in everything he does.

"Good," she says. "I hope someday that happens for me, because I think I deserve it after putting up with Josh."

I laugh so hard at that, I almost cry—not because it's that funny, but because it is so relatable. "You sure as hell do," I tell her when I get control of myself, "just, not with Jameson, please."

We laugh together, and it feels like the absolute most perfect *fuck you* to send out into the universe. I hope that, in whatever capacity Josh's spirit still exists, he knows that he didn't break us, and that we're both stronger for having lived through his lies.

"I have to get going," I say as I glance at my watch. I told Morgan I'd be home an hour from now, and I still need to go see Jameson.

"Is it weird if I say that I'm glad we met?" Sophia asks.

"If you'd asked me that yesterday, my answer would have been very different. But now, I'm glad we met too. I think it's good for both of us to recognize that just because he lied to us, it doesn't mean we're not worthy of something better."

"And also, I think this meeting confirms that despite his *many* flaws, he had exceptional taste in women," Sophia says.

"He sure did. Hey," I add as I hop off my stool and slip on my jacket, "Jameson told me what your job is. I work in marketing for the Rebels. I feel like there's a good chance our paths may cross again, given that your company is one of our newest sponsors."

Her shoulders shake with a silent laugh. "I'm pretty sure I have a meeting with the whole Rebels marketing team on my calendar for next week."

"I guess I'll be seeing you again soon, then," I tell her.

I walk out of that restaurant feeling like a hundred pound weight has been lifted from me—but I realize that it wasn't weight at all, it was pressure . . . the pressure to love the memory of Josh even though he wasn't a good husband, and to mourn him even though I don't miss him anymore. I'd been putting so much pressure on myself, and now I feel like I can breathe again. I feel free.

# Chapter Twenty-Six

## JAMESON

I swing the back door open a little too fast, and it ricochets off the door stop and flies back at my face. Luckily, I catch it in time, because I already have one fading black eye and a newly split chin—I don't need to look even more beat-up when I see Lauren.

"Where is she?" I ask Jules, who's standing at the kitchen sink looking at me like I've just broken into her house. I'll admit I came in a bit too quickly in my haste.

"I assume you mean Lauren?"

"Yeah, her car's outside." It's parked right where Jules's truck normally sits.

"She dropped her car off here, then walked over to Newbury Street to meet Sophia. I gave her my spot and parked my truck on the street."

My chest deflates with disappointment, even though it's probably best that I have a minute to collect myself—my emotions are all over the place, and my thoughts are running wild as I worry about how this meeting will go, and whether

Josh's infidelity will make Lauren afraid to trust me in the future.

Once I'm upstairs, I glance around, imagining how she'll see my place for the first time. It's monochromatic and sparse —exactly how you'd expect a bachelor pad to look. It's nothing like the warm and inviting space she's created in her house. After spending so much time there lately, my place feels kind of . . . cold. Lonely. Most of that is probably because she's not here. She has a way of bringing warmth with her wherever she goes.

I've just changed out of my suit and thrown on jeans and a fitted Henley when I hear a knock on my door. And when I open it, Lauren's standing there staring at me like she's never seen me before. Then she smiles.

"I'm so used to seeing you in a suit," she says, "that sometimes I forget how good you look when you're casual like this too."

I reach above me and grip the top of the doorframe with one hand, put my other hand on her hip, and lean toward her. "I'm also happy to take my clothes off, in case you need help remembering how good I look naked."

A laugh bursts out of her. "As tempting as that offer is, I need to talk to you."

I pull her close and kiss her forehead. "Why don't you come in, then."

I lead her straight through the living room of my sterile apartment, without giving her the full tour. She doesn't need to see my place, because I don't plan on living here much longer.

I grab a blanket off the back of the couch before I slide open the door to the small roof-deck. It's one of those rare early spring days where it feels like it's warm because we're so used to the cold and snow. I gesture for her to sit on the outdoor couch while I start the fire pit. She wraps the blanket around her, and when I sit next to her, she cuddles up to my side.

"You're a blanket hog, you know."

"I didn't know you'd want to share," she says.

"Like that would stop you. Even in bed, you steal all the blankets at night."

"Good thing you run hot," she says, looking up at me and tracing the line of my cheekbone, from my black eye down to the corner of my lip, with her finger.

"Good thing. How was your talk with Sophia?" There's no reason to beat around the bush.

"Surprisingly good." She snuggles in closer but doesn't give me any other details.

"Is that really all I get?"

"She told me her side of the story, which you've already heard. And she reminded me that what Josh did wasn't about me, it was about him being a narcissist who thought he could and should have whatever he wanted, no matter who he had to lie to or hurt in order to get it. Even though I knew that, hearing it from her was validating. And then, we decided that Josh had great taste in women, obviously." She looks up again and gives me an adorable eye roll.

"You're handling this so differently than I expected."

"I have wasted too much time already being upset about Josh. He gave me two beautiful girls and in spite of everything else he did—or maybe because of it—I now have a life I truly love. I finally feel ready to leave him where he belongs . . . in my past."

"I'm glad. And I'm sorry that I didn't tell you about Josh and Sophia right away. I know you felt like I lied to you, too—"

"You discovered the lie that trumped all of Josh's other lies—" She lets out a slightly bitter sounding laugh. "—and when you were keeping that from me, I . . . I didn't handle it well. I'm sorry about how I reacted, and I'm sorry that I left with my friends and didn't give you a chance to explain. I wasn't my best self last night. I was actually kind of my worst self, honestly."

I tighten my arm around her shoulders and kiss the top of her head. "If I can't love you at your worst, I don't deserve you at your best."

She tilts her head back against my arm and stares up at me. "Jameson Flynn, did you just say you love me?"

"I've been obsessed with you since your twenty-two-year-old self walked into my office, all sass and sweetness. But you were too young for me, and I knew it. And three years later, once I'd seen your determination, your openness, and the way you put your heart into everything you do, and once I finally opened up to you and you liked what you saw, I knew we could be good for each other. I'll forever be sorry that I didn't fight for us then, and that we had to wait five years to get to this point.

"But now . . . now I love the woman you've become—the kindness and empathy you show, the way you love your girls, the way you accept help when you need it, the way you've built a whole new life for yourself here in Boston, the way you've opened yourself up to another relationship even though you were burned badly before. I don't think there's anything I *don't* love about you, honestly. And there probably never has been."

In her eyes, I see those feelings reflected back at me, even if she's not ready to say she loves me yet.

"I love that you're always here for me," she says, "no matter what—that you are patient with me and great with my kids, that you are amazing with your sisters and nephew, that you have this soft side that you don't show the world, but that you've shown me. I love your protective streak, and that you only open up to the people you really care about. You make me feel like forever is a possibility."

"It is. You just have to be ready to take that risk with me."

"I'm ready." Her words are barely more than a whisper. "I think I've been ready all along, but I've let fear keep me from admitting it to myself or to you."

"What are you afraid of?"

"Loving again . . . getting hurt again . . . losing you again. . ."

I reach over and cup her jaw in my hand, promising myself that I'll always remember how lucky I am that she's choosing me, that we've made our way back to each other. "I'm committed to this. To us. I can't promise that neither of us will ever hurt the other, but I can promise you that we'll always work through it—that we won't give up on each other."

She grips my forearm with her hand and gives me a little squeeze that conveys so much. "That's exactly what I want in a relationship."

My lips meet hers tentatively, like the gentle first kiss we never had. We originally came together in an explosion . . . a firework with a long fuse that had been burning so slowly it felt like it might never light off. But now, I kiss her like I intend to cherish her for the rest of my life—because I do.

But too soon, she's pulling away, telling me she promised Morgan she'd be home fifteen minutes from now. I bite my lower lip in frustration, because I spent the last twenty-four hours without her, and I don't want to be apart another second.

"You want to come home with me?" she asks.

If I do, I might never leave. "Yeah."

"All right," she says, and she goes to stand but then turns toward me. "Will you stay?"

"At your house?"

"Yeah. Will you stay overnight?"

"You're not afraid it'll confuse the girls?"

She shakes her head. "They adore you. And I think they need to get used to having you around."

"Oh yeah? Why's that?" I need to hear her say it.

"Because I plan on keeping you."

———

"I seriously thought they'd never go to sleep." Lauren groans after she tiptoes back to the bedroom. I'm sitting against her headboard, responding to emails and wrapping up a few last things for work so I can pay attention to nothing but her tonight. I set my phone on the nightstand as she approaches. "You can't get them all riled up like that before bedtime."

"What did I do?" I know damn well what I did.

"From now on, you're only allowed to do your Flynn Rider impersonation before dinner. You can't expect them to laugh that hard, for that long, and then go to sleep."

Pretending to be Flynn Rider was not a talent I knew I had, but all I have to do is turn my head toward them and give them a big smile, and Iris and Ivy dissolve into giggles.

Their reaction was too cute, so of course I did it every time they asked.

I hold up both hands in a gesture of surrender. "I promise."

"You don't mean a word of that, do you?" She laughs as she comes to a stop right next to what I'm already thinking of as my side of the bed.

"I intend to mean it, but if they look at me with those big eyes and say 'pwease' like they were tonight, I may not be able to hold out."

"Cuteness is their superpower. You can't crumble in the face of that. I'm going to need you to back me up on stuff, you don't get to *always* be the fun one."

I reach over and pull her to the edge of the bed. "I'll always back you up." I hear what she's saying, and all the things she's not saying. I'll be there for her like no one ever has been. But I'll also have fun with her kids, because they deserve that too.

She swings one leg up and over me, settling herself right across my lap. "I missed you," she says, dragging her lips lightly across my forehead and her palms stroke across my shoulders and land on either side of my neck. "A lot."

"Did you miss me," I ask as she grinds herself against me, "or my dick?"

She leans down so her lips graze my ear as she whispers, "Is 'both' an acceptable answer?"

"Quite acceptable." My hands skim from her hips, up

along her sides, and to her breasts. "I missed you too. Maybe last night, most of all." I drag my lips along her collarbone as I say, "I don't like it when we're fighting."

"We weren't fighting," she says breathlessly, as she rubs herself along the length of my quickly hardening dick.

"You weren't speaking to me, which is worse. I wouldn't mind fighting with you," I tell her. "I used to live to piss you off at work, if you remember. Ever wonder why that was?"

Beneath my lips, her chest shakes with laughter. "Does making me mad turn you on, Jameson?"

"It did when I was younger, and pissed off that I couldn't have you. Now though . . . now, I think making you happy turns me on."

"You know what would make me *really* happy?" she asks, tilting her hips to run her clit along my dick. I shake my head as my own hips thrust up to meet hers. "If you stopped talking and fucked me. Four days is entirely too long to go without you inside me."

"Shut the door all the way," I say, nodding my chin toward the bedroom door. "Because I plan to make you scream."

She's off the bed and shutting the door so quickly I barely have time to fully sit up. On her way back to the bed, she pulls her T-shirt over her head then unties her flannel pajama pants and lets them drop to the ground. She's standing in front of me in nothing but a thong.

"Is that one of the pairs I sent you?" I ask. I promised her ten pairs for the one I ruined in the car, but she hadn't mentioned receiving them.

"The box must have come yesterday, but I didn't see it until this morning. Thank you for these."

"You can thank me by taking them off and letting me see you naked."

She hooks her thumbs under the straps on her hips, slides the thong down her legs, and then walks toward me, asking, "Why do you still have clothes on?"

I reach behind me and pull my shirt over my head in one motion, then swing my legs over the edge of the bed and I stand, dropping my jeans. Lauren reaches out to palm me through my boxers, and I groan as she fists the length of me—it's been days since I've come, and I'm so hard for her already. I need the sweet feel of her skin on mine, of her body taking me and making me a part of her.

I push my boxers off and watch the way she eyes my body appreciatively, then I sit back on the bed and pull her between my legs. "It's been days, and I need you. So here's how this is going to go. You're going to sit on my face so I can taste you, and after I make you come, I'm going to fuck you so hard you'll be screaming my name into a pillow so you don't wake up the whole goddamn neighborhood."

She raises her eyebrows in surprise as I lie back, situating myself on the bed so my head is on the pillow. "You want me to . . ."

"Get up here—one knee on either side of the pillow. I've missed the taste of you so fucking much."

She puts one knee next to the pillow, then swings her other leg over, and holding onto the headboard with one hand, she slowly lowers herself toward my face. "Like this?"

I grab her hips, pulling her down toward me as I say, "I didn't tell you to fucking hover, Lauren. Sit on my face so I can eat this pussy like it deserves."

Her breath leaves her in a whoosh, like it often does

when I say something unexpected and it's turned her on, and then she's sliding her hips forward and back so I can lick her clit. I slide my hands up her abdomen until I've got her breasts cupped in my hands and I can run my thumbs across her nipples, which has her bucking her hips faster.

The view from here, her breasts bouncing in my hands, her head thrown back so I only see her neck and chin, and her gripping the upholstered top of the headboard, has me aching to be inside of her. I increase the pressure with my tongue, sliding it faster and harder across her clit, and then she's moaning out "fuuuck" and moving her hips in tight, small circles over my face.

When she's just about to come, I slide my body out from beneath her and she whimpers in frustration, pushes off the headboard, and shoots me a look of pure rage over her shoulder. My dick jumps in response.

"I changed my mind," I say, "I guess it does turn me on when you're pissed off."

"I hate you right now," she grinds out between clenched teeth.

I kneel behind her. "I'm going to change your mind about that. Hold on to the headboard and try not to wake up the kids."

I slide into her slowly, and it feels like coming home. After years of doing what's best for everyone else, this relationship I have with Lauren is something that's just for me. That epiphany is interrupted by the way she slams herself back so that I sink into her all the way.

"Don't you dare fuck me slowly," she says. "I need you to make me come."

I rest one hand on the headboard next to hers, and lean

down so my chest is pressed against her back as I use my other arm to anchor her hips so she can't move.

"Ask. Nicely."

She turns her head to the side and locks eyes with me. "Please, Jameson. Make. Me. Come. *Now*."

I push into the deepest recesses of her body as she takes residence in the deepest recesses of my heart. And while she bounces her hips back into me, grunting out her pleasure, reaching one hand up and behind her and cupping the back of my neck, calling out my name as she tips over the edge to ecstasy, her body tells me what I already know. She is my endgame and always has been. She is the inevitable conclusion to my story.

# Chapter Twenty-Seven

## LAUREN

*Four Months Later*

"What the hell are cremini mushrooms?" Jameson's voice is bordering on annoyed as it carries through the phone, which is perfect— it means I've succeeded in sending him on a wild goose chase at the grocery store for "the last few items" I need for dinner tonight.

The man knows me inside and out and still believes that I am cooking him an elaborate birthday dinner—and I can't stop laughing about it.

"If you can't find them, you can just get baby bella mushrooms instead," I say into the phone, thankful that he can't see the way my whole body is shaking with laughter.

"And what, pray tell, are those?"

In the half hour that he's already been gone, his sisters, along with Paige and Morgan, have decorated the first floor of our house, and set up drinks and snacks on the back deck. Several of Jameson's friends, including a few current Rebels players, are hanging out in my kitchen. Colt is playing with the kids like he is one of them, and my best friends and their husbands just walked in a few minutes ago.

Our house is packed with the people who love us most— it's everything I dreamed about when I decided to move to Boston, only better. It's also why I'm standing on the back deck, because there's no way they could all be quiet enough for me to have this conversation inside.

"They're like normal white mushrooms, but brown." I have no idea how one even cooks mushrooms. Luckily, I won't be cooking. Jameson's favorite food truck, a BBQ place that has an amazing variety of foods, will arrive shortly after he gets home to cater his birthday party. The one he doesn't know he's having.

"If I can't find them, can I just get normal mushrooms?"

"You're asking because you already have those in your hands, aren't you?"

"Most definitely."

"Okay, fine. Hurry home, okay?"

*Our home.* Jameson came home with me the night I met Sophia, and he never left. Which has worked out well, since I've never wanted him to.

"I'll be home in fifteen minutes. Are the girls down for their nap yet?" He drops his voice low and says, "My birthday feels like the perfect day for some afternoon delight."

A laugh bursts out of me as I glance over my shoulder at our house full of guests, all here to celebrate him. "They're still awake, so we'll have to see."

We say goodbye, and then I head across the backyard to open the gate that leads to the driveway. I enter the code on the keypad to open the garage door and back my SUV down the driveway and park it on the street.

When I return to the garage, I pull out two portable sawhorses and the piece of plywood that Jules brought over. I lay the plywood across the sawhorses, then grab the packing tubes with the architectural plans I had Audrey draw up. I unroll the plans, flipping quickly through the extra-large pages to double-check that they are in order, and then I hold each corner down with paperweights I bought just for this occasion.

When I see Jameson's car approaching the driveway, I shoot off a text to the whole group inside, telling them to stay away from the windows and be quiet, and then I'm walking out of the garage to meet him.

"Hey, what are you doing out here?" he asks as he steps out of his car.

"I need to show you something in the garage. Come look at this."

"Okay." I can tell by his voice that he's confused.

"So, I did a thing. For your birthday," I say as I stop in front of the plywood. He stands behind me, his left hand resting on my rib cage, below my armpit, where my new tattoo resides. His hand always lands there, as if he's reminding me that we have matching dates inked onto our bodies: this year, when I came back to him.

"Are these . . . drawings of a garage?" he asks, reaching over my shoulder with his other arm to trace the lines of the two-car garage with his finger.

"Yeah, to replace this tiny one," I say as I glance around

the small freestanding garage that barely fits my SUV and some yard tools.

"You're giving me drawings of a garage for my birthday?" There's laughter in his voice, so I lean my head back on his collarbone and look up at him.

"Turn to the next page."

As he moves the paperweight, I slip my hand under the top page, holding the next one down. It's crucial that he sees these pages one at a time.

"Is this a fully finished room above the garage? This is a really big space." His eyes scan over the page. "Why would we need a bathroom and a kitchenette in this room above the garage?"

"I was thinking it could be an office space," I tell him, "for when you need to get some work done at home."

He tries really hard to leave work at the office, but it's the nature of his job that it isn't always possible. We set up one of the spare bedrooms for him to use as an office months ago, but it hasn't been ideal. If he needs to take a late phone call or something, he always ends up in the sunroom so he doesn't wake up the kids. Or, occasionally, he'll stay late at work because he knows he has a phone call that can't be interrupted.

"You really do want me here as much as possible, don't you?" he teases as he kisses the top of my head.

"Guilty. But I also want you to be comfortable here. Look," I say, flipping one more page and pointing at the next part of the plans, "this breezeway would come right off the sunroom, and then you could either take these stairs up to the office, or go through this doorway into the garage. So it would be separate from the house, but you wouldn't have to go outside to get there. And right here"—I point to an opening in the front of the breezeway—"is an exterior door so if you needed to meet anyone in the office, they could come in here and go right up the stairs without going into the house or garage."

He gives my side a squeeze, right over my tattoo, and when I look over my shoulder at him, he looks a little choked up. "Are you officially asking me to move in?"

"You basically moved in four months ago, Jameson. I'm asking you to stay . . . forever."

He kisses the top of my head again—the affectionate gesture he does almost without thinking about it now—then says, "But when—"

"I'm also thinking that it's time we both added another tattoo."

He stiffens a bit behind me. "Oh yeah, what are you thinking?"

"I'm thinking we add the Roman numerals for next year."

He dips his head down toward mine so his voice is low in my ear. "What's happening next year?"

"I was thinking that next year, we should get married."

"Are you . . . proposing to me?"

I flip to the last page of the plans in front of us, where the bottom page reads *Will you marry me?* in a beautiful hand-lettered design that I hired a local graphic artist to create.

"Lauren," he says, spinning me around to face him. Without me holding them down, I hear the papers roll up on the table behind me. "Are you serious?"

"You told me you'd wait for me as long as I needed you to. You told me you didn't want to push me. But I'm done taking this slow. I'm ready for this next step with you. And I hope that you're ready for it too?"

He cups the side of my face in his hand as he leans his forehead against mine. "I have to show you something."

"Okay," I say, wondering for a split second if I should be worried that he hasn't said *yes* yet.

He takes a step back, reaches in his back pocket, and pulls out his wallet. Then he slides his finger into it and kneels as he pulls out a ring. "I've been carrying this around for months, all the while knowing that the second you told me you were ready to marry me, I'd drop down on one knee. And here I am, finally. I love you, and I love this life we're building together. There is no one else in this world who I'd want to marry. No one else I'd want to raise two beautiful girls with. No one else I'd want to grow old with. It's only you, Lauren. It's always been you."

My hands are covering my mouth and there are so many tears in my eyes that I'm afraid I'm going to start bawling like a baby. "I didn't hear you ask me to marry you."

"Because I didn't." He smiles up at me. "You already asked me. This is me, saying yes."

He rises off his knee and holds the ring out, and when I hold my hand out for him, he slips it on my finger.

"You make me so fucking happy every single day," he says. "I can't wait to experience the rest of my life with you."

"Same." I laugh as I hold out my finger and examine my new ring while also wondering how it fit into his wallet all this time.

He wraps one arm around my lower back and pulls me to him, and his other hand tilts my chin up to him. "I'm going to spend the rest of my life making sure I deserve you." I'm about to say *Same, again*, but his lips descend to mine, and then he's lifting me and my legs are wrapping around his waist, and he's kissing me like he's about to take my clothes off.

An *ahem* sounds from right outside the open garage door, and we both look over to see Sierra standing there, camera in hand. "I'm supposed to be capturing the proposal, but I feel like this is going somewhere else, and I just wanted to remind you that the garage door is open and you're in full view of the street."

It's true. Jameson pulled into his normal space to the side of the driveway, so it's a clear view down to the street, where a woman is pushing a baby carriage while her partner walks next to her with their dog on a leash. And they've definitely noticed us, so I guess we're making a good impression on the neighbors.

I blush, and I can tell a deep crimson is staining my neck and cheeks just by how hot I feel. Or maybe it's the late-July heat. Either way, I drop my legs and Jameson sets me on the ground.

"What are you doing here?" Jameson asks Sierra.

She looks at me. "Lauren needed a photographer." She holds up her camera, as if to remind him that she and her husband run one of the most successful photography accounts on social media.

"Let's go inside," I say. "I can't wait to see the pictures."

Jameson grabs the two grocery bags out of his car, then follows Sierra and me into the sunroom, and the minute we step through the door to the kitchen, there is a chorus of surprise and a badly done rendition of "Happy Birthday" sung at an obnoxious volume.

But I'm not looking at our friends and family, I'm looking up at Jameson's smile as he takes in everyone we love, gathered here to celebrate him, and us. And when they finally stop singing, he says, "Did you all know Lauren was going to propose?"

There's shock and surprise and excitement rippling through the crowd, because Sierra is the only one I told. Even Audrey didn't know about the last paper added to the end of her drawings. Then everyone is surrounding us with their congratulations and well wishes and requests to see the ring. And everyone wants to hear how I ended up being the one to propose, but he already got me a ring.

And there's a moment, a tiny one amid the chaos and excitement, where I think about how I got here. I recognize that it wasn't an easy path, but it was exactly the one I needed to take. The heartbreak, the tragedy, the lies . . . the struggle to get here is what makes this moment—where I feel nothing but unconditional love from this man—even sweeter.

"I love you," I say, standing on my tiptoes to whisper in Jameson's ear.

"I love you, and I love our life together," he replies. "But I'll love it even more when your last name is Flynn."

# Epilogue

## LAUREN

*Two Months Later*

"I think that's probably enough," I say as I watch Jameson add yet another piece of wood to the stack he has going next to the fire pit. "We're not going to be out here all night."

I burrow my hands deeper into the fleece-lined pockets of my down vest. It's a clear and crisp late-September night, perfect for having friends and family over for s'mores and drinks around the firepit we just built into the new patio.

"Mama, look!" Ivy calls as she and Iris go down the small plastic slide in the corner of the yard. Jameson has big plans for this yard—a play structure and an in-ground trampoline for the kids, and a hot tub for us. But I've convinced him to wait until they're a little older before we do all that.

Right now, the entire new garage has been framed out, but it's still a construction zone over on that side of the yard.

Luckily, Jules was able to put up a temporary fence around the space to prevent the girls from accidentally getting into the area, or any construction debris from getting into the yard.

"Wow!" I say. "Can I see you do it again?"

Jameson laughs softly where he's kneeling next to the wood at my feet, and he caresses my calf. "Tire them out, please. We need some alone time tonight."

"Miss me while you were in New York?"

"You have no fucking idea."

"Oh," I say, reaching down and running my fingers through his hair, "I think I do."

He stands and, as always, towers over me. "You missed me, too?"

"You couldn't tell last night on the phone?"

"Shit, Lauren, the way you looked with your toy inside you . . . I wanted to record it and watch you over and over again."

"I would kill you if you ever recorded me," I tell him. Our agreement when it comes to phone sex—which happens now pretty much every time he's on a work trip—is: no evidence. The last thing I need is naked pictures or videos of me on my future husband's phone. I've heard of too many situations where people's phones get hacked and photos get leaked.

"I never go back on my promises," he says solemnly, then brushes his lips across mine. "You can trust me."

"I do. Implicitly."

"Ewww," I hear Graham's voice from the gate near the driveway, and when we glance over, he's walking into the backyard with Jules and Audrey. "Why are Uncle Jameson and Aunt Lauren *always* kissing?"

"Shut the gate," Audrey reminds Graham, who turns and takes care of it. He's really grown up this summer—he went from being a little kid to seeming much more mature. I don't know if it's the fact that he's grown several inches in the past few months, or that he started Kindergarten, but he suddenly seems like a real person with thoughts, ideas, and actions all his own.

"Trust me, buddy," Jameson tells him. "One day you'll fall in love, and you'll want to kiss that person all the time, too."

"Girls are gross," Graham complains loudly.

"Hey, what about Iris and Ivy?" Jules asks.

"My cousins are okay. But other girls are gross."

"Again," Jameson says, "you'll change your mind."

Graham looks at Jameson like he's crazy but doesn't contradict his uncle—he looks up to him too much to outright claim he's wrong.

Twenty minutes later, our backyard starts filling in. Morgan and Paige arrive together, and a couple friends we've made in the neighborhood come with their kids. Colt shows up by himself and makes a beeline straight to Jameson. He looks agitated, which is far different than his normal carefree demeanor, but I'm distracted from that conversation because there's someone at the gate I don't recognize. He's younger than me, and looks kind of lost, so I head over to him.

"Hey," I say, "I'm Lauren."

"I'm Drew. Jameson has said lots of great things about you."

"Well that's a relief to hear! Drew . . ." I pause, trying to place him because Jameson didn't mention anyone named Drew stopping by tonight. And then I realize who he is. "Oh!

You're Drew Jenkins"—I literally face-palm—"of course. I work in marketing for the Rebels. Welcome to the team."

"Thanks. I'm really excited to be back in Boston."

"Yeah, Jameson mentioned you have family here?"

"I grew up in West Roxbury," he says mentioning the Boston neighborhood that feels almost like a suburb and is directly south of our town of Brookline. "My whole family's still there. My sisters live on the same street as my mom." His lips turn down at the corners, but I can't quite figure out why and don't feel like it's my place to ask.

"They must be very excited to have you back here. Where are you living?"

"My family has a cabin up on Lake Winnipesaukee, so I was up there for most of the summer, but I just bought a place in the Back Bay. Moved in earlier today."

"You'll be right in the thick of things, then," I say, since the Back Bay is where many of Boston's best shops and restaurants are located. With two NHL contracts already under his belt, Drew has to be in his mid- to late-twenties, but with his wispy, light brown hair and his ridiculously long eyelashes, he could pass for younger.

Jameson and Colt must see Drew just then, because Colt shouts out, "Jenkins!" and waves his arm at him. Drew glances back at me.

"I think you're being summoned by your team elder," I say.

"Oh my God," Drew laughs, "do people really call him that?"

"Only if they want to piss him off. I wouldn't recommend starting off that way." I think I remember Jameson saying something about Drew getting off on the wrong foot with some of his teammates in Colorado. "In fact," I say, grabbing his forearm, "*definitely* don't do that."

"I won't. It was nice to meet you, Lauren."

"You too. I'll talk to you later," I say and turn back toward the house.

I know Audrey was headed toward the house to grab the platter of s'mores supplies a minute ago, and I want to make sure she found everything since I imagine Jameson will start the fire up soon. But I've only taken a few steps in that direction when I see her standing on the deck, frozen in place, looking like she's seen a ghost. And when I follow her gaze, her eyes are locked on Drew.

She doesn't even notice me until I'm right by her side. "You okay?"

"What's *he* doing here?"

"Drew Jenkins?" I say, just to be sure.

"Yeah."

"He got traded to the Rebels. I assume Jameson invited him over because he just moved into his new place in the Back Bay."

"What?" She whispers the word out so quietly it's almost silent. Her eyes still haven't drifted away from Drew.

"Why do you seem so shook?"

She exhales a ragged breath, then gives me a small, tight smile. "I'm not shook. I'm just surprised to see him here. We went to college together."

"Did you guys know each other well?" I know I'm prying, but it's not like Audrey to not spill all the info, and the fact that she's being a bit cagey has me wondering what the rest of the story is.

"Yeah, I tutored him in calculus my junior year."

"Is it . . . good to see him?"

Audrey presses her lips between her teeth as her eyes drift back to Drew again.

"Not really," she says, and then turns toward me suddenly, keeping her back to everyone on the patio and lawn and her head tilted forward so her hair covers her face on both sides. When I glance in that direction, Drew's eyes are focused on Audrey's back and there's confusion written all over his face. "Shit. I need to leave," Audrey mumbles. "I'm going to head inside. Would you do me a favor and send Graham in? He's going to be mad if I make him leave early, and I don't want to cause a scene out here."

"Audrey, what's going on?"

"I'll explain later. Please, just send Graham in as quickly as possible."

She makes a beeline for the glass doors and steps off the deck and into the kitchen, sliding the screen closed behind her. She must move farther into the house, because I don't even see her through the screen.

I glance once more at Drew, whose eyes are now focused on the door Audrey just went through. Then I find Graham, who is trying to catch my girls as they go down the slide. I hustle across the lawn to him. "Hey, bud," I say, "your mom needs to see you inside."

He complains a bit without outright refusing to go, then insists on giving both Iris and Ivy a hug. I haven't told him he's leaving, but it seems like he gets that sense.

"What's going on?" Jules asks as she approaches. She must see the concern written across my face.

"I'm not sure," I say quietly because I don't want Graham to hear me. "Audrey saw Drew Jenkins—he's a new player for the Rebels," I clarify because Jules actually goes out of her way to avoid hockey, "and now she's hiding inside and wants Graham to come in so they can leave."

Jules swallows so hard I'm surprised she doesn't choke. "Okay, well we drove together, so I'll go too," she says to me. "Graham, let's go, bud."

I glance over at Jameson, who's still engaged in conversation with Colt, but Drew's no longer there. My eyes scan the yard, but I don't see him anywhere.

"I'll walk in with you," I tell her, as Graham sprints ahead of us and into the house.

When Jules and I get inside a few moments later, Drew is kneeling down talking to Graham. Audrey's arms are folded across her rib cage and the look on her face makes it clear that she's not thrilled about any of this.

When Graham says, "I'm five and I'm in Kindergarten," Drew glances up at Audrey, and from this angle it's easy to see the confusion written across his face.

"It was good seeing you again, Drew," Audrey says. Her voice holds a certain level of finality—a permanent goodbye.

"Audrey," he starts, rising quickly to his full height. "We need to talk."

"We really don't," she says as she squeezes Graham to her side.

"We do." His words leave no room for negotiation. "And we can either do it here, now, or you can give me your number and we can talk later. But we will be talking."

I'm not sure how to interpret the look that crosses her face, but she doesn't look pissed. Jules moves to step forward, but I grab her wrist and hold her in place. I know Jules would never let a man talk to her that way, and Audrey is strong yet looks . . . interested?

"You can get my number from Lauren," she says. "We're leaving."

"I'll call you tonight. Make sure you answer your phone."

A scoff bursts out of Audrey. "Oh, like you did all those times I called you when you moved to Vancouver?"

"Audrey . . ." Drew says, his voice placating.

"Don't 'Audrey' me. I will answer my phone if I can. And if not, I'll call you back. That's what people normally do when someone's left them a message. Or twenty." Now she sounds pissed off, and she spins on her heel and heads toward the front door with Jules hot on her heels.

"Who was that, Mommy?" Graham asks when they make it to the front door.

"He's no one," Audrey replies right before the door shuts behind them.

My eyes meet Drew's and he's visibly upset. The way he looked at Audrey when he heard Graham's age, and then Audrey's comment about leaving him twenty messages and him not returning any of them . . . I'm trying not to jump to any conclusions, and failing.

"You want to help me carry the s'mores supplies out, please?" I ask Drew.

He shakes his head like he's trying to clear his thoughts. "Yeah, sure."

We head to the kitchen island where two large platters with graham crackers, chocolate bars, and marshmallows sit.

"So, how do you know Audrey?" Drew asks as he picks up a platter.

I hold up my left hand so he can see my engagement ring. "Future sister-in-law."

"Wait . . . Audrey is . . ." he says, and I watch him work this out, "Jameson's sister?"

"You didn't know that?" I ask.

"I had no idea."

"Weren't you already working with Jameson when you were playing hockey in college, with plans of him becoming your agent after you were drafted?" That's how it usually works with college players.

"Yeah, but I didn't know Audrey was his sister."

"Did she know Jameson was going to be your agent?"

"I don't know. I can't remember if I ever mentioned it specifically, but it was definitely public knowledge."

"How did you and Audrey know each other, again?" I ask as we walk outside.

"She tutored me."

I already knew this and admittedly was being nosey and hoping for a bit more information. But also, they clearly have things they need to talk about first, so it's probably a good thing that neither of them are blabbing to me.

Drew and I set the platters down on the table nearest the fire pit, and then I give him Audrey's number before he heads over toward Colt and Jameson. Jameson's eyes meet mine across the yard, and he looks concerned about whatever he sees.

In a few quick strides, he's by my side. "Hey, what's wrong?"

"Nothing." I don't want to say too much about the conversation I just witnessed, because if there truly is anything going on between Drew and Audrey, then Audrey should be the one to tell him.

"You sure? You look . . . I don't even know . . . which is what's concerning."

"I'm fine," I say, looking up at him, "really."

"Okay. But please tell me Drew wasn't just asking for your number?"

I laugh at the idea of giving my number to anyone. "No, he was asking for Audrey's. Apparently they knew each other in college, but haven't seen each other since—until tonight."

"Yeah, I guess their time at Boston University would have overlapped," he says. "Small world."

*Yeah,* I think, *especially for such a huge school.*

"You going to start this fire?" I ask.

"It'll be hard to make s'mores if I don't." He kisses my forehead before turning to grab the lighter.

Once the fire is going, people begin gathering around. We're passing out sticks for roasting, and kids are holding their toasted marshmallows out to me so I can sandwich them between graham crackers and chocolate. When I glance over at Jameson, who is now holding both Ivy and Iris so they won't get too close to the fire, the smile on his face takes me by surprise. This man who never wanted to settle down, who didn't want kids, ended up being the dad my girls deserve. He's also the partner I need him to be—supportive, protective, and loving.

He passes Iris off to one of our neighbors, a fifteen-year-old girl who's babysat for us a couple times, and gives Ivy to our babysitter's mom. Then he walks over, wrapping his free arm around me, and his lips are at my ear whispering, "How long until we can put the kids to bed and kick everyone out? I need you naked and on your back, or on top of me, or on all fours, or all of the above."

"Patience," I whisper back to him. "I'll make it worth the wait."

I glance at him in time to see his eyebrows shoot up. "I like the sound of that."

"You'll like the feel of it even better," I tease.

"I'm sure I will," he says, then leans closer and nips my earlobe, in full view of our friends, family, and neighbors.

"You two are sickeningly adorable," Paige says from my other side, and I can feel the flush creeping up my neck.

"Sorry, not sorry," I say.

Paige gives me a genuine smile. "Good, you shouldn't be sorry. You have what we all want, and you should be proud of the work you and Jameson have done to get here."

"I am," I tell her as he squeezes me closer, letting me know that he's proud of us too. "Also, I think we've nailed down a date and a location for the wedding."

"Oh yeah?" she says. "Do tell."

"Mid-June, and the reception will be at the building on State Street that overlooks the Customs House clock tower and the harbor." Paige had gone with me the first time I visited, and Jameson and I just went back last weekend.

"I think that's the best choice," she says.

I'd briefly considered having the wedding at Blackstone Mountain because both Jackson and Sierra's weddings there were amazing. But I attended both with Josh, and the idea of getting married somewhere I'd stayed with him felt wrong—even though Jameson and I have been up there multiple times making new memories with my friends.

"Me too," I tell her. "And really, I can't wait."

"We could just elope," Jameson mutters from my side. He'd floated that idea this past summer when we were in the Caribbean for Jackson and Sierra's babymoon, where we also found out that Petra was expecting. He'd argued that we were already engaged, and if we came back from our trip already married, we wouldn't have the stress of the wedding.

"Pretty sure our sisters would kill us," I tell him, "since I already asked them to be bridesmaids."

"And pretty much everyone is dying to see you get married," Paige tells him with a laugh.

"Because no one thought it would ever happen?" he clarifies.

"Because apparently you *insisted* it would never happen," Paige says.

"Yeah well, I was young and stupid then. But, I would still be holding true to that, if it hadn't been for Lauren."

With that, I snuggle into his side, thinking how I'll never stop being grateful for where we ended up, no matter how long it took us to get here.

## THE END

*Want more Lauren and Jameson? Get their bonus epilogue, set six years in the future while they are on vacation with Jackson and Nate, Sierra and Beau, and Petra and Aleksandr.*

*Scan here for*

Lauren & Jameson's
Bonus Epilogue

———

*Continue reading for a preview of Audrey & Drew's book, Center Ice, Book 1 in the Boston Rebels series. You'll continue to see Lauren and Jameson, as well as cameos from the other Frozen Hearts characters, in this new series.*

# Center Ice

## BOSTON REBELS, BOOK ONE

I've always been a wild card – the first to start a fight on the ice, and the life of the party off it – but appearances can be deceiving.

Being traded to the Boston Rebels could not have come at a better time. With serious family obligations to fulfill and a contract renewal with a new hockey team on the line, I have no time for anything else.

I return to Boston knowing I need to buckle down and focus on what really matters.

But the first night I'm back in town, I come face to face with Audrey, my college calculus tutor. We had a brief fling right before I was drafted into the NHL. Now, her five year old son is standing by her side, and I don't need a tutor to do *that* kind of math.

Audrey insists she doesn't want me involved in Graham's life unless I can commit to being a dad. With everything else going on, this is the worst possible timing.

But every minute I spend with Graham and Audrey feels

exactly right, and I'm left questioning everything I thought I wanted.

Because now my goals are shifting, and getting what I *really* want might come at the expense of the game I've given my entire life to.

# Books by Julia Connors

## FROZEN HEARTS SERIES

On the Edge

(Jackson & Nate's Story)

Out of Bounds

(Sierra & Beau's Story)

One Last Shot

(Petra & Aleksandr's Story)

One Little Favor

(Avery & Tom's Novella)

On the Line

(Lauren & Jameson's Story)

## BOSTON REBELS SERIES

Center Ice

(Audrey & Drew's Story)

Fake Shot

(Jules & Colt's Story)

# Acknowledgments

I'm filled with so many mixed emotions about wrapping up the Frozen Hearts Series, but mostly I feel profound awe and gratitude that so many readers have found this series, loved my characters, and spread the word about my books. I'm not sure I could have finished the series if I didn't know there were so many of you waiting on Lauren's story. Your messages of support and your enthusiasm for my characters really did lift me up when I needed the motivation to keep going.

For many reasons, this was an extremely hard book for me to write. I wanted so badly to give Lauren her happily ever after, and it took me quite a while to work out who the perfect man would be for her. There were many starts and stops, another whole book written instead of this one, and an unbelievable number of words scrapped as I tried to figure out Lauren's story.

In the end, I wrote my heart out with this book, and I could not have done it without the help of an entire freaking village:

*Melissa and Casey* – You both read every word of this draft (even the 5ok words I scrapped!) and pushed me to be better. You told me what wasn't working, made me rethink big and small pieces of my work, then believed in me and encouraged me when I doubted myself. There is no part of this book that isn't better because of your involvement. I'm not even sure this book would be what it is without the two of you! *Melissa,* I'll be forever grateful that you dropped into my DMs, took a chance on my books, and have become one of my biggest champions. *Casey,* I'm so thankful we connected and I appreciate your support, your hockey knowledge, and the honest and thoughtful way you give feedback. I'm so glad you were both on this journey with me.

*Danielle,* as always, you are my go-to hype girl. Our talks about books and writing and badass women really do fill my cup. I wish we lived closer, but for now I'll take all the phone calls and FaceTimes we can fit in amidst our crazy-hectic lives.

*Kait,* I'm not sure how I ever did this without you. Thank you for cheering me on while also keeping me on track. Thanks for dealing with my mini panic attack about things I thought I forgot to do, all while you're mid-flight, and then assuring me that I am not, in fact, a hot mess. Spoiler alert: I kind of am. Thank you for beta-reading this book, being my biggest cheerleader, and generally being an awesome person.

*Jenny,* thank you for reading and editing an early draft of this book. I seriously live for your reader reaction comments!

*Elizabeth,* thank you for being supportive and keeping all my secrets. I'm so thankful you wanted to read and edit this book before its release.

*Sarah,* thank you for being a genius when it comes to naming books, series, and hockey teams, and for being a great cheerleader for my books. Hearing your voice in my DMs always brings me great joy!

To my author friends who have offered support, advice, and friendship, especially *Lily, Victoria, Alexandra, Ashley, Jackie, Gina, Cate, Mary, Melissa, Cali, Elsie, and others I'm confident I'm unintentionally leaving out* –thank you!

To my husband, who literally picked up *all* the slack while I dove into my writing cave to get this book done. I could not have done it without you. Thanks for listening when times were stressful, and for gently suggesting (rather than insisting) that maybe I need to take a break from writing and publishing. Sorry that I continue to ignore that advice!

# Afterword

**Thank you so much for reading!** If you enjoyed the book, please consider leaving an honest review. Reader reviews mean so much to authors, and your time and feedback are appreciated.

**Sign up for Julia's newsletter** to stay up to date on the latest news and be the first to know about sales, audiobooks, and new releases!

www.juliaconnors.com/newsletter

# About the Author

Julia Connors grew up on the warm and sunny West Coast, but her first decision as an adult was to trade her flip-flops for snow boots and move to Boston. She's been enjoying everything that New England has to offer for over two decades, and now that she's acclimated to the snowy winters and finally found all the places to get good sushi and tacos, she has zero regrets. You can usually find her in front of her computer, but when she stops writing she's most likely to be found outdoors, preferably with a pair of skis or snowshoes strapped to her feet in winter, or on a paddleboard in the summer.

goodreads.com/julia_connors

amazon.com/author/juliaconnors

instagram.com/juliaconnorsauthor

tiktok.com/@juliaconnorsauthor?

facebook.com/juliaconnorsauthor

pinterest.com/juliaconnorsauthor

Made in the USA
Las Vegas, NV
11 September 2024

95149597R00204